...han was born in 1967 in Buenos Aires, where he lives
...ds Out is the first of his novels to be translated into
...iencias Morales, his latest novel, won the prestigious
...Novel Prize in Spain and will be published by Serpent's
...1.

SECONDS OUT

MARTÍN KOHAN

Translated from the Spanish by Nick Caistor

A complete catalogue record for this book can be
obtained from the British Library on request

The right of Martín Kohan to be identified as the author
of this work has been asserted by him in accordance
with the Copyright, Designs and Patents Act 1988

First published as *Segundos afuera* in 2005 by Editorial Sudamericana

First published in 2010 by Serpent's Tail,
an imprint of Profile Books Ltd
3A Exmouth House
Pine Street
London EC1R 0JH
website: www.serpentstail.com

ISBN 978 1 84668 637 5

Designed and typeset by folio at Neuadd Bwll, Llanwrtyd Wells

Printed in the UK by CPI Bookmarque, Croydon, CR0 4TD

10 9 8 7 6 5 4 3 2 1

For Julia

ONE

DEMPSEY KNOWS IT'S A ROPE, it's not made of rubber. It's a rope like the one in his training ring at the gym: thicker, of course, but still a rope. That means the fibres can stretch so far, but no further. Each fibre stretches, without tearing or breaking, protected individually and as a whole by the canvas sheath. Each fibre extends a few millimetres, a few centimetres: taken together, that makes quite a distance. But it's not rubber, not by any means, it won't break his fall then propel him back into the ring at the same speed. Dempsey knows this, and yet as he topples backwards in a daze he calculates that if the rope stretches thirty or fifty centimetres it might just be enough to hold him up, then he can bounce back onto his feet. This is what Dempsey is thinking, stunned by a tremendous blow from the Argentinian. He can't remember the man's name: Fripp or Flip, nicknamed The Bull. Dempsey is thinking this in the possibly not entirely misplaced hope that the rope will fit snugly under his shoulder blades. If that happens, he won't fall. If the rope will only give a little, just a few centimetres, even though it isn't made of rubber. That's what Jack Dempsey really needs: it would help break his fall and put him back on his feet again in the fight. That's his hope as he topples backwards. His face hurts, but he manages to concentrate, above all, on his back, on what he might feel on his back as he hits the ropes. How long does this last? A split second. His face is still burning and his jaw aches, but on his back, beneath his shoulder blades, just where he was expecting it, he can feel the rope. The rope (or more exactly the canvas with the rope sheathed inside it) is exactly where he had been expecting it, but it feels very damp, wet, in fact – and that's something Dempsey had not been expecting. The rope's wet. Possibly the seconds, his or his opponent's, overdid it in the corner before the bout, splashing water in his or his opponent's face. It may also be, Dempsey recognises, that it's his back rather than the rope that is wet, or rather that it's not only the rope, but also his broad, strong, muscular, imposing boxer's back. Or it could be the damp atmosphere, or sweat, or saliva from his opponent's mouth that dripped onto his shoulder while they were in a clinch or collided and the other man inadvertently leant on him. There are several possible explanations, but none of them matter: the fact is that the rope, or his back, or both of them, are wet. So that when the toppling Dempsey reaches the rope and leans against it, hoping it will propel him back into the ring, he slips off instead. He's wet, so is the rope, and he slides backwards with all the force of the punch that sent him sprawling. He's going to hit the canvas. There's no avoiding it. These things happen in boxing. But the rope doesn't even break his fall. It slides down from his shoulder blades to his kidneys to his waist. Instead of preventing him falling any further, the rope gives way. He's being knocked out – something unprecedented in his career as a boxer. There's more. It looks as though he's not going to slide down the ropes and land on the canvas of the ring as always happens. No: because of the slippery wetness everywhere, he is going to fall right through the ropes and out of the ring. But Dempsey does not know this yet.

◆

'Gustav Mahler used to say something very interesting. Gustav Mahler, the bohemian musician. He used to say that instead of giving the most expressive parts of his music to the most sensitive instruments – the violins, for example – he would write them for the harshest, the brass section, a trumpet or trombone. That's interesting, isn't it? The most expressive parts of his compositions were played by the least expressive instruments. I think that's interesting.'

'I really don't get it. Isn't that just plain stupid? Just imagine if, when he was going for a knockout, Firpo punched his opponent more softly rather than as hard as he could. What would you say about someone like that? That they're daft.'

'Please, Verani, don't be so crass.'

'But what you're saying is nonsense. It doesn't stand up.'

'I'm not the one saying it. It was Gustav Mahler.'

'You or whoever, Ledesma. Do me a favour. It's still stupid.'

'I don't get it, really, I don't know why you're being so pigheaded. Why do you insist on comparing the two things?'

'But what you say makes no sense at all.'

'A boxing match. Trying to knock another man down, to hurt him. And a symphony, in this case Gustav Mahler's *First Symphony*. You've no idea what I'm talking about, have you?'

'Yes I do. You say that the soft parts of his tune are played as loudly as possible. That doesn't make sense.'

'We'll never get anywhere, Verani, because you still refuse to listen to even a fragment of the work.'

'The thing is, Ledesma, I'd fall asleep, what more can I say?'

'I don't mean the whole symphony. Just listen to a bit, to hear what it sounds like.'

'Why don't you ask Roque?'

'Roque, well, he's a possibility.'

'There he is, why not ask him?'

'But what about you?'

'Please don't get me wasting my time. How long have we got before the deadline? I've barely started my article.'

'We still have a fortnight or so. What date is it today? We've got twelve or fifteen days still, I reckon. Look: we've got more than a fortnight. Sixteen days left, to be exact.'

'That's what I'm saying – don't make me waste time. Our friend Roque here looks really interested. Why not ask him?'

◆

I'm told that apparently he knocked over a glass of water just before he died. He either knocked it to the floor with an anxious swipe of the hand, or it fell off his bedside table when he groped for it. Nobody knows: if he felt ill, he might have wanted to take another pill out of the purple box, or perhaps, even though he could see it was late afternoon and the sun was still shining in through the window, he was trying to switch on his bedside lamp. It's less likely that he was trying to reach the phone, using the last remnants of his strength to dial a number to alert someone or to ask for help, forgetting that he never had a phone by his bed in this room, possibly confusing it with another one he had once slept in.

None of that matters now. These are just details mentioned to flesh out the meagre report that shortly after midday, alone in his house, flat on his back and entangled in his bedclothes, Ledesma died. They called me and told me ('It's Ledesma, Roque. He's just passed away'), avoiding the word 'died' as people used to avoid the word 'cancer' ('He's ill, Roque. There's no cure. He's got the big one'). When I said nothing, they began with the details. The broken glass, the spilled water, who knows what he was trying to do at such an odd moment, or what one might think is such an odd moment. The fact is, he died, and no one could say he hadn't warned them.

They give me the details: the vigil is tonight ('Around nine, half past nine') in one of the city's two undertaker's parlours ('No, not Vignazzi Brothers, the other one'). After that, there's not much else to do except get used to the idea that I'm never going to see Ledesma again. The funeral is tomorrow, after eleven.

Night falls, nine o'clock comes around, and I don't go to the vigil. I don't go to bed or to sleep either; I don't find something to do or to take my mind off it; I simply don't go. I spend several hours thinking about Ledesma, and that's enough. More than once I have my doubts, and wonder if I shouldn't be there, surrounded by wreaths, with the mourners, those who were his friends or colleagues. Each time I decide no, it's better to stay where I am ('Better not, what's the point?'), and at some moment or other I go over to the wardrobe and pull the bag down from the top shelf.

It's already light in the patio outside. I pull up the blind. I stuff a few essentials into the bag, wonder what death looked like on Ledesma's face, wonder if I didn't go to the vigil simply to avoid meeting Verani. The bag's quite light; I won't have to check it in. If I squash everything inside, I can take it on the plane with me so that when I arrive I won't have to wait for the luggage.

They rang Ledesma's daughter last night to tell her the news. They had trouble finding her – she wasn't at home, but had already left work, so that by the time they did manage to reach her and give her the bad news ('It's your father, Raquel. It's about your father') it was too late for her to catch the last plane. That's why she's arriving this morning for the funeral, almost twenty years since she was last here. I wonder if I'm going to miss the funeral like I missed the vigil, to avoid seeing the moment when Verani and Ledesma's daughter meet again.

It's eight o'clock in the morning.

◆

'Tell you what: why don't you sing a bit?'

'Me?'

'Just a bit, Ledesma, the bit you like best.'

'You're asking me to sing?'

'Of course. Just to give me some idea, then you won't have to bother with the record player. What's up, can't you sing in tune?'

'It's not that I can't sing in tune, Verani, it's just that you obviously have no idea what you're talking about.'

'Maybe I'm not expressing myself properly, but try to understand. OK, so perhaps I'm wrong to ask you to sing a bit, because it doesn't have words. But that doesn't mean you couldn't whistle the tune, or hum it, if you get me.'

'What do you mean, Verani: what on earth do you think we're talking about? What do you think Mahler's music is like?'

'I don't think anything; that's why I'm asking you to sing me a bit.'

'You've obviously got the idea it's like one of those cheap Rivero tangos, something you can launch into here in the bar and sing just like that.'

'Well, isn't it? That's why I'm asking you.'

'That's nonsense, Verani. Stuff and nonsense.'

'Don't get me wrong: I wasn't asking you to actually sing. Just hum the tune, or whistle. I know they're not songs with words that you can actually sing.'

'How on earth do you think anyone can sing anything in here, with all that racket going on outside? Besides, it's not so simple. Mahler has his symphonies, some better than others – it's a real shame you're so determined not to listen to them at least once in your life – but he also wrote songs.'

'You don't say!'

'Yes.'

'Songs with words?'

'Yes.'

'So I was right then.'

'No, not the kind of songs you mean. You think that if Edmundo Rivero or Nino Bravo pitched up here they could just launch into the songs. But it's not like that.'

'Are they songs with words?'

'Yes, of course.'

'And people sing them?'

'Look, Verani, why don't you come back to my place so you can listen to the records properly?'

'Can you sing them or not?'

'Of course you can sing them.'

'Well, sing one then!'

'The problem is you think they can be sung like a tango. Just like that, here in the bar with all that maddening noise going on outside. But these songs need a different atmosphere, different surroundings. Besides, they're very hard to sing. No amateur could do it.'

'No?'

'No.'

'Not even you?'

'Not even me.'

'But they do have words.'

'Yes, they have words.'

'What sort of words?'

'What d'you mean?'

'The words.'

'The words?'

'Yes.'

'Well, I don't know. They're in German.'

'In German?'

'Yes, in German. But I can tell you something about them.'

'Go on.'

'Mahler composed a series of songs, and just listen to the title: *Songs on Children's Deaths.*'

'My God!'

'The music is terrifying. A shiver goes down your spine when you hear it. Just think, a topic like that. The thing is, some time later, I'm not sure how long, Mahler's eldest daughter died.'

'You don't say!'

'Yes. A four-year-old girl called María. She fell ill, grew worse and then she died.'

'Poor little thing.'

'Just imagine what a devastating blow. Incredible grief. So then Mahler's wife Alma confronted him and said that in some way it was all his fault, that he shouldn't have set such terrible words to such tremendous music. She told him he was responsible for bringing the tragedy on them.'

'What can I say? I reckon his wife was right.'

'Whenever I tell that story I think of my poor Quelita.'

'If you ask me, I reckon she was right. With all the nice things to write about in the world, why on earth did he have to choose a subject like that? Women can sense these things. What did you say her name was?'

'Mahler's wife?'

'Yes.'

'Alma: the Latin for "soul".'

'Alma. With a name like that, of course she was going to sense it.'

◆

Donald Mitchell had to escape from his parents' house in Newark, but it was for the best. He was born in the last year of the century, in 1899 (if that was the last year of the century, and not the one following, as some people claim, probably with good reason). He never married and had hardly any friends. No one knows how or why he became so interested in optics, though the fact is that by the age of twenty he was pretty much an expert. His parents were poor farmers who foresaw a promising future for him making lenses and spectacles, and were pleased that once more the rule which says that children will do better than their parents was to be proved right. Prudent, provident, Protestant, month after month they patiently rather than greedily set aside what little profit they made from their farm. They stealthily hid the banknotes under a loose living room floorboard. Every so often they took the notes out to count and recount them, in order to reassure themselves of what they already knew: that over time, and in the same way as time, the amount was increasing slowly but surely. Yet one fine day – or rather, one dreadful day – every single one of those banknotes went missing. Afterwards they had to ask the Lord's forgiveness for the unfounded suspicions they dared entertain, if not express, about who might have been the perpetrator of such a despicable robbery. The fact was that, however difficult it was for them to accept the idea, it was their own son Donald who had commited it: the studious Donald, their only child (better to think it was on an impulse rather than a carefully premeditated plan), had prised up the famous floorboard when he was alone in the house, taken out the banknotes and at that moment realised (if he hadn't done so before) that this action meant he would have to leave the parental home. To his parents, used to living a life of poverty, the amount involved was quite considerable. Even so, as he started out on his escape to New York, it was only just enough for Donald to be able to purchase one of the sophisticated, newfangled photographic cameras that were still so rare and impressive. Having nothing else to do on his train journey into the unknown, he spent the time closely examining all the mysteries of the camera lenses and mechanisms rather than watching the landscape speeding past the carriage window. He also had more than enough time to go over in his mind the tale of the poor young man triumphing in the big city, trying to convince himself it applied to him. Subsequent events proved he was right to believe he would get ahead relying on nothing more than his gumption and his brand new acquisition. He was mistaken though (as subsequent events also showed) if he thought that once he had triumphed he would be able to return to his parents' house and be welcomed like the prodigal son. It was to be many years before he had to contemplate this return, and go back and be disillusioned; for the moment, he was leaving Newark behind, and felt that he was hurtling forwards (as in fact he was on board the train) to conquer the world. He did not feel overwhelmed by the city's inferno: it was inhuman, and therefore alien to him; he could only be affected by what was human. He had his share of what is known as beginners' luck; shortly after he arrived he got a job on *Sports Illustrated*. At first he spent all his time taking jolly portraits of smiling oarsmen. Then things improved a little: photographing the faces of weightlifters at the climactic moment of greatest effort opened up fresh possibilities for him. And finally, as though he had succeeded in making it his destiny by force of his belief alone, the great night arrived. It was 14 September 1923 and he was given the responsibility (with great insistence on what a responsibility it was) of covering the world championship boxing match. Donald accepted the challenge: to capture in still images the fleeting shapes of constantly moving bodies. Some of these images, perhaps most of them, will be nothing more than a sort of blurred blob, because in reality things happen much more quickly than his apparatus can accommodate. He is well aware, however, that all he needs is the sporadic perfection of a few clear images for him to achieve success in what he calls, or is starting to call, his photographic career. When he arrives at the stadium he refuses a position high up from where he could get a panoramic view of events. He is used to close-ups, and so asks if he can go nearer the ring. Thanks to his insistence, he gets what he wants: he's given a ringside seat, between a radio commentator and one of the judges. Instead of observing from a distance he's going to have to crouch down, but he hopes or senses that this closeness has to be to his advantage. He's a man who uses his eyes, he's a photographer, and yet what first strikes him when the bout begins and the champion and his challenger are in the ring are the sounds he can hear because he's so close, although they would be inaudible if he were a little further away: the grunts of effort or pain, the squeak of their rubber-soled boots on the canvas, the thud of gloves as they make contact. Mitchell tries hard not to lose concentration, waiting for the right moment. He mustn't be too quick or too slow, he mustn't waste the opportunity. It's impossible to anticipate the right moment: with rare good fortune, it can be intuited just as it's about to happen, or it can be recognised, almost miraculously, in the instant it is happening. It's a sort of vibration that runs through the body, through the hand holding up the magnesium flashbulb, through the finger poised on the button. Donald Mitchell feels it, or thinks he does, right now, at this second and no other, on the night of 14 September 1923, when the title challenger connects with all his might on his rival's face and the entire stadium seems plunged into a pit of silence or astonishment. Jack Dempsey, the champion, the holder of the world title, starts to fall, or is already falling.

◆

I can remember it all in bits and pieces.

The years have gone by, almost twenty – seventeen, in fact – and it takes a lot of effort to recall everything precisely.

The idea came from Arteche, the editor. He thought it was such a good one he was keen to hear praise from all the others: a special supplement commemorating the anniversary of the newspaper's foundation.

The fiftieth anniversary, a nice round number. In the town of Trelew and the province of Chubut, ours was the newspaper with by far the longest history in all Patagonia. Fifty years. He wanted everyone to go back to the beginning, to September 1923. According to the section they worked in, each of them was to choose a story from that month and reproduce it (or rather recreate it, said Arteche, correcting himself).

'The World As It Was Then', the supplement was to be called. It was going to come out in a month, but the articles had to be finished in a little over a fortnight. It was extra work on top of the usual daily stories that naturally took most of the time; but no one asked if they were going to be paid extra for it.

Showing more haste than real interest, they all came to consult the newspaper archives. I helped them as best I could, and I seem to remember some of them came back the next day. An archive is always far less rich than reality.

Ledesma and Verani had chosen their stories by that first afternoon. Verani was on Sports; Ledesma was Culture. I remember it as if it was today. When we left work, we did what we always did: went to have a coffee and a chat in the bar of the Argentine Touring Club Hotel. Outside in the streets people were cheering and shouting. Things were going on, some of which would become news.

Verani knew what he was going to do: in September 1923 Firpo and Dempsey had fought in the United States. The fight of the century. So he wasn't content with the month, or even the year. The fight of the century, no less. A good moment to launch a newspaper.

Ledesma also knew what he wanted to write about: in September 1923 Richard Strauss had been in Buenos Aires conducting the Viennese Philharmonic Orchestra. A kind of marathon that gave him the opportunity to play almost everything: Beethoven, Bruckner, Brahms; Wagner, Haydn, Schubert; Weber, Mozart, Mendelssohn. He also presented several of his own works: *Don Juan, Don Quixote, Salomé*; *A Hero's Life* and *Thus Spake Zarathustra*; the *Domestic* and *Alpine Symphonies*. I remember Ledesma was amazed that so much outstanding music could be rehearsed and played in under a month. But what to him seemed the most significant event, and what he had chosen as the subject for his article in the special supplement, was the premiere in Buenos Aires of Mahler's *First Symphony*. It had taken place in the Colón Theatre on the night of Monday 22 September, and Ledesma saw it as the most important cultural event not only of that month but of the whole year.

Verani thought he was exaggerating and wanted to know how big an audience there was in the Colón in those days.

I didn't say anything. I wasn't even twenty at the time, and preferred to stay in the background. I was used to being with people older than me, and so I always liked to listen rather than speak.

◆

'I can't believe you're being serious.'

'Why ever not? I'm being serious because you're always serious.'

'Yes, but you come out with such rubbish I think that deep down you're making fun of me.'

'Don't think that, Ledesma. Why would I make fun of you?'

'I'm sorry, but you say such ridiculous things that it seems to me you must be deliberately misinterpreting me.'

'I swear I'm not making fun of you.'

'I believe you, Verani, don't think I don't. It's just that sometimes it's hard to credit what you're saying.'

'I thought I was saying the same as you.'

'You may have thought so, but you're wrong. I called Mahler bohemian because he was born in a region known as Bohemia. With all the wars and rebellions, things are constantly changing in that part of the world: look at Germany today, I mean West and East Germany, look at Austria, or Czechoslovakia. It's all very complicated; in the past it all used to be different. If we say Poland today, we all know what we're talking about, but for a hundred years Poland didn't even exist.'

'That really is crap.'

'That's the history of the world for you, Verani, it's time you learned. Then you go and talk as if Mahler's a pop singer.'

'I didn't mean any offence. It looks like I misunderstood you.'

'Yes, it looks like that from a hundred kilometres away. To begin with, Mahler wasn't a singer.'

'But you said he wrote songs with words.'

'That's true, but that doesn't mean he was the one who sang them. What he did was compose.'

'Compose.'

'Yes, compose. And he was a great orchestra conductor.'

'You don't say.'

'I do. Do you see how wrong you were: you were imagining some drunk in a bar singing off-key as he blabbed onto his accordion.'

'I never said he was a drunk.'

'You make me laugh. What did you imagine: a guy on a spree standing on a table singing, with a chorus of drunken sailors?'

'I never said a thing about drunks.'

'Did you know Gustav Mahler rose to be director of the Vienna Opera? Did you know that?'

'No, I didn't.'

'You don't know anything, but that doesn't stop you shooting your mouth off.'

'I may have misunderstood you.'

'The problem is, you don't understand because you don't want to. You're pig-headed. And now I'm sure you've come away with the idea that there's nothing popular about Mahler's music, but that's not true either.'

'It isn't?'

'Of course it isn't. He has lots of things taken from popular traditions, melodies directly inspired by folklore.'

'You don't say!'

'Of course, if I talk about folklore you immediately get a picture of Jorge Cafrune on his horse.'

'Is that wrong too?'

'Of course it is. Verani, sometimes I don't know what to make of you.'

'It couldn't have been Cafrune, anyway. He hadn't been born yet.'

'Even if he had been, Verani, that's not the folklore I'm talking about. Do you really think that by playing your country zamba tunes you can reach the top at the Vienna Opera?'

'I wasn't the one who mentioned folklore. It was you.'

'Yes, it was me, Verani, and I'll say it again. You can't imagine to what extent Mahler's exquisite music draws on themes and even forms from popular music. That's why I mentioned folklore.'

'But when I say folklore, you tell me that's not what you meant.'

'I say that because you get carried away and lose sight of the fact that we're talking about a great musician, an avant-garde composer. You get it all jumbled up and start to think that a Mahler symphony is just the same as any old tune, played any old how.'

'You were the one who mentioned folklore.'

'I was trying to help you understand, Verani, but you won't.'

'I'm not going to deny I may not understand what you're talking about. But you have to admit you're not explaining it very well.'

◆

Verani did not read the page devoted to the fight very closely. I remember, because I was watching him all the time and it caught my attention. He was never comfortable reading anyway. He muttered the words as he struggled with them, and followed the lines of writing with his finger or a grimy fingernail. Anyone reading with him would always finish long before he did, and then have to wait or pretend he was still reading so as not to hurt Verani's feelings.

Even so, it only took him a couple of minutes to get through the account of the fight. I remember because I saw him. He can only have taken the most cursory of notes: that our man should have won, but that the other one did. Either that was enough for him or he got bored, or decided to leave a more thorough examination to another day. I saw him turn the page and get absorbed in other articles.

A little further on, he came to a halt. This time I saw his chin trembling as if he was at prayer: he was reading something. Curious, I tried to spy what the article was about. All I could see was that it was a short piece on the crime page. I was sure he read it all; I even think he took some notes. At that moment, I had no idea what the story was. I didn't want or didn't dare to ask him: I thought I was bound to find out all about it a while later on in the Touring Club Hotel.

It didn't happen though, at least not that day. That day, Verani didn't say a word about it, and in the days that followed there was nothing to suggest he would become so talkative about something he seemed to want to forget. Once again, I didn't want, or didn't pluck up the courage, to ask him. Ledesma too was more than usually preoccupied with his own affairs that evening. He was nervous and slightly upset because it was around then that he had to start looking after his daughter Raquel.

◆

As soon as he hits the floor, the count begins: from one to ten. In a clear, strong voice so that even in his groggy state the fallen boxer can hear that his defeat is being counted out. So that everyone by the ringside can hear. And for those in more distant seats, or up on the terraces, he swings his arm to and fro as though trying to teach the possibly already beaten man.

It's better when they fall full length, on their back or headlong, amid a shower of blood, sweat and snot. It's better when they fall full length, when they are stretched out on the canvas, because that makes it easier to establish the exact moment (and, after all, it is only a question of moments) to begin the count.

Sometimes, however, they hit the canvas less cleanly, they fall in less of a heap. Instead of toppling over, they sit down, their legs splayed out from under their crumpled body, until their backside touches the canvas. That's a knockdown too, and therefore Mr Gallagher has to begin counting. Or they may collapse to one side, completely senseless, and yet stop themselves falling by reaching out a glove: they touch the canvas and so prevent themselves falling. As far as the count goes, though, this is still a knockdown, because it is defined as touching the floor with anything that isn't the sole of their boots, the flat part of their feet. The boxers do it to stop themselves falling, and yet he, Mr Gallagher, has to see it as a knockdown. And start to count.

As soon as he hits the canvas, the count has to begin: that's what Mr Gallagher tells himself, Mr Jack 'Slowest' Gallagher, when he sees the champion falling. Both he and the challenger can get knocked down lots of times and get back up again; the fight goes on until one of them doesn't get up again, or doesn't get up quickly enough.

The non-expert will say that it's easy to tell when a man, boxer or not, is on his feet and when he has fallen. Of course, put like that, seen like that, it is easy; but when what's important is the instant the man and the canvas come into contact, the exact moment when the two finally meet, then it's necessary to be very precise.

All this means Mr Gallagher has to be supremely attentive at all times, to concentrate as hard as he can. Now, for example, the champion is falling. He's falling just like the other man fell, more often than him. As soon as he hits the canvas, the count has to begin. The moment he hits the canvas.

TWO

AS WITH ALMOST EVERY CITY, the airport is on the outskirts. But as is the case in every small or not-too-large city, it's also quite close. Even though it's on the outskirts, it's very close, because, in all small or not-too-large cities, the outskirts are close. Travelling by car, it's no more than a quarter of an hour away. Anyone with more time or patience can take the bus for Puerto Madryn which passes close by, but if you choose to do this, as well as time and patience, you need to be prepared to walk, because the bus does no more than pull up at the roadside, and from there to the airport building you have to walk seven or eight hundred metres, if not a thousand.

I don't have much patience, and I don't want to walk into a head wind, even though I'm not pressed for time. So I stop in at the Touring Club and get them to call a taxi for me. The driver is Abel. He talks at me, because he always does, because we all talk, and the topic is one that will dominate Trelew today and also, although gradually less and less, in the days to come ('Like everyone, he had his good side and his bad side, but he lived his life. The important thing is that he passed away at peace'). I agree and say nothing, or something in passing which is pretty much the same as saying nothing ('Who are we to judge others?'). Every so often, Abel looks in the rear-view mirror ('Is his daughter coming?') and sees me in the inverted rectangle ('Yes. On this flight'). Then we arrive.

This is the new airport, where nothing happens. The old airport, where things did happen, where everything once happened, has been abandoned. All that's left of it are a few scattered ruins, dry weeds and the bare rocks of the surrounding desert. This panorama only serves to increase the sense that nothing is going on at the new airport. You can have a coffee by the big window on the upper floor and this view, so flat it seems to go on forever, reinforces the idea that time is standing still. There aren't even any planes on the runway, because there's only one aircraft that comes and goes. The one that in a few minutes is going to take me to Buenos Aires is the same one that must now be approaching Trelew. It's probably over Viedma or on its way to the Valdés Peninsula, and the fact that there are no other planes but this one makes the empty runway look even flatter and more desolate.

As I'm having my second cup of coffee, the question missing with the first is finally asked ('Tell me, Roque, is it true that Ledesma died?'). The coffee they serve at the airport is too strong, and I forgot to ask for a bit of milk in it ('Yes, it was yesterday afternoon. There must have been something about it in today's newspaper'), though I could ask for some this time ('You're right. The truth is, I didn't look'). I don't though ('I didn't look either, but there must be something').

The waiter's holding the tray tucked under his arm, a sign

he's settling in for a long chat ('And you must be in a hurry to get to the capital. To miss the funeral, I mean'). I neither encourage nor discourage him ('To tell you the truth, I would never have gone while Ledesma was alive') but at that moment a guy from Buenos Aires comes in, sits down and calls the waiter over ('Tell me, Roque: Ledesma, before he died, I mean, did he make it up with Verani?'), then the man raises a finger and calls out again ('Not as far as I know') and the conversation is interrupted.

If it wasn't for the wind, which occasionally twists and lifts the tips of the longest blades of rough grass, you might think that the view through the window was a photo, one of those gigantic murals that some bars display, not realising they look so cheap, rather than part of the reality outside, that empty nothingness, as though nobody had died, as though I wasn't leaving.

It's nine in the morning.

◆

'Did you know Jack Dempsey is the foreign boxer who appeared most often on the cover of *El Gráfico*?'

'No, I didn't.'

'Well, that's what I read the other day. Eighteen times. Jack Dempsey.'

'You don't say.'

'I'm talking about foreign boxers, mind. If you're talking about Justo Suárez, Eduardo Lausse or Pascualito Pérez, that's a different matter.'

'Or "Tiger" Gatica.'

'"Little Monkey" Gatica, you mean. Yes, they're all Argentine boxers though. I'm talking about foreign ones. Among foreign boxers – and that means, above all, American fighters – the one who was on the cover most often is Jack Dempsey. Eighteen times.'

'I didn't know that.'

'And there were plenty of them, Verani, I can tell you. You might have thought it would have been Joe Louis, Rocky Marciano, Jack La Motta, or even Cassius Clay in more recent times. But no, it was Jack Dempsey.'

'Jack Dempsey.'

'Yes, Jack Dempsey. Eighteen times. And just think what *El Gráfico* was in those years.'

'I can imagine.'

'That's what I read the other day. I saw it and thought of you. I said to myself: I'm sure that'll interest Verani.'

'Yes, of course it does.'

'That's why I'm telling you. I would never have imagined it.'

'Nor me.'

'See how wrong you can be?'

'That's true.'

'To tell you the truth, I would have said it would be Joe Louis. But no: it was Jack Dempsey. Jack Dempsey! I saw it and thought of you.'

'You don't say.'

'It's true though.'

'I would never have thought you liked boxing.'

'I don't. Probably at some other time I wouldn't have noticed, but not now. I saw it and said to myself: I have to tell Verani.'

'Yes, but you say you were reading about boxing.'

'I was reading, yes. I can't even remember what exactly, would you believe? But you read a bit of everything, don't you? A bit of everything.'

'But this time you were reading about boxing, so I figured you must like it.'

'As I say, Verani, one reads a bit of everything. But I wouldn't really say I liked it.'

'You don't like boxing?'

'No, I really don't. To be honest, I think it's disgusting, a disgrace. Putting two men in a ring together so they can beat each other to a pulp! I can't imagine anything more horrible.'

'But lots of people enjoy it.'

'Well, Verani, if it comes to that, the masses enjoy many things. I don't understand how you can ban cockfights out of concern for animals, and yet allow boxing, which, in the end, is exactly the same thing but with human beings. Just think, Verani, it's disgusting, two men punching each other until one of them collapses senseless. It's ghastly, barbaric.'

'No, what I was talking about was the fact that you were reading about it.'

'One reads a bit of everything, Verani. Or don't you know the meaning of a "broad culture"?'

'I thought you liked it.'

'Well, the truth is, I don't. I don't like it at all: I think it's a disgrace. But, for example, I read a lot about the wars in Europe, yet that doesn't mean I like war.'

'No, not war, of course. War really is disgusting.'

'War, Verani, is the most inhuman part of the human condition.'

'Yes, war is really disgusting.'

◆

The victim was found in a fourth-floor room at the City Hotel in

Buenos Aires, the same room he had been staying in until then. What might have been in that room? Easy to imagine: two single beds, made up or very tidy; a table and chair, a wardrobe, a heater and a small armchair by the window. What could be seen from that window? The domes of the most imposing buildings along Avenida de Mayo; further off, an even more imposing dome, that of the National Congress, visible because the buildings that would later come to block the view do not as yet exist; and the historic City Hall, which can still be seen in its entirety by anyone determined enough to open the window and lean out to the right a little way.

In the centre of the room, a fairly plain iron light fitting with three lampshades and three bulbs. The fitting was attached firmly to the ceiling, firmly enough to support a man's belt, plus the dead weight of that man hanging from the belt. That was how they found him, hanging from the belt, strangled by a slip knot in the slippery leather that required no more than a bit of effort, his face scarlet from the pressure, from the effort, the lack of air, the onset of death.

The chair was neither close to nor far away from the spot where the body was hanging. This was by no means a mere detail, because the man must have used the chair first to stand on and then to hang himself from. A very simple chair, of the commonest kind, not far away enough or detached enough to be able to say for sure that somebody else must have been involved in the arrangement of the furniture, but not near enough either, not on its side or directly beneath the body, to be able to say for sure that the victim was the only person involved.

Clothes: outdoor suit. In other words, the victim had just arrived, or was about to go out, and if in fact there had been someone with him, that person was not necessarily someone he knew well. As was the fashion in those days, he wore the knot of his short tie tight around his neck, and this might have lessened the pressure from the belt and helped avoid or at least postpone the moment of death; but when, as apparently happened, that pressure was increased, it must have helped advance it.

Verani came back to the archive twice that same afternoon. The others had all made notes and chosen their stories, and each of them was more or less enthusiastically getting on with their article. Verani was the only one who came back for more, but he wasn't reading about his piece, which didn't seem to interest him: he was more concerned with this story he had found outside the sports section, which had nothing to do with his article.

◆

One day, although not as yet, there will be such a thing as (although there isn't as yet) the protection count. As yet there are only two alternatives facing Mr Jack 'Slowest' Gallagher: to count until the moment the fallen boxer gets up again, or, if he does not get up, to count to ten and, by reaching that number, put an end to the count, the fight, everything. The length of time the fallen boxer takes to get up after that is of no importance to the fight, and therefore to its referee, although the matter might continue to interest him out of a sense of compassion. It's no longer important for the fight: the other man, the one who knocked his opponent down, will be either waving his arms triumphantly in the air or draping them around his seconds' shoulders: the seconds will be either crestfallen or triumphant, the doctor will come bustling into the ring.

One day there will be what doesn't yet exist: the protection count. Although he has no clear idea about this kind of measure,

Mr Gallagher calculates, or perhaps only guesses, that there might be the need for some tempering of cruelty in the sport's regulations. In the end, that's what progress is all about, in this as in so many other areas: a greater consideration for the dignity of human beings.

When it exists, this is what the protection count will consist of: first of all, imagine a boxer being knocked down. He falls the way they all fall: groggy, shaken, out of it, nothing more than an object. As soon as he hits the canvas, the count begins: one, two, three. Then imagine, for the sake of our example, that although when he was knocked down he seemed to be out of it forever, all of a sudden he recovers, like a sleeping person waking up with a start. He gets up quickly, before the count has gone beyond four or five. He looks conscious, completely conscious, and perhaps exaggerates his state of readiness in order to impress the judges and his opponent, trying to prove in all kinds of ways (laughing, winking, shrugging his shoulders, slapping his gloves together) that he's perfectly able to resume the fight. It doesn't matter how sincere the smiles or the glove-slapping may be, the referee has to continue the count to eight. He can't go on to ten, because that would mean the end of the bout, but nor does he leave it at the four or five seconds it took the boxer to get to his feet again. He has to go on to eight so that he can help the fallen boxer clear his head before returning to being punched or punching again, suffering or meting out punishment.

For the moment, however, that is not how things stand. Humanitarian progress, though inexorable, takes its time and cannot be anticipated. Mr Gallagher has to follow different rules tonight and in the subsequent nights when he is officiating: he has to count the time a boxer is on the floor, and stop counting as soon as the man gets up again. God protect the fallen boxer, and if there is no God, nobody will protect him (but Mr Gallagher doesn't believe there isn't a god).

Something else which doesn't yet exist is what will be called the neutral corner. Mr Gallagher also has an intuition about that: he can vaguely sense that there is something unnecessarily cruel about boxing in his own day, something that ought to be mitigated or completely eliminated. So what happens at this period, or to be more precise, tonight? The boxer still standing, jubilant at having knocked his opponent down and feeling he now has more of a chance of winning than losing, strains to get at the fallen man. Sometimes the referee even has to push him away so that he can get close and start to count. The boxer on his feet looks particularly erect, he stands tall, supremely strong. He is threatening, seeing his chance to put an end to things. As soon as the other boxer gets to his feet, if he manages to, he will repeat the flurry of blows to his face. He won't hit the man on the canvas because, apart from being expressly forbidden by the rules of boxing, it's one of the most shameful signs of cowardice. He will hit him though, as hard as he can, as soon as the other man gets to his feet, trying to knock him senseless again as soon as possible.

When the neutral corner, which does not yet exist, becomes part of boxing, things will be different: there will be no raised fist just waiting for the fallen opponent to get back to his feet. The standing fighter (even though it's against his instincts) will have to retire to the corner opposite the one where his opponent has fallen, or the corner furthest from the part of the ring where he fell, as knockdowns don't always happen in corners. He will have to wait there for the other man to get back to his feet, keeping his desire to attack in check. When he does, the attacker can punch him again, if he so wishes, until he knocks him down again, if he is capable of it; but he won't be able to indulge in the vicious cruelty of someone who rather than starting the fight anew goes in for the kill.

All these doubts, which, within reason, occasionally keep Mr Gallagher awake at night are, without a doubt, the main problem: for the boxing authorities, they are the main event, just as in boxing one particular fight becomes the main event. However, as of now, as has been amply demonstrated, they belong to the future, to a time yet to come. They are not something to be taken into account tonight, in this part of the events of the night of 14 September 1923. What Mr Gallagher has to decide now is the exact moment when the champion, who has already been knocked down, actually touches the canvas with his body, or, as is sometimes said, with all his humanity.

◆

I can remember Verani reading persistently, and if I remember it it's because it was not something you would expect of him. It was so odd it caught my attention then, and that's why I still remember it after all these years.

The article was very short, either because it was a precis of an original article published somewhere else, or because not much was known so there was not much to write. In any case, Verani took far too long to read it through, too long even for him, who found it so hard to read. From that I deduced he was reading the information over and over again.

He came, left, came back again. I'd never seen him in the

archive so often. He still didn't make any comment, and had said nothing in the Touring Club. He took more notes. I asked him in passing how he was getting on with the article about 1923, and he said he hadn't started it yet.

The crime story was so short his insistence made no sense. There was hardly anything to it: a dead body in a hotel room, nothing more. Scarcely anything to justify the passion Verani was dedicating to it. But he persisted, writing things down, rejecting them, obviously questioning himself.

After that he handed me back the copy of that day's edition. I concluded he must have finished delving into such shallow waters. But I was wrong: a little while later he was back, asking for copies from the following days. He wanted to know what had happened next. I gave him seven or eight editions, which he took away and soon brought back. He asked for another ten, for the days after that, skimmed through them, brought them back; and so on, until he had looked at all the newspapers up to two months after the day the discovery of the body was first reported.

There was no further mention of it: not a single one. As anybody would, Verani was expecting the story of the case to continue with details of how the investigation was progressing. And if, as so often happened, there was no progress in the investigation, then there ought to have been more reports about the mystery or enigma of the death. There was nothing like this in the crime section on any of the following days: neither that the case had been solved nor that it hadn't been solved – which might have been even more interesting for the newspaper readers. There was nothing more, nothing at all, no reference, no clarification, no rectification. The story of the dead man seemed to have vanished, disappeared into thin air, as might have happened (although it didn't) to the dead man's body. To judge by the coverage or lack of it in the paper, something more than silence must have led to the complete disappearance of this isolated incident.

This lack of clues only increased Verani's interest, even though he had no idea what to do next.

◆

'Think about it, Verani, just imagine that hail of blows on the head of some kid, from a poor family, no doubt, from the provinces, who, even before he took all that punishment, was not exactly a bright spark. Because boxers aren't exactly brilliant, are they?'

'They're all sorts.'

'Boxers are dim though, you can't deny that, can you, Verani? They can't be very bright if they become boxers. Then, on top of that, just think about all the blows they receive on their heads, punch after punch after punch.'

'The bloodthirsty boxer only aims for the head. The more intelligent ones go for the body.'

'I don't care about all that technical stuff, Verani. To me, they're two dimwits beating each other to a pulp. If, on the way, they get a ruptured kidney or broken ribs that changes nothing. What I want you to do is to imagine what happens to their brain with each of those blows, with all the ones they get in a fight, then all the fights in their life. Each one of them scrambles the brain, upsets it, it bleeds, it cuts out. It's revolting.'

'No one can touch Locche.'

'Who?'

'Locche.'

'What about him?'

'You don't know who he is? Nobody can touch him, Ledesma. No one can hit him.'

'Don't give me that, Verani, I'm trying to be serious here. I'm going to the heart of the matter, to the philosophy of the sport. But you give me an example, the example of one particular boxer, whom I'd like to see in a few years' time anyway. Don't let's get sidetracked with individual stories.'

'It's not a story. I can tell you stories about him if you want. Before the fight with Fuji – the fight for the title, I mean – they got Locche to lie down on the bed in the dressing room. This was ten minutes before the fight: they wanted him to relax. But Locche was so relaxed he fell fast asleep there and then. Ten minutes before the fight for the world championship! And Locche was so relaxed he fell asleep.'

'What are you trying to say?'

'I'm telling you a story, Ledesma, so you can see what a story about boxing is. The other thing I mentioned isn't a story, it's something else: the fact is, no one can touch Locche. Don't you know what they call him?'

'Yes, I do. And I also know what a story is. I don't need you to explain it to me.'

'A boxing story, I meant.'

'About boxing or anything else. Don't rile me, Verani. A story is a story, you don't need to explain it. I know what a story is. I also know that you think you can undermine a whole argument just by giving me one example. That's where you're wrong, Verani. Don't even think this is the exception that proves the rule. I'm trying to get you to look at the fundamentals, to make you think, and all you do is tell me a story about Locche. What can I say? Sometimes I wonder why we waste our breath with all this conversation.'

'Roque's interested.'

'Roque, yes. Roque's interested. Roque's a good lad.'

◆

Every good fighter, and that's what Dempsey is, fights clear-sighted, with his eyes wide open. He knows that if his sight is clouded in any way, he's going to lose. He has to spot every attack as quickly as possible, every ruse – the real and the pretend punches – and has to be able to see when his opponent offers a chink in his defences – a chink he can only take advantage of if he's seen it in time. But when he receives a blow, at the exact moment when the fist hits him, this rule no longer applies. If he wants to avoid the blow, which he does, he has to see it coming, but once it's arrived, as in this case it most certainly has, there's no point watching it. Better to shut your eyes, which is what a fighter will do, just as anyone else would, fighter or not, if he was punched in the face. This means that as a rule a falling boxer will have his eyes shut or, if they're open, his sight will be clouded, because it's a question of instinct and reflexes to shut them, it's not a matter of choosing or deciding, will power doesn't come into it. And there's not much point opening them again if you're still stunned by the blow, because precisely as a result of that blow, even if you open them, you won't see much. Jack Dempsey is well aware of these rules and of all the others in boxing, because if he wasn't it would be hard to win fights and become world champion, which is what he has achieved. So it's the fist of the other man, whose name he has completely forgotten but whose nickname is The Bull, which is the last thing Dempsey sees. He sees it coming very fast from the left-hand side, straight for his face, and although he manages to see it and to think he ought to block it with his own fist, he doesn't succeed in doing so – which just goes to show that the hand is not always quicker than the eye. Dempsey sees the fist coming, then sees a shadow, and then nothing. After that he sees, or rather imagines he sees, himself falling. At this precise moment he must have his eyes shut, his eyelids sunken and the pupils rolled back in his head. That's why he can see himself, imagine himself falling – because to do that you have to have your eyes shut. Despite this, Dempsey quickly recovers (his capacity for recovery is extraordinary, and never more so than tonight). He's toppling over, and yet his eyes are already open again. He's falling, and he knows it. Therefore, when he opens his eyes he doesn't expect to see, as he would if he was upright, his rival's face, or his raised gloves. He might, as he falls, get a last glimpse of the other man's sweaty chest, or his midriff covered by the raised belt of his shorts, or, in the worst case, glimpse his knees flexed to launch another attack. But when he opens his eyes again Jack Dempsey sees none of this. He sees something else, something he wasn't expecting. The other man (what was his name?) is nowhere to be seen, although he has to be there somewhere, doesn't he? What Dempsey sees is something else entirely: it's a rope, or rather canvas wrapped around a rope. Until a second earlier, he had been thinking of that, of a rope. He was expecting it across his back. Now Dempsey sees it in front of his face (not the one at the height of his back, the next one up). He opens his eyes and sees it: wet, quivering. He sees it go past him. Sees it go past his battered face, in a flash. It's not the rope moving, of course, it's him falling. Dempsey understands all this. But if he sees the rope going past him, in front of his face, he ought to see it rising from his chin to his mouth and then level with his eyes, until he finally loses sight of it somewhere between his forehead and his hairline. But now the opposite is happening: the rope goes from his forehead to his eyes, then is level with his mouth, and he loses sight of it down below his chin. Something strange, really very strange, is happening in his fall.

◆

'Do you know what Dempsey said to Jack "Doc" Kearns?'

'No.'

'But you know who Kearns was.'

'No.'

'Jack "Doc" Kearns was Dempsey's manager. In fact, he was in his corner on the night of 14 September 1923. You can imagine why they called him Doc.'

'No.'

'Come on, Verani, think about it. They called him Doc because he was a doctor.'

'Yes, of course.'

'That's also why he was in Dempsey's corner.'

'Yes.'

'And do you know what Dempsey said to him?'

'No.'

'It was in the break between the first and second round. That was the only break there would be, because, as you know, the fight finished in the second round, but they had no way of knowing that. It was the break. Firpo had been knocked down seven times in the first round. Seven times, no less!'

'Now, after three knockdowns, it's a K.O.'

'Yes, now it is, but we have to look at this historically. We're in 1923, fifty years ago. Firpo has been knocked down seven times in the first round. Seven. Dempsey only once. Of course, you could say that his once was more than equal to the other seven.'

'You don't say.'

'So much so that at the bell Dempsey went over to his corner, sat on his stool and asked Jack "Doc" Kearns: "What round did he knock me out in?"'

'What d'you mean "what round"? There was only one.'

'That's right, Verani, but don't you see? Dempsey was completely befuddled. That was what I wanted to talk to you about. Just think for a minute what the state of his brain must have been like, and he was a young, healthy man. Just imagine what must have been happening to his battered neurons, the blood clots preventing him thinking straight. At that moment Dempsey didn't have the slightest idea what was happening to him.'

'He asked what round it was, and there'd only been one.'

'That's right, Verani! We're talking about someone who is completely confused, because on top of the confusion about the rounds, there's something even more important, terrible even: the thing is, Dempsey thought he had lost. He could stay on his feet until the end of the round, but when he reached his corner, just imagine what state that poor lad's brain must have been in for him to think he had lost by knockout.'

'But he hadn't lost.'

'Of course he hadn't lost. That's what a furious, red-faced Jack "Doc" Kearns tells him as he douses him with a sponge of freezing water to bring him around. He tells him he hasn't lost. Not just that, but that he's winning the fight. Whenever Jack "Doc" Kearns got angry, his face puffed up and turned bright red. That was how he looked when he told Dempsey he was winning. But he warned him to keep his guard up or the other man would knock his head off.'

'All that in English.'

'In English: yes, of course. But just look at how damaged a person can be because of the punches he's taken. Just think, Verani, how bad Dempsey must have felt, how groggy that man must have been to have imagined he had lost the fight by a knockout. Don't you think that's terrible?'

◆

You have to think twice before you take each photo. Because although the technological advances, in cameras with rolls of film, for example, offer new and better possibilities, these are not boundless. Taking photos can be wonderful, and no one knows this better than Donald Mitchell, because Donald Mitchell has sacrificed everything, or nearly everything, to buy a camera and start a career as a photographer. If he had his way, every feint, every attack, every blocked or successful punch, every clash of gloves or shoulders, every explosion of sweat or water from a head jerked back by a blow, would be worth trying to capture in a still image. But you cannot and should not abuse the means at your disposal, or time itself, which is just as finite as they are. Every spent flashbulb leads to lengthy preparations to make the camera ready for the next shot. Sometimes, by the time you've finished, the smell of magnesium in the air has already vanished. Each round lasts three minutes, and they are still in the first one. There's a minute separating each round from the previous or next one. The Argentine challenger has already been on the canvas seven times. Donald Mitchell thinks he has a good shot of at least two of these knockdowns, although he can't be sure until he's developed the negative, thanks to the dark chemical arts. For now, everything is between the eye, his finger and the camera's optical memory; or between all this, which is his skill, and hope. Once, unfortunately, one of the referee Gallagher's legs got in the way. A second time, a sudden movement by the challenger left the shot out of focus, possibly even out of the frame. A third time, for no apparent reason, it was the flash that failed. Even so, thanks to his persistence, two or three of the images might be all right. They all capture the numerous knockdowns the challenger suffered during that first round. One of them (would to God it came out) shows, or ought to show, one of the Argentine's gloves resting on the boot of the champion standing above him. It's only a tiny detail, nobody in the entire stadium can have seen it in the fury of the fight or the excitement of seeing that one of the boxers was on the canvas. It may only be a detail, but that makes the photo. In outside reality, this is only a detail, because a lot more is going on, and that glove on that boot went unnoticed. They will notice it in the photo, however, because in the photo the glove and boot are not details; in the photo they are everything. If that knockdown had been the end of the fight, it could have been the defining image of defeat and victory, but things didn't turn out that way, because, on that occasion, as on the other six, the challenger recovered and went on fighting. Now the one who's falling is the champion, Jack Dempsey. It's always more exciting when the person knocked down is the champion. And from a journalistic point of view the defeat of a champion is always more newsworthy than a victory, as if victory was something to be expected, and defeat, only defeat, could really be news. Besides, when a champion wins things stay as they were: nothing has changed and, therefore, in some sense, nothing has happened. When a champion loses, on the other hand, a new champion is crowned, so that there are at least two lives which will not be the same as they were before. Now it's Dempsey who's falling. He may or may not get up again, but for the moment he's falling. The knockdown is a fact, and that fact is news. What happens with Donald Mitchell is odd: on the one hand, before he takes a photo he has to think twice. This precaution comes from the need to reflect, to contain his impulse. On the other, the possibility Donald Mitchell has of taking a good photo is due entirely to his intuition, to his instantaneous reaction, to the speed-of-light reaction of eye and finger. It's a split second that does not allow for any doubts or thought. Now, for example, as Dempsey falls, he has to take a photo of that fact without any hesitation. There's a religious gleam in Donald Mitchell's eyes. His finger is poised on the button.

◆

Ledesma seemed preoccupied at that time. He had been on edge ever since his daughter had come back to live with him after not seeing her for almost eight years. It wasn't that this made him unhappy, quite the opposite, but as well as being pleased about it he was also touchy and nervous.

His wife had not yet died in far-off Buenos Aires, but she was in her final illness. I had heard the story whispered about her and Ledesma: nobody in Trelew had escaped hearing it at least once. I had found it hard to believe, because it didn't fit with his unflappable, reserved image. Now that I was seeing him in a much more irritable state though, sometimes even rude, it seemed more plausible that he could have once completely lost control and tried to shoot his wife.

His daughter, little Raquel, appeared among the tables in the Touring Club. Sometimes she went behind the bar, where she could talk to the waiters, or she would wander along to the hotel hairdressers, where every so often a traveller would ask for a trim or someone from Trelew would have a shave. Verani meanwhile finally told us the story of the crime (murder or suicide) at the City Hotel. What was most striking, he insisted, was the way the news had disappeared from the papers after that first mention.

In other circumstances, Ledesma would have let him talk without encouraging or discouraging him, or would have stared out of the window at the throng of people shouting slogans in the street outside. In other circumstances, Ledesma would have preferred to remain aloof. But in those days he grew irritated easily, and snapped at everything. He barely let Verani finish before he demolished every one of his conjectures, and ended by asking abruptly if he didn't realise the story must have been invented to fill space in the newspaper, which explained why there was nothing more about it in the days that followed.

Without a word, Verani poured more sugar into his milky coffee and stirred it.

Ledesma raised his head and looked around for his daughter. He still couldn't get used to having to take care of her.

THREE

'**HOW CAN I PUT IT?** His *First Symphony* comes out of silence. That's how Mahler's *First Symphony* starts, the first movement of the *First Symphony*, in other words, the beginning of his entire symphonic production. It comes out of silence. Of course, you'll say: "That's how all symphonies begin." What else could there be before, a second before the start, just before the first sound, if not silence? You'll say to me: "That happens with all symphonies" (including, I could add, the start of Beethoven's *First Symphony*, which has the unexpected, miraculous sound of a finale). That's what you'll say, and apparently you're right. Apparently. Because what I'm saying is not that Mahler's *First Symphony* starts after silence. No, it comes out of silence. Do you follow me, Verani? It's not that it cuts into silence, like any sound might do, but it rises out of it. It begins with a very slight, very gentle sound, which little by little becomes audible. His *Ninth Symphony* ends in exactly the same way – and that was the last one he completed. (You might say: "So that he wouldn't outdo

Beethoven, who wrote nine too" (I also like to think Mahler was superstitious in that way too)). The last movement of Mahler's *Ninth Symphony* (don't be surprised, Verani, but it's an adagio) ends with the strings playing. The sound dies away, dies away, dies away, until it merges back into silence, until it becomes silence. That's the end point of Mahler's symphonic production. And it starts in precisely the same way, except in reverse: the sound doesn't dissolve into nothingness, it rises out of it. That's how Mahler's *First Symphony* begins: believe me, you'd really like it if you heard it. It starts in this state of suspension, Verani: I don't know if I'm making sense to you, it's not easy to put into words, you have to listen to it. It starts in this state of suspension (which is also the way his *Ninth* ends), then comes the gentle introduction of the strings in A, followed by the woodwinds playing a simple fourth: the chords A and E. I don't know if that means anything to you, Verani, but it's important. Don't forget this is the starting point for all the drastic ruptures of atonalism. It's where they come from, but they're not really present as yet (least of all in his *First Symphony*). Then the first theme appears: a hunting call in the distance, which curiously Mahler scores not for the trumpets or horns, but for the clarinets: two clarinets. Put like that it might seem a bit confused, but you should see how precise it all sounds when you listen. If you pay close attention you can hear it: it sounds like the call of a cuckoo. Then the main theme of this first movement comes in: it's a theme drawn directly from one of the songs Mahler composed. It's an example of what I was telling you about, Verani, as plain as the nose on your face: the tune from one of his songs is transferred almost wholesale to the *First Symphony*. You'll say, or could say: "But what hunting are you talking about. Ledesma? What cuckoo?

Music doesn't represent anything!" And you would be right. Absolutely right. Except that it was Mahler himself (it has to be said) who allowed this kind of ambiguity to arise, at least in his earliest compositions. He himself wrote on this first movement "like a sound from nature". Does that mean then that the composer started from ideas outside music, and therefore was writing programme music? Or should we, in spite of everything, stick to our convictions that music is an absolute, that in the end it is pure form, pure form and nothing more? If you say to me, as you did say, or were on the point of saying, that you couldn't care less about the cuckoo, and that a symphony doesn't represent anything at all, that's because you've made your mind up about it. So have I, Verani, and I can sense that we agree.'

◆

I'm falling, thinks Jack Dempsey. He doesn't think, as he might do soon, a short while later, or as the Argentinian might think, I'm falling and I'm going to get up again. Not for now. For now, it's all about falling. He isn't thinking about getting back up in time. I am falling, he thinks. He thinks of it in this way, with the idea of duration, with the feeling of how long it is taking. Anyone who's been knocked out knows that a fall like that is instantaneous. Since the person falling is usually unconscious, or nearly so, because, if he wasn't, he wouldn't be falling, what he feels is a sudden collapse, which takes no time at all: first there's everything, then nothing, the world isn't there anymore, in a split second all there is is the canvas, the count, the grogginess and the imminent throw of the towel. It all happens at once. When the man being knocked out opens his eyes, if he does, and renews his links with the outside world, he discovers the referee busily counting: one, two, three. When he comes round it may be that he's further on in the count: he could be up to six or seven. That's how the fallen boxer knows that time has kept on going, that what he thought was no more than a second was in fact several seconds. That's how the person being knocked out knows that a period of time has gone by, without him realising it, that it has passed him by, that time was compressed into an instant and lost its duration. But on this occasion, things are different for Jack Dempsey. The difference can be seen in his reaction, however limited, to what is happening to him. It's enough that he's thinking I'm falling, rather than I fell, because there are some kinds of events that can only be understood once they've happened. But Dempsey thinks, I am falling. He thinks this while the stadium starts to erupt with astonishment and it seems as though some people are clambering into the ring. Dempsey senses the passage of time: it's an instinct a boxer carries inside him, because he knows what it means to knock someone down or to be knocked down. This passage of time is part of his body's instincts. It's the falling body that senses how long this fall is, and his body is telling Dempsey: this is longer than usual. He does not succeed in asking himself why this fall is taking so long. The answer, if he had succeeded in asking himself that question, is as simple as it is disturbing. It has to do with an elementary rule about the equation between time and space which, despite being a rule and despite being elementary, might give an unexpected result on this occasion: this fall is taking longer because it is a longer fall.

◆

Of course Verani had invented stories in his time, and more

than once, just like any journalist. The day the cheque from Salustiano Ltd (the sports emporium) bounced, for example, and the newspaper had to pull their advert, Verani found himself adding ten lines to his report on the match between Independiente of Comodoro Rivadavia and Gaiman FC. He wrote a lengthy description of a dribble by 'Pistol' Rigante that probably never happened. But he felt, one could almost say instinctively, that this case was different. It was one thing to add a dribble to reality, or a missed penalty, but it was a much more serious affair to add a dead man and a mystery.

Verani didn't think the story of the crime (murder or suicide) in the City Hotel could be merely a journalist's invention, as Ledesma had claimed (at the time, he also put it down to Ledesma's being on edge). The dead man in the hotel had to be true. The rest might have been a fabrication, including the fact that there was no more news about it in the subsequent editions of the paper. But a body hanging from a belt in a hotel bedroom was too concrete a detail, too real, not to be true. That was how Verani saw it.

The time allotted to write the stories for the fiftieth anniversary of the newspaper was rapidly vanishing. By now there was only a fortnight left. This is quite a while, especially for a journalist, but, as with reading, Verani found it hard to write. That afternoon for the first time he suggested to me what later became an open request: that I write the article on the Firpo–Dempsey fight for him. He explained that he was completely preoccupied by the story of the dead man in the hotel.

I didn't say yes or no, but I wanted to lend him a hand with the story of the murder or suicide that seemed so important to him. I gave him the number of someone I knew, Valentinis, who worked in the archive of a Buenos Aires newspaper. That seemed to me the easiest way to find out whether the article in question had been invented or not by the crime reporter on our newspaper. I was well aware of what Ledesma could say against this – that the story could just as easily have been invented by the journalist in Buenos Aires and simply copied by the local man, because Buenos Aires' newspapers weren't above that kind of trick either (although he was born in the capital, Ledesma had quickly adopted the provincial habit of hating everything to do with Buenos Aires).

Valentinis devoted a lot of time to the matter, which had obviously interested him too. After receiving our call, he rang back later that same afternoon. The story had been published in his Buenos Aires newspaper. It appeared in a side column of the crime page on 16 September 1923 (a day before it appeared in the Trelew paper, confirming the hypothesis that this was simply a shortened and adapted version of the original). The article reported an event which had happened two days earlier, on the 14th. This first article was not very long, because there wasn't much information: the dead man, the belt, the hotel room.

On the following days, although only sporadically and briefly, there were further references to the case in the Buenos Aires paper. They all said the same thing, however: that nothing was known. Not a thing (the Trelew journalist had obviously decided there was no point repeating this news about a complete lack of news, and had abandoned the story). Not once or twice, but three times, reference was made to this same unchanging lack of information. But how often can you write about nothing before it becomes pointless? As the days went by, and lacking any useful leads, the police gave up their investigation, the journalists gave up writing about it, and the affair slid into oblivion.

◆

Donald Mitchell has absorbed the photographer's way of viewing the world: he looks at it and sees a photograph. But his imagination goes beyond that: it's cinematic too. Now he is looking at the champion Jack Dempsey's back. It's the back of the heavyweight champion of the world: it rises from the waistband of his shorts in layers of firm muscle, knotted toughness that shows no hint of softness. You know that wherever you touch, it will be solid. In the centre, of course, you would touch the spine and its hard bone, as you would along the curve of every rib. But if you felt beyond them it would be almost as hard, thanks to the perfectly toned muscle, which seems as solid as bone to the touch. It's a massive, worked-on back. Mitchell is staring straight at it. He can appreciate it as an anatomical treasure. Given the chance, he would probably feel the same about a Rodin sculpture, where he could admire every fibre and nerve. But now his cinematic imagination supplements his photographer's eye. This is the back of a falling man. He sees it for what it is, but he can also anticipate what is going to happen next. There is the massive back: everything is back. But as Dempsey goes on falling as he is now, behind his toppling back the other half of the scene will become visible, the half that gives meaning to the whole: the challenger's fierce, arrogant stance after he has hit and knocked the champion down. Mitchell knows he has to wait until both figures are visible: the possible victor and the possible vanquished, for the lens to capture the complete event (victory and defeat). He has to wait for this absolute back to continue on down before the other balancing figure appears. That is the moment for him to press the button. Donald Mitchell waits, but something happens. He looks and looks, but to his astonishment what he sees is more and more back. He looks as hard as he can, but all he sees is back.

◆

'If I said "*agitato*", Verani, what would that mean to you? What does it suggest? In all likelihood, nothing. You'd sit staring at me without saying a word, just like you're doing now. And yet, my friend, if you'd agree to learn something, to relax listening with a drink, a few olives, some cheese, you'd learn how this magnificent music really sounds, you'd understand it all as clear as day. I'd stake my life on it. That's how the second movement of Mahler's *First Symphony* begins, Verani: *agitato*. And it starts by quoting from another song – a *lied* from 1880, on a subject you must know: Hansel and Gretel. Oh, come on, Verani, don't tell me you don't know that, where have you been all your life? What bedtime stories were you read as a child? Anyone who has heard that terrible tale of those two children and the witch's oven has to remember it their whole life. And Gustav Mahler, who was always fascinated both by the world of childhood and that of popular music, composed a song on the subject. After that there's a trio, Verani, you'd really like it: a trio in F major, a slow waltz that ends in D major, which exquisitely quotes from sentimental popular music. But hold your horses, Verani: I said he "quotes" it: he uses two trumpets as a wonderful counterpoint to the sumptuous main theme. If you can be a bit patient, Verani, and I hope that you can, you'll be very impressed with the third movement. It's – how shall I put it? – it's a funeral march in

D minor. I don't know if you follow me. If you heard it you'd understand, I promise you. It's a funeral march in D minor. It's hard to describe in the abstract like this. But at home, over a glass of wine... and if need be, we could compare it to the funeral march in Beethoven's *Third*. I'm guessing that of the two you'd prefer Gustav Mahler. Do you know why? Because here too you'd recognise some of the popular tunes Mahler always turned to. For this part – you won't believe it! – Mahler based the theme on a popular round, *Frère Jacques*, in its German version. In southern Germany it's a children's song about a hunter's funeral where all the animals of the wood come to pay their respects: the deer, hares... it's so delightful! I know, I know, you're going to tell me again that music doesn't represent anything. You've already said that, or were just about to, and I completely agreed with you. If you like, you can forget all about the deer and the hares, I'll go along with that, no problem, let's just enjoy the music as the pure interplay of forms. Or is there a better way to describe the echoes here of popular melodies? You should hear how joyful it makes the symphony, even though it starts from a funeral march. Aha! You don't agree? I can see you're raising your eyebrows. Or is that because of the noise out on the street? You won't really be able to appreciate how abrupt a contrast can be until you've heard Gustav Mahler's music. It's a funeral march, and yet it's joyful. And don't tell me that's how life is, because I can assure you that's not the case. In the space of two bars in Mahler's music you go from one state of mind to another. In life that can take days, weeks, sometimes even years. But in this symphony you're listening to a funeral march and suddenly everything has become joyous. Yes, it's a slightly suspect joy, I'll grant you that. A joy we could attribute to the characteristics of popular music, or of popular culture in general, if you prefer. But if we wish we could also see the lilting air of the music in this passage as the slightly ironic, or even entirely ironic, way in which Mahler quotes and incorporates these elements from popular music. Please, Verani, don't ask me to give my verdict on such a delicate matter. What we need to do is sit down and listen to the symphony, then we can all reach our own conclusions. Roque here has already said he's up for it.'

◆

Seated at a nearby table was Arregui, the editor in charge of our crime page. He hardly ever came to the Touring Club Bar, but he was there that day. I can remember what he was drinking: Gancia with no ice. He was on his own.

Verani took advantage of the few moments Ledesma was absent, taking Raquelita to his sister's. He excused himself, said he'd be right back and went over to the table where Arregui was sitting. I could hear snatches of their conversation: I didn't hear everything Verani was saying, but I can clearly remember what I did hear.

Arregui was busy with a wooden toothpick, trying to get rid of something stuck between his teeth since lunch. He carried on at this while he answered Verani's questions. He asked him if he knew who wrote the crime section back in 1923. None of the articles were signed. Arregui said he hadn't the faintest idea: there could have been more than one person, or nobody at all. There weren't many staff on the paper in those days, so it was most likely that everyone turned their hand to everything. To have one person responsible for each section was a sign of progress that probably didn't exist back in those days.

This seemed to convince Verani to give up his already rather vague notion of trying to find, after all these years, the person who had followed or tried to follow the case. Even if that person were still alive, he would doubtless have forgotten all about it. Instead, he tried to persuade Arregui to use the episode for the article he was going to write for the anniversary issue. Although it was far from being a famous case, the very fact that it had been so quickly forgotten at the time might prove interesting.

At a certain point they were talking over each other: I think Arregui prevented Verani from finishing his proposal. As he saw it, things were very clear: a case that nobody had paid any attention to fifty years earlier could not possibly attract his now. Besides, he had already chosen his article. It was a crime that had caused such a big splash when it happened that it had been all over the front pages. It had taken place in Rosario, which Arregui called Argentina's Chicago, and it contained all the most vital elements: violence, lowlife, some macabre details, the secrets of the night, mafia wrangling. And instead of the appearance of just one dead body, there had been five. Five appearances, Arregui explained, though not five bodies. There had been only one dead body. It hadn't appeared five times either, but it had appeared in five different locations, in five wooden boxes in five different places in the Port of Rosario. The torso in one spot, and then each of the limbs separately: first an arm, then the other one, a leg, then the other leg. All of them hacked off by what was apparently a blunt saw. A macabre detail: the head never appeared. At the autopsy, the forensic experts ruled that the victim had still been alive during the dismemberment. The police detectives discovered the victim's fingerprints had been obliterated with acid, and they had no face or teeth to help them establish a credible identity. By pursuing other clues, however, they successfully resolved the case. They had never believed Sentinelli when he assured them that Sentinelli-Waisser and Co. had been dissolved after Waisser had said he was giving up the liquor business to go and lead a quieter life somewhere in the interior of the province. Like everyone else, they were aware it was common for Waisser's accounts to repeatedly show inaccuracies that were hardly coincidental. They also suspected, like almost everyone else, that Sentinelli was perfectly capable of violent reactions. The fact that the wooden crates where the pieces of body appeared were identical, or very nearly, to the ones used by Sentinelli-Waisser and Co. to unload the often irregular shipments they made of fermented eggnog or mandarin juice was, in the police's view, the final, irrefutable proof as to who was guilty of the crime. The judge, however, and subsequently the appeals court, ruled that this did not prove anything, that there wasn't even any proof that Waisser was dead (although he was never found again) and that therefore there were no grounds on which to convict Sentinelli.

That's the kind of story our public is interested in, said Arregui. Sentinelli went on living a comfortable existence in Rosario, until one evening at the end of the forties his latest-model Chevrolet veered off a road in the north of Argentina and ended up head-first in the waters of the River Paraná.

Verani came back to the table where I was waiting for him. He didn't say another word until Ledesma returned.

◆

'I suggest you don't wait, as you might reasonably expect to do, for a silence between the third and fourth movements: the silence which in concert halls is usually filled with coughing or even applause from the untutored members of the audience. Don't wait for it in this instance, because there isn't one. The fourth movement follows on from the third without a gap, as if they were one and the same thing. There is a noticeable difference, however, which I could point out to you as you're not exactly an expert on this kind of thing. This fourth movement, which, as you quite rightly suspect, is the final one, stands out from the previous three both because of its length and because of its apparent formal complexity. It begins in F minor. At that stage of his career (we're in 1888, remember) Mahler could not conceive of the possibility of finishing a symphony in a different key to the one in which he had started it. Not that he was abandoning the idea of evolving tonality, which brought him such spectacular results, but he still hadn't taken the leap of applying it to the complete structure of an entire symphony. The time wasn't yet ripe, Verani. So for the moment he starts the fourth movement in F minor, and it's marvellous to hear just how he manages to return to the D major and the optimistic world of the first movement (Mahler said that the D major chord here should sound as if it had fallen from the heavens, or from another world. Explain to me if you can, Verani, how you're not dying of curiosity to come back to my place to hear the records). In the final part of the symphony we hear phrases and repetitions of many other themes, especially from the very beginning. Up to here you could say that the symphony was moving forward. But at this point, Mahler feels the need to call a halt and look back. I don't know if I'm giving a clear image of this, I think I am. It's the perfect example of a recapitulation. He moves forward, progresses, develops things. But before the finale, at the start of the last section, there's a moment of retrospection that reviews all the ground covered. It is only then that Mahler can embark upon the apotheosis that is the climax of the symphony. If you wanted to be really nitpicky (which I hope you don't) you might say that there is a slight echo of late romanticism about this finale. Naturally, I'm referring to the idea of "triumph after a struggle" which Mahler skilfully avoided in each of the first three movements, but which surfaces here in the fourth. But we're not going to fight over that, are we, Verani? Don't forget, we're talking about the first ever symphony that Mahler composed, when he was nothing more than a lad of twenty-eight. And anyway, it could be argued that these traces of musical romanticism aren't necessarily a fault. No, please, don't tell me what you think until you've actually heard the symphony. Mahler can sweep away all preconceived ideas, although he might have a hard time with you if you won't even sit and listen to him. I can't deny that the fourth movement is long, and that life is short. But I can assure you that you won't feel you've wasted your time. When the symphony was first performed in 1889, some of his contemporaries said it was tedious. But it almost goes without saying that our contemporaries never understand, especially when what they hear is so innovative. There are countless examples of this: Mahler himself was frequently a victim. All too often they didn't understand what he was trying to do, or misunderstood, or closed their ears to the best examples of his formal breaks with the past. Of course, that was his contemporaries. Now we're in 1973, Verani, and things have changed: it's more than eighty years since the symphony was first played in Budapest, and fifty since it was first heard at the Teatro Colón in Buenos Aires.'

◆

How to explain it? The rule is simple: a boxer has been knocked down when he touches the floor with a part of his body other than his feet. That's why Mr Gallagher bends his left knee slightly to get a better view of Jack Dempsey's downward trajectory and the part of the floor that he is likely to come into contact with. But it's also obvious that if Dempsey has been knocked down, he's fallen much further than is normally the case, and yet Mr Gallagher has not yet seen any part of his body touch the floor. The strange thing is that his feet (his boxer's boots) are not touching it either. Mr Gallagher is confused; he doesn't know what to do next.

This is because what has happened is extraordinary, it's unbelievable, impossible. Jack Dempsey has not only been knocked down, he's been knocked out of the ring. The other fighter literally propelled him out of the rectangle where everything happens or should happen. Without a doubt, this event will become part of boxing history. Even at this moment, Mr Jack 'Slowest' Gallagher is well aware of this. It is so unusual, so unique, it will not only become part of that history, but will be talked about until the end of time. Above all because this is a fight for a world title, held in no less a stadium than the Polo Grounds of New York. It's not some undercard bout in an unknown gym, one of those fights where two wretched no-hopers climb into the ring and lay about each other wildly and mercilessly. Not only is it a world championship fight, it's for the heavyweight title. If it was between two flyweights or two featherweights, you might expect to see one of them fly through the air – that's why they're given such names. But to see this happen when two heavyweights are fighting is improbable, almost impossible. And yet it is happening.

That's why Mr Gallagher already knows this moment will go down in history forever. Mr Gallagher can calibrate this macro-view of time, measured in years and decades, quite easily. But the micro-view, the one right in front of him now (and perhaps for that very reason) completely escapes him.

◆

Even as a little girl they called her Quelita. As far as I know, nobody ever called her Raquel. Quelita, and sometimes to poke fun at her, Quela, which is what she was called when she grew up. Her mother had taken her away from Trelew when she was little more than three. I didn't remember her from those days: I hadn't yet started working at the newspaper, and only knew Ledesma by sight, like you know everybody. I didn't remember her at all; in fact, I may never have met her if, as they say, she was hardly ever let out of the house. Verani remembered her. Of course he did. Verani played with her before she could even speak properly. She would run around him, and he would lift her up, pretend to let her fall, then catch her at the last second.

Then what Ledesma's friends always referred to as the 'argument' happened. Even the calmest people sometimes lose their temper, and when that happens, it tends to be even more explosive than with people who are always doing so. Apparently, Ledesma kept a secret notebook about his wife's earlier life; the mere existence of such a thing was terrifying, and suggested that something wasn't quite right in Ledesma's head. Nobody ever read any of these notes (and some say that in fact they never really existed) about the years and events that had happened before the two of them met. So when someone went and told Ledesma things about those years, what could you expect? Gossip like that abounds in small towns: it's up to each and every individual whether they believe them or not. Ledesma believed them.

He never talked about it. Perhaps with someone he was closer to; with his sister, probably, when the two of them were on their own together. But normally Ledesma never mentioned it. Once an indiscreet person apparently made an allusion to it in his presence, but Ledesma didn't react in any way, as if the man was talking about someone else. He was winding up his Seiko watch and making sure it was telling the right time. He leaned towards the window (it goes without saying they were in the bar of the Touring Club) to check with the clock on the Banco Nación Tower. All he said was: these things happen. He said it in a low voice, not really wanting to be heard.

Now, eight years later, Quelita was doing her school homework on one of the bar tables where she could spread out her things. Every afternoon her father ordered her a hot chocolate with biscuits, not realising that the coldest days of winter had already passed. With the excuse that the chocolate had not completely dissolved yet, Quelita let it grow cold.

On this particular day, Verani came bustling in excitedly. He had just been on the phone and had news from Buenos Aires. Valentinis had unearthed something. The dead man at the City Hotel had been a foreigner. That was his news. Verani saw this as significant, not with regard to the death itself, which was the same for a foreigner as for an Argentinian, but with regard to the way the case had dropped out of the news afterwards. I also thought it made more sense that the death of a foreigner, of a man who dies in a place that doesn't belong to him, could slide into oblivion much more easily. Someone who dies in the midst of all his own things, his own people, is surrounded by traces of himself which can only continue after his death. But a person who dies somewhere else, as a foreigner, has already been detached from his own world and his death is also detached in the same way.

A foreigner is someone who's isolated. That's what I said. A foreigner is someone who's isolated. If he dies, he dies a foreigner, and that's an isolated incident too. The news of this death can also be isolated. Verani agreed, Ledesma didn't.

Verani and Ledesma had known each other more than ten years, yet still addressed each other formally.

The desert makes the sky look bigger. Mountains don't; the sea doesn't. Mountains make it look higher, and cut it in two; the sea competes with it. The desert – a desert like this one, which doesn't have any sand or grass, this nothingness I'm looking at because I always do and because I've nothing else to do, makes the sky look even bigger. To make this worse (or perhaps better), there isn't a single cloud in the heavens today. Nothing but sky, from here to eternity, with an aeroplane somewhere.

You'd think that with such a sweeping view you would see the plane in the distance. But that doesn't happen. In such a huge expanse of sky, the tiny detail of a plane in flight is even more easily lost. You look and don't see a thing. Even if you know, as I do, that the plane is coming from one direction and not another, because it's coming from Buenos Aires and not from Ushuaia or Comodoro Rivadavia, and so make sure that's where you're looking, even then you won't see it in the distance.

It's ten o'clock in the morning.

The arrival is announced for seventeen minutes past ten. It may sound like boasting to give such a precise time, but the fact is that this kind of flight, which has no stopovers and therefore is less likely to run into any kind of trouble, is not usually late. Sometimes they even arrive early, if, for example, the skies are clear or there's a tailwind. And sometimes they arrive on time, at the exact minute announced, which almost seems the fulfilment of a prophecy.

At last the plane comes into view. It doesn't look very far away ('Your attention, please'): it gives the impression of having appeared all of a sudden rather than having been approaching all the time. In fact, when I eventually spot it, the plane is quite close, as if it had somehow managed to avoid being seen in the distance. For a long while it wasn't there, for all that time it was absent, and then all at once there it is ('Your attention, please').

As it comes in to land, it seems to be floating rather than flying. It's hard to admit it is no longer travelling at a high speed, because that is not how it seems ('Aerolineas Argentinas announces the arrival of its Flight 1814 from the city of Buenos Aires'). It seems to be suspended in mid-air, almost at a standstill. Yet it is approaching. If you stare at the sunlight glinting on the grey wings for a few moments, you can tell it's getting closer ('The passengers will disembark through Gate No. 6').

You hear the noise of the engines later still, when you can already see the writing and the blue-and-white stripes on the side of the aircraft. It's then you understand it was this silence which increased the sense that the plane was floating. Now that you can hear the roar of the jet engine, the plane's movement and speed are obvious. A puff of white smoke as the wheels hit the ground shows it has landed.

After that there's a lengthy trundling towards the terminal, a final blast from the engines, a turn off the runway, and finally the plane comes to a halt. It's right in front of the window I'm looking out of, quite close by. Soon there's a YPF fuel truck next to it, a tractor with a cage for the luggage, and two white sets of steps being wheeled out towards the aircraft exits.

Slowly, cautiously, as if they have just woken up from too little sleep, the passengers start to leave the plane. The metal steps are swaying slightly in the wind, and their structure is precarious, so they need to be carefully negotiated: everyone looks down at the step they are putting their foot on. At the bottom, they have to walk about fifty metres across the tarmac from the plane to the terminal building. I watch the line snaking towards us.

I fix my attention on a woman with long blonde hair, because I sense she has dark eyes and that if she were to smile (which she doesn't), wrinkles would appear at the temples. I think I know her name, I know who she is. She comes towards the building carrying a blue bag. But then I spot another woman, who's coming down the front steps, and realise I was mistaken about the first one. It's not easy trying to work out how a girl of eleven might have grown into a twenty-eight-year-old woman. You have to concentrate on the things that don't change.

She's walking, head down (that's understandable, she's here for a funeral after all), and although she has on only a thin overcoat, she doesn't show any sign she's cold or that the wind upsets her. She doesn't know who I am. There's no reason she should recognise or even remember me. I could tell her my name, and it would mean nothing to her. I could tell her who I am, what job I do, and it would still mean nothing to her.

I, on the other hand, know she is called Raquel Ledesma, also known as Quela, and that she was born in Trelew, province of Chubut, in 1962 – in the same month that Frondizi was kicked out of office; that when she was three, that is in 1965, something very serious happened between her father and mother, so serious in fact that her mother decided to move away to Buenos Aires, taking her daughter with her; that eight years later, in other words in 1973, her mother died of cancer, and that when it was diagnosed she decided her daughter should, despite everything, return to her father so that he could look after her. She came back to Trelew at the age of eleven, after eight years of not having seen her father, while in the capital her mother was in the final stages of her illness. The intention was for her to come back to live here forever, making her life in this town (which in those days was prospering), but something else happened, which must have been as serious as the earlier incident, because, after only a few weeks, what was meant to be a definitive return was cut short. Her father sent her back to Buenos Aires to live with her grandparents on her mother's side, a move which had the added advantage of helping them get over the death of their daughter. In the years that followed, father and daughter saw each other only occasionally, with him always travelling to Buenos Aires, whereas she never came to Trelew, or rather to Gaiman, where her father had moved. Time went by until it became the present, this bright morning or yesterday afternoon, because it was yesterday afternoon that her father Ledesma died, also of cancer, although his last days were worse because he was that much older.

She has come for the funeral that is taking place now, or rather in an hour's time, in Trelew's old cemetery, a funeral which doubtless Verani and all the others, friends and acquaintances, will attend, people from past and present, everyone, that is, except me, who is going to leave, who is leaving at this very moment.

Raquel Ledesma passes very close to the window. I pay and stand up ('Your attention, please. Aerolineas Argentinas announces the departure of its Flight 1816 for Aeroparque Jorge Newbery in the city of Buenos Aires'). The last thing I want to do is bump into her.

FOUR

LEDESMA WAS CONVINCED VERANI WAS so slow and I was so wet behind the ears that both of us were wrong. To him, the fact that the dead man was a foreigner didn't seem important. Thinking about it, what else would you expect from someone staying at a Buenos Aires hotel? It wasn't very likely that it would be someone from the city itself. It was far more likely to be either a traveller from the provinces or a foreigner. Those are the people you find in a city centre hotel: people who are not from that city. Obviously he wasn't talking about small family hotels in outlying neighbourhoods, or boarding houses, the kind of places where the desperate or the destitute seek shelter. Ledesma gestured a lot as he spoke; after all, we were in a hotel too, or rather the cafeteria in a hotel, the oldest and most traditional in Trelew.

In 1923 as now, the Buenos Aires City Hotel stood right in the centre, only a block away from Plaza de Mayo, the city hall, the cathedral and the presidential palace. The ideal place for a tourist. For a provincial, it had a further attraction: the proximity of the brand new underground railway. It was the first in Latin America, and reached Plaza Miserere. For the provincial as well as any foreigner, there were also the tombs of the two most famous national heroes: one on the side of the square, alongside the nave of the main church; the other at the opposite end, in the entrance to another, open-air church.

Ledesma insisted there was nothing odd about all this, and he was right. It was all very predictable. What he couldn't or wouldn't admit, however, was that it was this very predictability which could give rise to the unpredictable. A foreigner in a central hotel was entirely to be expected. But that made it all the more intriguing to speculate how someone could go from this normality to a sudden death, whether by his own or someone else's hand. How could something so unremarkable turn into a decision to take a belt and tie it to the light fitting and bring about somebody else's or your own death?

Ledesma shrugged.

He didn't look outside.

◆

With your legs high in the air, the world looks different. For a boxer, the legs are the launch pad, the balancing point. They are what define his stance and his style. Naturally, heavyweights are slower, but that doesn't mean their legs aren't the fulcrum for all their efforts. Those who know next to nothing about boxing think it's all in the hands: a punch here, a punch there – simply hands and face. Those who know more look at the feet, the legs, the way they move and dance, the angle of foot and heel, the way the two feet are never parallel, or the legs completely straight at the knee. Those in the know realise it's the legs that are the fulcrum, the springboard for all boxers. And now Dempsey's legs are in the air. It's literally the world turned upside down, because he has literally been turned head over heels. He's literally been turned upside down. At first he finds this hard to comprehend, as always happens when metaphors become reality: they are too crude, too obvious. At first, Dempsey cannot understand how his feet can be higher than his head: he reacts by kicking his feet and boots frantically in a cycling motion. He's trying to find the floor. He should touch it with his feet if he's been knocked down, or with his back, if he's been really flattened. But neither has happened. As a child, he used to take the down pillow he loved to bury his head in, plump it up carefully, and lay it beneath his feet. His mother said it would help his circulation. Twenty years, a whole lifetime – his whole lifetime – has gone by since then. In a flash of memory, for a split second he recalls that feeling from his childhood, when his feet were higher than his head. He also does something similar in the gym, to help make abdominal exercises tougher. But on those occasions, as he lies on a bench with his feet in the air, he is helped by Jack 'Doc' Kearns. His trainer holds his feet so that he can push up with his body. Is it the Doc he is seaching for with this brief, frantic, kicking motion? It looks somewhat similar to his efforts in the gym, except that he's not lying down on anything and there's no one holding his feet. The lights are full in his face. The powerful floodlights of the Polo Grounds are still streaming down on the ring, but now they're right in his eyes as well. He sees them and is dazzled. He's blinded, so he screws up his eyes. He does this only because the lights are blinding him, and yet it looks as though he is in pain.

◆

Outside, down below, everything looks the same: one long monotonous glare. Shortly after take-off there were lots of different things that caught my attention: first the curve of the bay at Madryn, which looked as forlorn as all ports do. Then the Valdés Peninsula, so clearly defined that anybody looking at it could recognise the shape from the map and almost believe that maps and reality can be the same thing. But soon, partly because the plane had gained height, and partly because it was further out to sea, everything became this same indistinct mass, sometimes sky-blue in colour, sometimes white.

The stopover at Trelew was so short (getting the passengers off, the new ones on, filling the plane with fuel, then taking off again) that the inside of the plane was given only a rapid clean. Passengers always need to feel they are the first to sit in their seat, to use the table, or to turn on the air above their head. A passenger wants to feel nobody was ever sitting where he is before him. But there are too many signs on my seat of the person who flew here from Buenos Aires to Trelew. As I travel I can sense the presence of someone here just before me. I imagine it was Ledesma's daughter and that I am in the seat she travelled in. I touch everything (the window blind, the light button, the lid on what was once an ashtray, the buckle on the safety belt) and think to myself that she touched them only a few minutes earlier. I remember seeing her walk wearily to the terminal. I remember her sixteen years ago, doing her homework at a small table in the Touring Hotel bar, or whiling away the hours in the hotel hairdresser's on one side of the dark corridor leading to the bathrooms.

It's eleven in the morning.

By now they'll have dug out the spadefuls of rough earth. By now Ledesma's burial must have started. The two lanky youths who always look so serious and are perhaps a bit simple-minded, and who routinely carry out what is after all the routine task of digging and filling in again, must by now be sweating a little. They look absent-minded (possibly also because they aren't that bright) which seems entirely appropriate to the kind of work they do. However cold the weather is, they never wear anything more than threadbare pullovers. In summer they wipe their brows with a cloth which is always grimy with dirt.

Once they have cleared away the soil, the two of them stand back. That's what they must be doing right now. Then comes one of the most painful moments: they pick up the ropes to lower the coffin into the grave, making sure they coordinate their efforts so it doesn't tilt or sway. There will be the sound of stifled sobs. Then the two youths will remove the by-now unnecessary ropes, with a wrenching movement that must seem violent. Now the dead man is in the ground, as he should be. It is the start of a lengthy process that only time can complete, a process by which the idea that it's really Ledesma who is in there, down in the ground, gradually comes to seem unreal. The first handfuls of earth drop onto the coffin. Thrown by the family, the loved ones. They hit the lid with a harsh thud. If they still think it's Ledesma in there, they must really feel abandoned. I hope that isn't what Quela is feeling. Hopefully Quela, who is taking a handkerchief out of her bag to wipe the tears from her eyes, has already understood that what is down there was once Ledesma but is no longer him.

As if they have suddenly come back to life, or realised where they are, the two youths set to work again. For a few minutes they had been left out of the picture, forgotten and forgetting why they were there. Now they step forward again, spades in hand, ready to undo what they did only a short while before, to cover up the hole, return the earth to the earth. Whereas before there was only a trickle of earth from people's hands, now it falls in rapid, rhythmic spadefuls, giving the impression that things are speeding up. Some or all of those present will be thinking it's better that way. Get the whole thing over and done with. Bring an end to the brief ceremony, the procession, the farewell, faces buried in hands, 'ashes to ashes, dust to dust'. Now all that remains is to cover up the hole, fill it in, flatten the earth without making it seem the grave is being trodden on, conceal the fact that the earth has been freshly dug, conceal the fact that there is earth left over, that there is more now than there was before, because before Ledesma wasn't down there and now he is.

The believers among them are crossing themselves and murmuring their prayers. For them, Ledesma is already on his way to heaven. I'm really in the heavens, and I realise this has to be false. Completely false. I'm in the heavens, and I can tell them there's nothing here. Ledesma died. He's being buried. They must have finished burying him by now. His daughter Raquel must be taking it all in, standing next to her aunt or her cousins in the centre of the scene. Verani (who I know was present) will have been discreet and stayed to one side, taking advantage of his sadness not to have to look up.

◆

'Do you know what they called Firpo?'

'Of course I do, Ledesma, what do you take me for? They called him "The Bull".'

69

'Not just "The Bull".'

'Yes they did, they called him "The Bull" because he was as big and strong as a bull, and because he charged like one.'

'Yes, I'm not denying they called him "The Bull", but that, or rather "Little Bull", was also Justo Suárez's nickname.'

'Yes, "Little Bull". The "Little Bull of Mataderos".'

'That's right, Verani, "The Little Bull of Mataderos". I can see you've read the Julio Cortázar story.'

'Who hasn't heard of Justo Suárez? "The Little Bull of Mataderos". What a time that was, eh, Ledesma?'

'Yes.'

'Those were the days all right. Justo Suárez: "The Little Bull of Mataderos".'

'That's what I'm getting at, Verani. That's what I mean about Firpo, Luis Angel Firpo. They called him something more than "The Bull" because "The Bull" or "The Little Bull" could also mean that other boxer, who was called "little" because he was in another category. Firpo was head and shoulders above him. There's a photo in *El Gráfico* of the two of them together, Firpo and Suárez, they're shaking hands. Remind me to show it to you some day.'

'That's some scoop, isn't it? Those two together – it would be like having Bonavena and Monzón in the same photo nowadays.'

'Yes, but you have to add the weight of history to the other meeting, Verani. The weight of history. The 1920s, Verani: do you remember the hopes there were for Argentina in those days? President Alvear had his siesta while the country grew around him.'

'Those were the days.'

'But nowadays, just look what a mess we're in. Sometimes it gives me a headache simply thinking about it.'

'They used to call Firpo "The Wild Bull".'

'"The Wild Bull", that's right. What a nickname, eh?'

'Just hearing it makes you go weak at the knees.'

'You're right there.'

'Incredible!'

'But don't forget that's what they would call Jack La Motta as well.'

'"Wild Bull".'

'Yes, "Wild Bull".'

'Just like Firpo.'

'No, not quite. Not quite the same as Firpo. That's what I'm trying to tell you. Because Firpo wasn't just "The Bull" or "The Wild Bull"; no, they called him "The Wild Bull of the Pampas".'

'I knew that! What do you take me for, Ledesma? "The Wild Bull of the Pampas". Just hearing that makes you tremble with fear.'

'"The Little Bull of Mataderos" was something else again. You've read the story by Cortázar, so you know what I mean. Imagine, from Mataderos, where all the slaughterhouses are! Just think of all that death, those animals being slaughtered.'

'The sad thing is neither of them got to be world champion. Monzón did though. And I'm convinced Bonavena is going to get there too.'

'God willing. Come back to my place one day and I'll show you the photo. The two of them are there: Firpo and Justo Suárez.'

'"The Bull" and "Little Bull".'

'Just think of it! Firpo was much bigger, and a lot older too.

That's why they called the other boxer "little". Still, when you hear "The Little Bull of Mataderos" that's scary too, isn't it?'

'Who wouldn't go weak hearing a name like that?'

'OK, but it's worse being called "The Wild Bull of the Pampas". First because there's no "little". Then because of that "wild". And finally because they use the word "pampas", Verani, which was the same as calling him "barbaric".'

'The Pampas are very Argentinian.'

'You're telling me! The word conjures it all up: Echeverría's "Slaughterhouse", the Unitarians and the Federalists in the nineteenth century, Sarmiento's "Facundo". It implies all that.'

'So what patriot thought up a name like that for him?'

'You think he was a patriot?'

'Of course. "The Wild Bull of the Pampas"!'

'Why do you think it must have been a patriot?'

'Think about it, Ledesma! "The Wild Bull of the Pampas"! The Pampas! There's more patriotism there than in the national flag.'

'D'you think so?'

'Of course! More than in the national coat-of-arms.'

'Perhaps, but don't forget that in boxing these things are mainly used to promote fights. It's all about selling things. It's a business, isn't it?'

'And isn't selling records a business too?'

'What I'm trying to point out is that nicknames like that were invented for purely advertising purposes.'

'But this one's dripping with patriotism: "The Wild Bull of the Pampas". I wonder who first thought of it?'

'D'you really want to know? It was Damon Runyon.'

'Who?'

'Damon Runyon.'

'Say it more slowly.'

'Damon Runyon.'

'A Yank?'

'That's it.'

'A Yank?'

'A young journalist from the *New York Tribune*. A friend of Dempsey's, by the way.'

'You're pulling my leg, Ledesma. You say these things just to get me riled.'

'Don't say that, Verani, you know how fond I am of you. If you don't believe me on this, come around to my place and I'll show you the copy of *El Gráfico* where it's all explained. And you'll also be able to see the photo where Firpo and Suárez are shaking hands.'

'It was a Yank who came up with "The Wild Bull of the Pampas?"'

'Yes, Damon Runyon. A young journalist from the *New York Tribune*.'

'I don't believe it.'

'What d'you expect? A gaucho? Every Argentine gaucho knows that the bulls on our Pampas are as gentle as lambs.'

'So it was a Yank who gave him the name.'

'Yes, a Yank. A Yank who obviously mixed up our Pampas bulls with buffalo from the Wild West of California.'

◆

There were three versions of what had happened. In Trelew, all three were told with the same degree of certainty or uncertainty. The first was that Ledesma had never intended to shoot: all he had done when he heard or suspected his wife was visiting the house in the Malvinas neighbourhood was raise the revolver and point it at her. This threat had been enough for her to leave for Buenos Aires with the girl, who must have been three years old at the time, with the intention of never coming back.

According to the second version, Ledesma had meant to shoot her, and had pulled the trigger, but that for some reason or other – rust, chance or some other cause – the gun had failed to go off. For her, though, it was as if it had done, or perhaps even worse: as there had been no shot, the matter had not really been resolved, and that was what she could not bear. That, and her desire to protect Quelita, was what had led her to leave Trelew.

The third version of the story was that there had been a shot, and that she had been hit in the shoulder. If the bullet had gone a little further to one side, it could have ruined her face; a little lower, and it could have destroyed a breast. But either because he was such a bad or a good shot, Ledesma hit her in the shoulder. She decided not to go to the police. She waited until the wound had healed and she felt better, then she moved to the capital with her daughter. Those who saw her said she had completely recovered, apart from some discomfort, especially in wet weather. They also said she either felt sorry for Ledesma or was simply too drained to press charges against him.

For years she wanted nothing to do with Ledesma: they never even spoke. Then eight years later she wrote him a letter. In a few lines she told him the bad news the doctors, in their usual cold manner, had given her. She was dying, and felt that, in spite of everything, their daughter ought to be with her father.

♦

What happens when a man who depends on looking suddenly cannot see a thing? A situation like that would leave anyone feeling lost and confused. But for a photographer it's far worse. For him it is no compensation that he can still hear clearly, that he is still balanced on his feet, that he is well aware of his body. Donald Mitchell needs to see. As long as he can see, he can control the world, but if for some reason that is denied him, he is nothing in the world. And now he cannot see a thing. He goes on looking through his camera viewfinder, which is almost like the prolongation of his eye. A natural prolongation, just as for a boxer the glove is the natural prolongation of his clenched fist raised to land a punch. For Donald Mitchell, the camera viewfinder frames the life going on beyond him; it orders everything, endows it with meaning. That was how he saw the challenger being knocked down seven times and getting up again seven times. That was how he was seeing the champion being knocked down for the first time. So many remarkable events in the space of two and a half minutes! That's life: afterwards there might be hours, years even, in which nothing at all happens. Yet tonight, in those first two and a half minutes of the fight, in what could seem either the everlasting or the fleeting length of time that the first round has taken, one amazing thing after another has happened. Donald Mitchell not only saw it all, he photographed a lot of it (as much as he could, limited only by his camera's capacity to capture still images). Now he was watching the tremendous fall of the heavyweight champion of the world, Jack Dempsey, who had lowered his left arm and dropped his guard, allowing the challenger, like a phoenix rising from the ashes, to hit him square on the chin with a tremendous right. Donald Mitchell was seeing it and was about to photograph it (far too many photographs for a single round, but how could he stop taking them when reality was being so generous with its opportunities for images?) But his finger hesitates on the button, because all at once he cannot see a thing. Not a thing: only darkness. Shadows, darkness, nothing at all except for the dark. At first, he's afraid his camera is broken. It's understandable this is what he is most afraid of: after all, to buy it he has sacrificed his family and his honour. Perhaps, he thinks, or fears, something has happened between plates and lenses. He is as afraid of that as he would be to think there was something wrong with his eyes. If the camera is broken, his career is finished, and so is his life. The same would be true if it were his eyes that were the problem, but he does not think of them. He thinks of his camera. Possibly one day the fascination with technological progress will be free of the fear of new inventions breaking down. But not yet. In those days people still felt there was something miraculous about the motor-car engine when you cranked it and it moved off, about the aeroplane which rose into the sky and disappeared into the distance, about a light machine that could capture a scene and reproduce it, or the metal needle producing a voice from a revolving disc. All of them could fail: it still seemed incredible they did not do so on every occasion. That is what Donald Mitchell feels about his camera, which has now apparently failed, because all of a sudden it no longer allows him to see reality, and only offers him a dark, unmoving expanse of black. He is about to learn that it is reality that has broken down, completely disintegrated, that it is reality which has gone dark and ceased to move. The camera Donald Mitchell is holding up is working perfectly, and so are his eyes.

◆

'Just imagine for a second if we could bring those two hulks here to Trelew.'

'Don't even think it, Ledesma. A few boxers might leave Trelew, but none come here.'

'I don't mean they would have to come here, to the Touring Club Hotel, right in front of our eyes. What I mean is if we could somehow be near them.'

'I'd get all emotional.'

'I know you would.'

'I'd have tears in my eyes.'

'I bet you would. And if we could see them up close, what would they be like? Two hulks.'

'As big as two barns.'

'Yes, as I was saying, two huge hulks. Bigger than any basketball player. Because a basketball player can be more than two metres tall, but they're like an obelisk or a giraffe. I don't deny they look impressive, they're huge too. But they look streamlined.'

'It's jumping up to the hoop that makes them so tall; it's like the giraffe's neck for reaching up to tree branches.'

'Something like that.'

'Isn't nature wonderful?'

'You're right again, Verani. Wise and wonderful. Just think of those two heavyweight boxers, the highest category.'

'That's why they call them the top weight.'

'Yes indeed, top weight. You can't get any higher. You look and what do you see: two huge hulks. All muscle and sinew. Their windpipes, Verani: as big as this. Not even you with those huge hands of yours would be able to get them round those windpipes. All muscle and sinew. And the breadth of their backs! Unbelievable! You'd have to spread your arms wide to reach around them. From behind, your arms probably wouldn't even reach their chests. Not even if you stretched them out. Just think of that! And try poking your finger into their abdomens. Go on, just try, Verani, try and you'll see. Try to push your finger into their abdomen. You've got thick fingers. D'you know what? They wouldn't go in an inch. Stick your finger in as hard as you can, Verani, I bet it won't sink in at all. That's a fact. It's like touching a wall, but one made of pure muscle.'

'A lot of hard work in the gym.'

'That must be it.'

'Hours every day with the skipping rope and punch bag.'

'Just imagine having them here: Firpo and Dempsey.'

'Don't go on about it, it breaks me up.'

'If you saw them together, both so huge and strong, you might think they were the same.'

'How do you mean, the same?'

'The same weight, I mean. Huge hulks like that, Verani, they would probably look the same to you.'

'Two huge barns.'

'That's right. But don't forget that Firpo had a big weight advantage over Dempsey.'

'Is that so?'

'Yes, it is. Keep it in mind when you come to write your article, because it's an important point. Firpo weighed in at ninety-eight kilos.'

'Ninety-eight?'

'Yes.'

'What about Dempsey?'

'Dempsey weighed eighty-seven.'

'That's some difference.'

'Yes, it's twelve kilos: count them.'

'Between two boxers it seems even more.'

'That's right. Because they were the same age. Think about it: you must have seen it in the archives. Firpo was twenty-seven. Dempsey twenty-eight.'

'Almost exactly the same age.'

'Yes, almost exactly. Both of them were born at the end of the nineteenth century. By 1923, the year of the fight, they were both at their peak.'

'What do you mean?'

'At the peak of their profession, Verani. They weren't youngsters anymore.'

'Hang on a minute. Yesterday you were saying that at twenty-eight you're only just getting started.'

'Yesterday, yesterday, Verani: that was then, this is now. We're talking about two completely different things. Don't try to compare things that can't be compared. A composer's artistic maturity is one thing. The way a sportsman's body develops between adolescence and maturity is another.'

'Twenty-seven, twenty-eight. It's a great age.'

'Roque's the one to know. He's still got that to look forward to.'

'Yes, Roque's the one.'

'So the two of them were the same age, but not the same weight. Firpo was several kilos heavier.'

'Twelve, did you say?'

'Yes, twelve. Ninety-eight compared to eighty-seven. That will have meant Firpo was slower. Dempsey was lighter on his feet.'

'But Cassius Clay was heavy, and light on his feet.'

'Agreed, Verani, but you're talking about the modern day, whereas I'm referring to history. And in history there are things that survive: for example, the fact that Firpo knocked Dempsey out of the ring. The extra weight that made Firpo slower around the ring meant his knockout punch was heavier too. Because you know far better than me what the great Frascara and the great Borocotó used to say. A boxer doesn't hit just with his hand, or with the strength of his arm. A boxer hits with the whole force of his body thrown forward. That's when the physique of someone like Firpo becomes really impressive. It must have been like being hit by a railway locomotive.'

'But of course it was the other one who won the fight.'

'The other one?'

'The fight. Dempsey was the winner.'

'Dempsey, yes. Jack Dempsey.'

'That Yank had some guts, didn't he? Being that much lighter and yet knocking a far bigger man out.'

'Yet he managed it.'

'But he didn't knock him out of the ring, like the Argentinian did.'

'No, he didn't knock him out of the ring.'

'Not out of the ring.'

'Yet he won the fight.'

'I know he did, Ledesma; what do you take me for? That's what I'm trying to tell you. He was older, although only slightly. He weighed a lot less, and he was hit with a haymaker that sent him clear out of the ring. And yet he was the one who won. That was what was so unfair, Ledesma, at least that's how I see it.'

♦

Can it be true that basically a boxing referee is a failed boxer, in the same way it's said, for example, that an art critic is a failed artist? A referee also is there on the threshold, or in the proximity, of what he once wanted to be, censuring and legislating. Some people would see the connection, as well as the rule that makes it possible.

It's true that as a young man Jack Gallagher put on the gloves. Tenaciously, he turned up day after day at a gym in Queens, and spent hours shadow-boxing against the wall, or pounding a heavy punch bag he could barely get to move. He even climbed enthusiastically into the ring to exchange wild blows with someone else as keen as him on the sport.

It would have been hard for anyone to claim he had a natural ability for boxing, but our hopes tend to feed off themselves, and pay little attention to evidence from the world outside. Besides which, in general people prefer not to discourage others, leaving it to someone else to give them the bad news. That is why Jack Gallagher's desire to become a boxer seems to have lasted for quite some time. Not only was he too skinny and lacking in skill, he had a slight limp: hardly an ideal situation for anyone wishing to carve out a future in a sport where the main aim is to hit without being hit. But he needed to kiss the canvas (as they say in the business) more than once before he realised boxing was not for him. Once he even suspected he had seen laughter (had he seen it or heard it? He had just been knocked down, so his mind wasn't entirely clear) at the ringside from those men who smoked cigars and came to visit neighbourhood gyms in search of hidden talent.

By becoming a referee he could stay in this world. He could

also develop a certain innate sense of justice which, according to his family, he had possessed since childhood. It seemed to him the closest thing to his true desire – that of being a boxer. Not the most similar, but the closest. After all, it meant he climbed into a ring and lived the fight from the inside, or very nearly.

Whenever he thought of it in these terms, he was happy. But at other times he saw it in a different light. At other times he felt that being a referee, precisely by putting him so close to what he would have loved to be, was the perfect formula for constant frustration. If he had pursued any other kind of activity – selling land, processing fish products or whatever – he might eventually have recovered from the stigma caused by the failure of his ambition. As a boxing referee he was constantly and cruelly reminded of it.

It was this which sometimes led him, while he was actually refereeing a fight, to stand there staring at the two boxers while fantasising about what might have been. He did his utmost not to neglect his specific tasks – making sure they did not headbutt each other or throw low punches, pushing them away from each other in a clinch, forcing them to stop boxing when the clang of the bell came. He was very good at his job: the sporting press was virtually unanimous about this. Yet deep down inside, without admitting it to anyone, not even his closest friends, he knew that sometimes when he thought of his life (of what his life might have been) during a fight, he lost concentration for a few seconds, was no longer there.

◆

'I know you're not someone who has travelled a lot. But perhaps for some reason or other life has taken you to Junín.'

'You're right, I'm not much of a traveller. I prefer to stay where I am.'

'You're not a man of the world, shall we say.'

'I was born here. It's not that I never want to leave Trelew – sometimes I take a break in Gaiman, or have some business to do in Rawson, or if I want to see the sea I might travel as far as Madryn or, better still, Playa Unión. But never very far: an hour's journey at most. Why go any further?'

'So you've never been to Junín.'

'Junín? Where is that exactly?'

'It's a long way off. In the west of Buenos Aires Province.'

'Oh, right, all the way up there. I hardly ever head north. But I do know people from Junín. So do you.'

'Who are you talking about?'

'Do you know Becerra?'

'Becerra? The man who runs the general store?'

'That's the one. He sells a bit of everything, and is doing well.'

'The other day he sold me a plug that didn't work.'

'That must have been a slip – he's a good lad. Anyway, he's from Junín.'

'From Junín, in Buenos Aires Province?'

'The very same. Him and all his family.'

'I never knew that.'

'See, Ledesma? You learn something new every day.'

'I mentioned Junín because that was where Luis Angel Firpo was born. I don't know if you've already taken note of his early biography. He was born in Junín in 1896. That may be the reason why they called him "The Wild Bull of the Pampas". You can't imagine what Junín must have been like in those days: still much more like a small frontier town than the modern, vibrant city it was to become.'

'What do you mean, a "frontier town"?'

'A frontier with Indian territory on the Pampas. I don't mean with Chile, do I? Before you reach Chile there are all the other provinces: La Pampa, San Luis and Mendoza.'

'That was what I was wondering about.'

'It was there, in Junín, Buenos Aires Province, in the heart of the Pampas, that Luis Angel Firpo was born.'

'Do you know who else was born in Junín?'

'No.'

'You don't know?'

'No.'

'No idea?'

'You're not talking about Becerra, the one from the general store, are you?'

'No, I already mentioned him. Do you really not know, Ledesma?'

'I've really no idea.'

'It was in Junín that Evita was born. The saint of the poor.'

'Eva Duarte?'

'Yes, Evita. The fairy godmother to Argentina's dispossessed.'

'Eva Perón?'

'What a coincidence, eh? And you didn't even know.'

'It's not that I didn't know, Verani. The fact is, you're wrong.'

'Me, wrong? How am I wrong?'

'Eva Duarte wasn't born in Junín. She was born in Los Toldos.'

'You're not going to tell me where Eva Perón was born. She was born in Junín.'

'No, sir. She wasn't born in Junín. She was born in Los Toldos. A crappy little hamlet.'

'Tomorrow, without fail, Ledesma, I'll bring you a copy of *Mundo Peronista*, where it states for a fact she was born in Junín.'

'Don't be so naive, Verani, that's what they want you to think. She used to say she was born in Junín, but it was a lie. One lie among many. She said it to try to put a decent gloss on that murky past of hers. She wanted to hide her obscure birth in Los Toldos, along with the fact that her mother wasn't married, and what her real name was – because her father never recognised her. He recognised her seven brothers and sisters, but never her.'

'Eva Perón was born in Junín, or my name's not Verani.'

'Eva Duarte was born in Los Toldos, and her name was Ibarguren and not Duarte. She was born in Los Toldos.'

'You're not going to tell me where Evita was born.'

'I'll tell you and whoever else doesn't know: she was born in Los Toldos. The other version is a fairy story. She was ashamed of her birthplace, and tried to put a gloss on it. She was born in Los Toldos.'

'In Junín, or my name's not Verani. And I won't allow you to contradict me. I'm not going to listen to you.'

'If you're such a Peronist, why don't you go out into the square and start beating a drum with the rest of them?'

'That's what I ought to be doing, instead of sitting here in this stupid café listening to all the stuff and nonsense you're coming out with.'

'Don't be so offensive, Verani, or so impolite. Just because you can't admit Eva Duarte was born in Los Toldos.'

'She was born in Junín.'

'In Los Toldos.'

'In Junín.'

'In Los Toldos.'

'She was born in Junín.'

'She was born in Los Toldos, I tell you.'

Verani must still have been smarting from their argument, because the next day he was in the Touring Club Café, absentmindedly poking at the coffee grounds in his cup of milky coffee when he saw Arregui going by outside. He jumped up, went out and intercepted him. He was in such a state he forgot what everyone in Trelew knows: that you have to push the Touring Club Café door away from you, not pull it towards you. He pulled it, and the door got stuck: that usually only happens with people who are not from here.

I know they talked to each other, because afterwards each of them gave me their account of it. Verani was trying to renew Arregui's interest in the story of the dead man at the City Hotel. He told him the new bit of information, which he was sure would fascinate him. The dead man was a foreigner. But this did not seem to excite Arregui in the slightest. Instead he went on and on about the well-worn stories surrounding deaths of this sort: the enigma of the room locked from the inside, the monkey, the skylight, the mystery of the yellow room. Verani had no idea which of the two of them had not understood: was it him or Arregui? What he was sure of was that the other man was determined not to listen to him, or to listen to him properly. He had never said it was a yellow room. Or that it had been locked, let alone locked from the inside. He had never mentioned any skylights. If he had mentioned anything like that, it had been the window – and a big window at that – which looked out onto Avenida de Mayo. That wasn't a skylight. He hadn't mentioned windows, and still less any monkey. What monkey could there have been on the loose in Buenos Aires, apart from 'The Monkey' Gatica, which was a long time later anyway? Sometimes Arregui lost the plot: that stuff about the monkey sounded absurd. Besides, the nickname for Gatica was 'The Tiger', never 'The Monkey'. That was what Prada's fans called him, because they hated him.

FIVE

HE HAS TO SAVE THE APPARATUS. He has to save his camera from the crash. Donald Mitchell can't think of anything else. In fact, he doesn't even really think it, in the sense of mentally framing a phrase or image or clear idea. It's a defence mechanism, an instinct of self-preservation. Except that this instinct, which ordinarily involves protecting his own life or physical integrity, in this case refers to rescuing the apparatus which he uses to capture images. Perhaps it would be more accurate to speak not of an instinct but of the exact opposite, a purely cultural gesture. It might even be best to say that Donald Mitchell feels obliged to repress his instinct for self-preservation in order to do what he does: to realise that a huge ninety-kilo boulder is about to topple onto him, and yet to be more concerned about his camera being damaged. After all, it could cost him severe bruising or even a broken bone or two. Dempsey falling out of the ring is like a grand piano falling from a balcony. So how does Donald Mitchell react? He stretches out his right hand to protect the camera. Although he is a beanpole, his right arm is the strongest part of his physique. And he still has his weaker left arm. He thrusts it out in front of him, pointing slightly upwards, in a gesture that a decade later would become very popular in many parts of Europe. He spreads his hand and holds it as stiffly as he can. He's trying to do the impossible: to halt the champion's fall. To hold it in mid-air, with one hand, as if he were holding up a torch or a white flag. Wouldn't that be a miracle, a real miracle, such a miracle that not even God would be able to perform it? God couldn't, and he can't. Even so, he stretches out his arm and opens his hand, stiffening them both. He may not be able to stop the fall, but perhaps he can soften it. Then Jack Dempsey's downward curve from the challenger's glove to the Polo Grounds floor will meet with some resistance. There's no need to be an expert in physics to realise that this will slow the toppling body down, and so lessen the impact with the ground. This is what the photographer has become at this precise instant: nothing more and nothing less than an obstacle. An obstacle. But for once a welcome, useful obstacle, not the unwelcome agent of some kind of difficulty. A true blessing, at least from Jack Dempsey's point of view. What is most likely to happen is that under the boxer's weight the photo-journalist will crumple and try to shield himself, but even so he will act as a spring, or a featherbed, and be of some use to Dempsey. There's no denying the fact that Dempsey is falling. He's falling, or has fallen. Tens of thousands of people can see it, hundreds of thousands more are hearing the news. Donald Mitchell is aware of it in the most extraordinary way, because he feels it in his whole body; his crushed fingers, his soaked hand, trembling arm, hunched back, his quaking knees, his sliding feet, his unseeing eye.

◆

Valentinis had been busy in Buenos Aires. To look the story up in the newspaper archive would have taken him little more than half an hour, plus the effort of hauling two or three stepladders along some damp corridor or other. But now, of his own accord, he had carried out further and necessarily more difficult research. Even in Buenos Aires the police or judicial bureaucracy must have been pretty inefficient, especially since it was fifty years since the events had occurred. There was no reason to think he would find any convincing document.

Yet Valentinis, either intrigued or with time on his hands, had succeeded in unearthing more information about the dead man in the City Hotel. The event had happened, and was recorded at the time. The hypothesis, which Ledesma believed or appeared to believe, that the newspapers had invented the whole thing, was obviously wrong. Someone had indeed died in that hotel room on the night of 14 September 1923.

A forensic expert by the name of Tapia had established that the cause of death was asphxyiation. The police experts had to discover how this had occurred, but were unable to go beyond the initial suppositions or reach any definite conclusions. The original description of it as a 'death in unclear circumstances' could not be improved upon. The search for clues in the room proved inconclusive, not because there were no fingerprints, but because there were so many: several people had been there in the hours leading up to the death. For motives that were hard, if not impossible, to discern, anybody could apparently have put an end to that life. Even the dead man himself.

Valentinis permitted himself a commentary on that expression 'death in unclear circumstances'. He was talking on the phone, and took his time. The motive for the death might be unclear, he said, but it was clear a death had occurred. There was nothing so certain as death. He too was under the impression there must have been some reason for the police to close the case so quickly. Usually, following the violent death of a foreign citizen, diplomatic representations from abroad tend to increase the pressure for a case to be solved. But in certain circumstances they can produce exactly the opposite. Someone abroad can be seen as representing their country. If there is any unpleasant aspect to their death, therefore – something that might produce an uproar or a scandal – then all the diplomatic efforts will be directed towards hushing the whole thing up as quickly as possible.

Valentinis thought this was what had happened in this particular instance.

◆

'Look, Verani; look what I've brought you.'

'What's that?'

'A magazine.'

'Don't tell me you brought *El Gráfico*.'

'No, not *El Gráfico*. I've got that at home. This is a very interesting publication, an educational publication, I'd call it, that you're probably unaware of. It's called *Music for Everyone*. D'you know it?'

'I must admit I don't.'

'I thought as much. It's a very interesting magazine, with very good illustrations. Feel it, Verani, just feel the quality of the paper.'

'What are those little drawings?'

'Those "little drawings", as you call them, are what I wanted to show you.'

'They're cute.'

'They're a little more than that, my friend. They are eighteen silhouettes made by Otto Bohler which show Gustav Mahler conducting an orchestra. As you can see, they're nothing but outlines and shaded bits, which is why I call them silhouettes. Aren't they wonderful?'

'They're striking all right.'

'In his own day everyone recognised Mahler as a great conductor. What he found more difficult for them to acknowledge was his greatness as a composer. We've already talked about that, if you remember. Here you can see him conducting.'

'Cute little drawings.'

'Did you know Mahler conducted sitting down?'

'No.'

'Yet despite that, just see how much energy and movement he put into it. Come closer and look here, Verani. Look at this silhouette: one arm arched above his head, fingers clenched, while in the other the baton is pointing upwards like a sword. Mahler's face is turned to the right. (What is he staring at? The tubas?) Now look at this one. Look, and compare them. Perhaps you'll conclude, like me, that it is the reverse image of the first one. This time Mahler is glancing to his left (and this time there's no doubt about it, he is obviously communicating with the first violin). This time it's the baton which is raised above the genius's head: it's stabbing the air. This time it's his left hand which is lower: it's barely higher than his waist, and the fingers look like an iron claw.'

'It's all very interesting, Ledesma. Everything you brought.'

'To help you put it into context, Verani, these are from his early years in Vienna. Come closer: books don't bite. Look closely at his gesture here: his left hand is in the air, but to one side; his head is down, and the baton is straight up in the air. And don't miss this one: this time the silhouette shows him from the front. You're looking straight at him, and what do you think about that? I mean, because you can't see his features, and yet you look at it and say straight off: Gustav Mahler, it's Gustav Mahler. How do you know? It's the glasses, that's how you can be so sure. Those two clear white ovals, standing out from the shaded parts of the silhouette: they're what tell you it's Gustav. Isn't that amazing?'

'It is.'

'Don't tell me you're not impressed. I can tell from your face you find all this fascinating.'

◆

He still has one alternative, however: he can identify with the loser. He has done this quite often in the past, at the moment when one of the two men fighting so near to him is knocked down. He sees him fall to the floor, bleeding, dazed, mouth twisted, glassy-eyed, and thinks: that could be me. And it's true. The natural reaction, the much easier and more tempting one, is to see himself, arms aloft, being carried shoulder high, while in the other man's corner his seconds douse him with cold water and ask him to repeat his name, his mother's name and the name of the city he was born in. It's natural to want to identify with the one kissing his glove and blowing kisses to the crowd, then letting the referee raise his arm up towards the stadium floodlights. But the fact is that two people have been fighting in the ring, and if there's a winner it's because there's a loser as well. It's very rare for the balance at the start of the fight, that perfect equality which precedes the action, to be maintained, so that when the three judges tot up their scorecards they declare the bout a draw. Far more usual is a lack of balance: one fighter prevails over the other.

But as some kind of consolation, some sort of compensation, Mr Jack 'Slowest' Gallagher (once a future boxing prospect, now a referee) usually concentrates on the man losing. He thinks: that could be me. The man trying unsuccessfully to stand up, the one whose eye is closed because of the huge swelling over it, the one with blood pouring from his eyebrow, the one suffering, the one in pain – that could be him.

Tonight, for example, at the Polo Grounds in New York, it is Dempsey who is falling. And it's an ugly fall: he's been sent sprawling out of the ring, through the ropes. On top of a flailing photographer and an unsuspecting spectator. The last thing anyone saw of him were the soles of his boots: the white rubber soles which, until a few seconds before, had been scraping across the ring. Dempsey is sent sprawling, and he probably hasn't the faintest idea what is happening. There was the flash of his rubber-soled boots, and then nothing. His face must be aching from the challenger's final punch, but on top of that he must be feeling all the different blows he's received in this unheard of fall against something that is neither the canvas nor the ropes of the ring.

However you look at it, at this moment you would count yourself lucky not to be him. Even though, technically at least, he's still the heavyweight champion of the world: something everyone would love to be. But it definitely seems preferable (and

Mr Gallagher thinks so too) not to be him in this situation, not to have to be in his place. He's going through hell. It doesn't matter that it may provide him with an interesting story to tell his little grandchildren when he's an old man. Right at this moment Dempsey is having a hard time.

Other people fall in the same or a similar way: soldiers at war, drunks in taverns (death greets the first; hilarity the second). Yet these comparisons are not applicable here, because nothing can compare to the dreadful way a knocked-out boxer falls to the floor. It's epic and ridiculous at the same time. It's like death, but it isn't irreversible. It's a unique moment in a man's life.

This is the moment when Mr Jack 'Slowest' Gallagher finds himself projecting his own life onto the scenario. If he had gone on with his career as a boxer (something his Uncle Dick encouraged but his mother was against) it could easily have been him who now finds himself with only a foggy notion of what is going on, who feels only a stabbing pain. Perhaps it isn't so bad being a referee after all. Apart from rare accidents when a punch goes astray, the referee usually climbs out of the ring in one piece: no bleeding, no mass of bruises.

Mr Gallagher is normally embarrassed about the clothes he has to wear. The short-sleeved light blue shirt and blue bow tie make him look like a clerk or a waiter, especially compared to the two great hulks whose actions he has to control. At times like this, however, it feels to Mr Gallagher as though his clothes are a protective shield.

◆

Twice in the past I've hesitated and not done what I'm now determined to do. Twice I thought of doing it, and was sure I would, but on both occasions I backed out. To call Valentinis, to find him and meet him to talk about something which hadn't been mentioned for years might have seemed strange. On the other hand, it could seem perfectly natural, since that is precisely how things are rescued from oblivion. Plans, ideas, grievances, intrigues, all disappear and reappear in this unexpected, random fashion. Something different can happen as well: you think that, over time, these things will be diluted until they completely disappear, and when this doesn't happen, you have to get used to the idea that what had seemed destined to vanish without trace is still quietly there.

Perhaps I would have liked to forget the whole thing. By this time, Ledesma was in Gaiman, living the life of a recluse, a suspicious, exhausted figure who did not miss any of us a bit. Verani was still in Trelew, but was more distant, even from his friends, giving the impression he was the one who should feel offended when the time came to venture out from the corridor leading to the bathrooms at the Touring Club and get on with life. I somehow felt that everything had started to go wrong when the story of the dead man first came up. I admit, as I admitted at the time, that things might have happened as they did anyway, with or without the dead body to argue about and get angry over, but the topic had become so important for all of us that on occasions even I, who never normally spoke, allowed myself to speculate, and later refused to believe that anything in that distant story of the hotel and the hanged man could be left unresolved.

That is why when I found myself making a trip to Buenos Aires in early 1980, I thought of trying to find Valentinis. I finished all I had to do well before time – although often we run into unexpected difficulties, it sometimes happens we also find quick solutions quite by chance as well. I had two free nights in the capital. On the first, I hung about outside the newspaper office where Valentinis worked or had worked. It was in one of the dark areas of the city down near the port, which was perhaps what led me to change my mind: the fact is, I preferred to spend the evening under the gloomy street lights rather than enter the newspaper building and asking for him. On the second night I prowled around the block where Valentinis lived, somehow imagining that simply by being there I might see him and go up to him. Naturally, this didn't happen. Nor did I pluck up the courage to ask any friendly-looking neighbour. I returned empty-handed to my hotel that night, and to Trelew the next morning.

I went to Buenos Aires again two or three years later. This time (as it had possibly been the first time, although I never admitted as much to myself) my main objective was to meet Valentinis. I thought this meant I wouldn't invent any excuses to avoid doing so. However, I took so long over my other reasons (or rather pretexts) for being in the capital that I found I had almost no time to spare. All I did was call the newspaper a couple of times, and felt a great sense of relief when the line was busy. Once again I came back to Trelew without having seen him, and it was only when I gave in to self-deception that I began to imagine I had really tried.

I did (or rather didn't do) all this without having any clear idea of what Valentinis and I had to talk about, seventeen years after we had become interested in the case, which in turn was fifty years after the death itself. I was unsure what I wanted out of any such conversation: I didn't even know what question I would ask to set our discussion in motion.

Nor was I clear about my reasons for twice avoiding a meeting I was so anxious to have. Like everything else, they remained shrouded in a sort of limbo of vague intuitions. It took Ledesma's death (which happened yesterday) for me to make up my mind to finally seek Valentinis out. I knew I would probably not find him. I knew that if I did find him he would probably not want to speak. And if he did speak, I thought I knew he would have nothing fresh to say. I thought I was avoiding our meeting precisely to avoid that 'nothing'. But now Ledesma has died – he stretched out his hand, knocked over the glass, writhed in his bed for a while, then died. And I'm beginning to think that my real intuition was that Valentinis did have something to say, and that I didn't want to hear it as long as Ledesma was still alive. If there was nothing new, the simplest thing would be not to question the doubtful hypotheses Ledesma had ventured all that time ago – although he had not seen them as doubtful at the time, convinced as he was that they helped him resolve the mystery. If there was something new, however, something that disproved what Ledesma had seen as his clinching proof, I would have to control the impulse to board a bus for Gaiman so that I could tell Ledesma the truth. He would have a lower opinion of me, as I would of him if things happened in reverse.

Now Ledesma is dead, and I'm arriving in Buenos Aires.

It's midday.

It can happen that a traveller arriving from the provinces feels swallowed up by the big city. But this is most likely with someone arriving by bus or train, coming in through suburb after suburb, until there is a solid line of houses with no green in between, and then taller buildings, a build-up of traffic, more people thronging the streets, polluted air. In that case it's true: if you reach Constitución or Retiro after a long journey from the provinces, the city seems endless and engulfs you. But I came by plane, I've literally fallen from the skies, so that before I was in Buenos Aires I got a good view of it all. I saw its edges, its limits. I saw when and how the patches of green ended, or continued inside the city, and although I'm slightly overwhelmed when I walk along the streets, I manage not to feel lost simply by telling myself that the image of the city is just one of many things you can see if you are only a little bit higher.

◆

'Look at this, Verani. Don't miss it.'

'What do you want me to look at?'

'This photo, Verani. It's marvellous.'

'Which photo?'

'This one, Verani, can't you see where I'm pointing? The problem is you're not paying attention.'

'I am, Ledesma, I swear it.'

'No, don't deny it, you're not listening. You're looking (despite yourself, I admit) out of the window. What d'you think you're going to find of interest out there? The same old drums banging, and people shouting: my head's aching from it. They march along the street outside the window, and you don't listen to me. It wouldn't happen if we were at my place.'

'What photo do you want me to look at?'

'The one I'm pointing to. It's wonderful. Can you guess who they are?'

'No.'

'Not even the one without a hat?'

'Not even him.'

'Make an effort, Verani, don't give up. Let the riff-raff outside make their noise, and concentrate on this. Take a good look. What can you see?'

'I can see two women and four guys standing around on a pavement.'

'Is that all you can see? Nothing more? Sometimes you surprise me. If you've no objection, I'd like to explain a few things so you realise just how blinkered your view of the world is. Do you mind?'

'Go ahead.'

'You're right, the photo does show a pavement. But not just any pavement. This is one of the exits to the concert hall in Graz.'

'An exit because they're coming out.'

'That's right. This is the Graz Concert Hall in Austria on 16 May 1906. That probably doesn't mean anything to you, but I'll explain: it's the first performance in Austria of *Salomé*, composed by Richard Strauss. Strauss is this one here, coming down the steps wearing a light-coloured hat. Don't get him confused with the waltz composer. That was Johann.'

'As in Johann Cruyff.'

'This one is Richard. Richard, as in Richard Wagner, and that's no coincidence. The world première of the work had been in Dresden, on 9 December of the previous year. Mahler couldn't attend, and Strauss missed his presence keenly. He wrote to him a few days later: "Where were you on the ninth? I greatly missed you."'

'They were friends.'

'Yes, in a manner of speaking. The Viennese censors condemned *Salomé*. They saw it as riddled with heresy and sexual pathology.'

'Tell me more!'

'I am telling you, Verani. As I've said before: you can't create anything new in art without meeting resistance. That's a fact proven time and again by history, my dear friend. That's why Mahler and Strauss gave each other so much support.'

'They were friends.'

'They had a special kind of friendship. Just look at them here: Strauss is taller, a more imposing figure, and Mahler is staring at him. The others on the pavement, the woman in a white dress and the man with the cane, are also staring at him. Strauss is the centre of attention. Take a good look at Mahler, glancing at him from the sidelines. Today we know which of the two is more important, and I'm saying that without meaning any disrespect to Strauss. Whenever I hear *Zarathustra* a shiver goes down my spine. If you came home and listened to it, it would affect you too.'

'I'm afraid I don't have the time.'

'That's right, go on making excuses. You haven't even listened to Mahler yet, and I've got all his records at home. Did I ever mention Bruno Walter? Today we know who should be centre stage and who should be looking on from the sidelines. But all this happened in May 1906, if you follow me?'

'Yes.'

'At that time, although Strauss was often questioned, even pilloried, he had won greater recognition as a composer.'

'People liked him more.'

'He was more appreciated. As an orchestra conductor, no one could match Mahler. He was the most outstanding conductor of his time, believe me. But the music he composed did not win recognition in the way that Richard Strauss's had, even though some people still resisted its aesthetic novelties.'

'That must have irritated the other guy like hell.'

'Nowadays we know Mahler was the greater composer. But this is now, and that was then. May 1906: just look at how Mahler is staring at him.'

'He must be all choked inside.'

'Please don't always believe that kind of nonsense, Verani. They helped each other a lot. In fact, after all the criticism *Salomé* received from the Austrian press, Mahler immediately set out to learn the score so that he could put it on at the Vienna Opera, where he was conductor.'

'That's why I said he bottled it all up inside.'

'And Richard Strauss did the same. He put on and championed Mahler's music, even after his death in 1911.'

'Mahler died young.'

'He was fifty.'

'A spring chicken.'

'Only five years after this photo was taken. And he looks so healthy here.'

'That's life.'

'So here the two of them are: Mahler and Strauss. They were friends. In a manner of speaking. Five years later, in 1911, Mahler was out of the picture. And in 1923, around the middle of September, Richard Strauss conducted Mahler's *First Symphony* in the Teatro Colón at Buenos Aires.'

'An event.'

'As you so rightly say, an historic event.'

◆

Valentinis called me at home the next time. At home, and late at night: he had something urgent to tell me. He thought he had found, or deduced, some important information, and did not want to wait until the next morning to ring the paper, where he could have bypassed me and spoken directly to Verani. He phoned my house and spoke to me. He left it up to me to decide whether or not to disturb Verani, who went to bed early, and give him the news. In fact, I did wake Verani up, because I called him immediately, and he had already been asleep for some time. But not only was he not upset, he thanked me for it.

What Valentinis had established seemed merely anecdotal initially. At first, I thought he was exaggerating. The police had found the dead body hanging in the hotel room some time after midnight. The corpse wasn't stiff or cold, which led them to conclude the death was very recent. The forensic experts confirmed this, with greater accuracy; they calculated, in their detached way, that death must have occurred either a few minutes before or a few minutes after midnight. In other words, the last minutes of 14 September, or the first of the 15th. The margin of error was not huge, but just enough to make them uncertain as to the actual day of death.

This wasn't the main news, however. The fact that he had died one day or the next was unimportant, according to Valentinis, provided he had died during that period of approximately ten minutes. This had apparently been proved. If it was on the fourteenth, it was right at the end of the day; if it was the fifteenth, it was just beginning. All of which simply meant one thing: the man had died during the Firpo–Dempsey fight.

It had been staring us in the face the whole time: that's why we hadn't seen it. Not only had the dead man been found on the night of the fight, but at the exact same time that the bout, which did not last long, had begun and ended. The two events happened at precisely the same moment. Valentinis had even taken into account not only the time difference between Buenos Aires and New York, but also the delay with which Argentinian radio broadcast the fight (the death had occurred at the exact time of the radio transmission, that is to say when the fight was being listened to in Buenos Aires, not the real time it took place in New York).

Valentinis ventured to suggest that this exact overlapping might not be a coincidence. I told Verani as much, and I know that far from being annoyed at having been woken up during the best hours of sleep, he was unable to close his eyes again that night.

◆

'Now take a look at these photos. A family album.'

'Your family?'

'No, not mine. Gustav Mahler's.'

'Sorry, I misunderstood.'

'Look at this one, for example. The four of them: the whole family. They're all dressed in white. Maiernigg, 1906. Gustav Mahler, Alma Schindler de Mahler, and their two girls.'

'Good-looking. The wife, I mean. A looker.'

'You're right there. Just ask Mahler, Gropius, Werfel or Oscar Kokoschka. Just ask them.'

'A bit on the heavy side, if you ask me, but not too plump.'

'Don't forget that was another time, with other tastes.'

'A fine-looking woman.'

'And these are their two daughters. This one here is the younger one: Anna Justine. She's still alive.'

'Still?'

'Yes, she was born in 1904, don't forget. She must be seventy-eight or seventy-nine now.'

'Getting on a bit.'

'She's not young anymore, that's for sure. They used to call her "Guki". Who knows what she's called now. This other one is Maria Anna, nicknamed "Putzi". Alma is resting her hand on her shoulder. I think it's her Mahler is gazing at.'

'Is she still alive as well?'

'This one?'

'Yes.'

'No, Verani – don't you remember what I told you? This daughter died aged five.'

'My goodness!'

'She was born in 1902 and died in 1907. I told you Alma blamed Gustav for composing the *Songs of Children's Deaths*, because she thought he had brought the catastrophe on them.'

'Don't you agree?'

'Here's another one of Maria Anna. Isn't it a wonderful photo? Mahler and his daughter. Maiernigg, 1905. The little girl had only two years left to live: who would think it? Just look how happy Mahler is. Look how he's laughing – that's very unusual for him. It's because he's about to greet his young daughter: who wouldn't be happy at that? You can see: the coat round his shoulders is about to fall off. Look at the way the girl is holding out her arms to her father: it's really moving. And he's bending, so happily, to take her face in his hands. In the photo at least, his left hand is covering her face. You could see that as an evil omen too.'

'Poor little thing.'

'Poor parents. Just think: Alma lived until a few years ago, the youngest child is still alive. But these two here, looking so happy, with the sea in the background and a bright sky above, how soon they were gone! Gustav Mahler in 1911; Maria Anna Mahler in 1907.'

'It really was a tragedy.'

'I often think somebody ought to write that little girl's biography.'

'His daughter's?'

'Yes.'

'But she died when she was five!'

'That's right, Verani. Just five.'

'But if she only lived for five years, what biography could you write?'

'That's just it, Verani. The story of those five years. There's an awful lot of material in those five years. Just think, Mahler and Alma Schindler's daughter, in the Vienna of those days. A whole era in five years.'

'You're pulling my leg.'

'Why would I do that, Verani? I'm being serious.'

'But it's an absurd idea. The biography of a little girl who died aged five.'

'Yes, but that little girl was the daughter of those parents, she was where she was, and saw what she saw.'

'But she only lived five years, Ledesma!'

'That's just the point, Verani. This is one of those exceptional cases when time is concentrated. Something that doesn't happen in the space of several centuries can happen in a few years. What doesn't happen in years can happen in a few days. What doesn't happen in days happens in a few hours. And what doesn't happen in hours can happen in just a few seconds.'

'That's absurd.'

'No, it's a case of time being concentrated. You have to learn to spot these instances and decipher what they mean. Concentrated time, Verani: in short, even in extremely short periods of time you see a whole era, or even a change of era. History can change just like that. Concentrated time, Verani. That's what we should write about.'

'You're winding me up, aren't you, Ledesma?'

'No, I swear I'm not.'

'The worst of it is you think I don't realise it.'

◆

Jack Dempsey knows very well what vertigo is. After all, he lives in a city, the city of New York, which even in the 1920s has its fair share of tall buildings. Not only that, but because of his profession he has crisscrossed the skies in aeroplanes. He knows what height is, and the void. He does not agree that vertigo is the attraction of that void. To him it's something different. To him, vertigo is a fall that lasts too long; so long that it goes far beyond the mental calculation, the expectation, the idea of how long it might take. Falling from a tree, for example, does not produce vertigo, because it's easy to imagine the distance from the branch to the ground and measure it. He has never felt the attraction of falling or jumping, either leaning over a balcony or out of a window. It's not the void that attracts him; it's something very different. It's when he calculates the distance a fall should take, but somehow cannot measure how long it will take. That's what vertigo is for him: a fall that takes too long to measure. Falling, falling, falling, seemingly to take forever. To be waiting for the fall to finish, and to find it never does. It's this kind of vertigo he feels now. A strange, unexpected vertigo as he topples backwards. A boxer being knocked down takes at most two seconds to fall. After that, he finds himself sprawling on the shiny canvas of the ring. If there is still some resistance in his knees, or if he stumbles as he falls, it will take him at most two seconds. But this fall seems to be lasting twice as long as that. Dempsey knows as much, he can sense it, he feels vertigo, the void swallowing him up. He desperately wants to reach the end of it: and it's this desire that he calls vertigo. Now, at last, he crashes into something, though heaven knows what. The fall is finally over, after he has toppled backwards against the ropes, slipped through them, turned on his side, flown head down through the air. He drags all sorts of things with him, like a river in flood; he smashes into this and that, breaks and scatters more things, sends them flying or crushes them. He's been felled, brought to the ground. And finally he hits it: not the shiny and by comparison welcoming canvas of the ring where he was fighting, but the real ground of the Polo Grounds. The floor at last: the fall is over, and so is his vertigo, and Jack Dempsey, the world champion at all weights, starts to wonder what can have happened to him, and what he should do next.

◆

I have a vivid memory of Verani at that moment: he was triumphant. He was convinced he had discovered the key to the enigma, fifty years on. After all, he said, the death at the City Hotel had remained unsolved not because the person responsible had never been found. Or rather yes, that was the reason, but in a sense that was of secondary importance. What was more important was that they had never uncovered the motive behind the death (or what is loosely called a motive, because it is usually linked to some absolute reason). The death was the effect of a cause that at the time nobody had been able to identify. That and only that was the reason why they had been unable to find the culprit. If it had been suicide, that person might have been the dead man himself. But even in that case, there had to be a cause which would explain everything. And it was precisely this cause that those who had investigated the death fifty years earlier had been unable to determine.

But now, Verani insisted, trying to convince Ledesma he was right, they were in a position to establish the connection that had inexplicably gone unnoticed through all the intervening days and years: the connection between the death at the City Hotel and the Firpo–Dempsey fight. By bringing together these two events they could link cause and effect, and so solve the problem that had eluded the investigators at the time. After fifty years, no less. As Verani said: a whole lifetime.

SIX

WITHOUT TAKING HER EYES OFF her nails or cuticles for one second, Melody Nelson quit him. What he quit was boxing. He said to himself: this isn't for me. As a result of what he said, she said: this man isn't for me. Until then she had always seen him as a hero: a gladiator or a giant. Even when he lost, which was frequently, she saw him as her hero, because heroes, whether gladiators or giants, can also sometimes suffer defeat. She would tenderly press an ice pack against the purple crescent of his worst swellings and whisper to him: my champion, my champion, my beautiful champion. She forgot, or pretended to, that he had lost rather than won the fight, usually by knockout.

He finally grew tired of so many defeats, of always losing, and took the decision to quit (or almost: to stay on as a referee). From then on, Melody could not help noticing what she had apparently not seen before: that her boyfriend was getting a pot belly and losing his hair. Falling out of love can be that simple. It can vanish into thin air that easily.

She left him for 'Buffalo' Dick: the dumbest of the dumb. He was a rough, possibly retarded young boxer from the poorest neighbourhood of north Manhattan. He was taller than Gallagher, and, also, it has to be admitted, somewhat better-looking. But those weren't the reasons which led Melody to hand Gallagher back all his love letters in a shopping bag, telling him that from now on 'Buffalo' Dick was her boyfriend and the man she was going to marry. Gallagher would have liked to tell her that 'Buffalo' Dick was someone who would find it hard not only to write a love letter, but to write his own name in letters that didn't look as though they had been laboriously traced like a drawing. He realised this would not go down very well, and so restrained himself.

'Buffalo' Dick was a boxer. And he had no plans to quit boxing.

◆

Verani was absolutely sure of himself. I can remember being envious of this, the way he insisted that he was right and never doubted it, because in those days I was still very young and only rarely managed to feel sure about anything. Verani was convinced that the way the death in the hotel and the fight in New York overlapped precisely meant the two events had to be connected. He was unconcerned that they had happened several thousand kilometres' apart. To him, the key was not in this non-existent proximity in space, but in the fact that they had happened at exactly the same time. He rejected out-of-hand any suggestion that this was mere coincidence, pure chance. Verani did not see it that way: to him, these two events, the fight and the death, could not have happened at the same time if it was simply a question of meaningless chance. They had to be related; one had to be the cause, the other the effect. That was how everything made sense. Because, as with any other death, or any other event, the death at the City Hotel could not be inexplicable. Everything had an explanation, absolutely everything. Verani slapped the table with the palms of his hands. What sometimes happened, he admitted, was that some things were not self-explanatory, so you had to look elsewhere for an explanation. Some things could only be explained by something else. In the case of the dead man at the City Hotel in Buenos Aires, that something else was the fight in New York for the heavyweight championship of the world between Luis Angel Firpo from Argentina and Jack Dempsey from the United States.

Verani's reasoning was simple but convincing. As its name indicated, a world-title fight was an event of worldwide significance. It covered the whole world, and therefore affected or was important to the whole world. While this event was going on, nobody and nothing could remain uninvolved. Other events that had happened in the recent past, he argued, were equally important to the whole planet: the moon-landing in 1969 (and Neil Armstrong's words: *That's one small step for man, one giant leap for mankind*) or Brazil's goals against Italy in the 1970 World Cup final (especially the one Pelé scored with a header, leaping up, arching his whole body and seeming to hang in mid-air for two or three seconds, as if gravity didn't exist, as if instead of being in the Estadio Azteca in Mexico City he was the one strolling around the moon, sticking flags in the ground and sweeping moon dust into his pan).

That was the essence of it. Nothing and nobody could be uninvolved. That was what was meant by a worldwide event. Nothing and nobody could help but be a part of it, could be left out, because an event like that embraces everything. There is no outside. That night in Buenos Aires, for example, while Firpo and Dempsey were fighting in New York, there was no possibility of being involved in anything else. That something else did not exist. Anything that happened, however apparently remote, had necessarily to be linked to the title fight, because at that moment in time the only thing that could exist was the fight and the myriad repercussions it created.

A death at the City Hotel, for example. Although it had not been one of those deaths commonly called 'natural', it could not have been caused by one of the usual motives: jealousy, revenge, despairing love, terminal illness, robbery, blackmail or betrayal. At that time on the night of 14 September 1923, while the two men were in the ring in New York, anything else going on had of necessity to be linked to that fight. Without that, it couldn't have any meaning. If someone died in Buenos Aires in that short space of time, it must in some way be because of the fight. The fight had to be the reason for the man to be killed, if he was killed, or for him to have taken his own life, if that is what he had done.

◆

'Go on, Verani. Take a guess.'

'The thing is, I've no idea.'

'Go on, give it a try.'

'I swear, Ledesma, I haven't the faintest idea. I couldn't even guess.'

'But someone like you who is so interested in crowds and their behaviour, someone who is always confusing the quantitive with the qualitative, surely you must at least be able to hazard a guess?'

'It's true, I've got a good idea when it comes to crowds, but I've no idea how big they are.'

'But the one is linked to the other, Verani. Otherwise, how do you know it's a crowd?'

'I know because it's simple: I look and I know.'

'That's just tautological.'

'You want numbers because you have a statistical view of things. I don't.'

'If you don't see it in terms of numbers, how do you see it?'

'I see it in terms of knowing what I'm looking at. Say for example I'm at the San Lorenzo ground in Almagro. Let's imagine I'm in Buenos Aires and I want to go and see Ayala "The Mouse" play. So I go to the stadium, look at the terraces, and say to myself: there's a lot of people here today; there's not many people here, or there's quite a few here.'

'Just by looking.'

'Just by looking.'

'But you wouldn't know how many.'

'Yes, I would: a lot, a few, or somewhere in between. You want a number because you're statistically-minded. Not me. What I need is to be somewhere and to take a look. I can even tell you beforehand. An hour before kick-off, for example, by the number of people coming in, or already there, I can tell you: today the stadium's going to be full; today it's not; today some people aren't going to get in; today it'll only be three men and a dog. It's quite simple, Ledesma: when something is worth it, there'll be a crowd.'

'You say that because you think the size of the crowd is what's important.'

'I do, Ledesma. If Monzón is boxing at Luna Park, if Ayala is playing at the Gasómetro ground, if Troilo is performing at the Malibú, or Perón is speaking in Plaza de Mayo, then the place will be full. Crowds of ordinary people want to go.'

'You're mixing oil and water, Verani. You're talking about two very different things.'

'No, I'm talking about the same thing, Ledesma. People aren't stupid, and know when they should go along to something. I know that for a fact, so don't bother arguing with me.'

'Well, if you know it for a fact and are so clever about crowds, why won't you tell me how many people you think saw the Firpo–Dempsey fight?'

'I won't tell you because all you're interested in is numbers, and I couldn't give a stuff about numbers. I couldn't care less. What I know is something else, something much more important; I know when two or three lost souls turn up, when there are only half-a-dozen crazy guys, and when there's a real crowd. A real crowd of ordinary people, Ledesma.'

'Don't shout, Verani, please don't shout.'

'How am I supposed to get you to understand if I don't shout?'

'You can say whatever you like. But don't shout.'

◆

The boxer is on top of him. He's slow to respond, to realise what's going on, because everything was happening really slowly and then suddenly speeded up. He can't find any other explanation for how alarmed he feels, the way he's being crushed, how impossible he finds it to breathe or move. The only explanation, the one going through his mind right now, is that the boxer is right on top of him. The boxer is Jack Dempsey, world heavyweight champion, and he must weigh around ninety kilos. How can he, a skinny photographer weighing only fifty kilos, get those ninety off him? He considers himself a photographer and thinks in terms of photographs. He's just missed the photo of his life, the photo which would have justified everything, even the scorn, the parental rejection. He missed the chance because he didn't think to press the button, and now it's too late. Although he managed to shield the camera from the full impact, it has been knocked out of his hands, and, even if he did manage to pick it up again, it's no use now. It was a great picture: the champion flying out of the ring. He should have caught it on camera. An image of this world-shattering event. Perhaps at this very moment someone else is taking the photo. Someone else, but not him. Because now he is part of the picture, part of the image. He's not sorry that he tried to get as close as he could to the action, but in order to be able to see and take photos, being too close can sometimes be a problem. What's needed is the minimum amount of distance: the step back that painters take to judge perspective, or that boxers take to calculate their next punch. He hadn't managed to take it, and now he's part of the picture. If somebody else is taking the photo, the one he would have liked to take but didn't, then he will be in it. Not very clearly, no doubt: a hunched, blurred figure at most. Possibly no one will even be able to tell it's him underneath, but he will be in the photo. This really worries him: to have gone so rapidly from being the observer to being observed. Nobody was looking at him: he was the one doing the looking, but now everybody is looking (not at him, at Dempsey, but the fact is, Dempsey is right on top of him). To be honest, he'd prefer if nobody was taking a photograph (in fact, there isn't anybody). He has to admit that the main reason for this is professional rivalry. The other reason is a far more private one: Donald Mitchell doesn't like having his photo taken. It's well-known that some primitive peoples refuse to be photographed because they believe that whoever takes their picture also takes part of their soul. Those who like to take photographs always try to refute such a primitive belief. Yet although he is not one of these primitive men, Donald Mitchell shares this idea, and this in fact is why he loves taking photos.

◆

'Since you don't know – and it's obvious you don't – I'll tell you.'

'Fire away, Ledesma. Take a chance.'

'No, Verani, no. I'm not taking a chance. I'm giving you an accurate figure, taken from a reliable source.'

'But that's easy. Anybody could do that.'

'Write it down, my friend. This is something you ought to put in your article. Especially in an article by you, Verani, because you're such a believer in the more the merrier.'

'Forgive me if I don't write it down, I haven't got a pen with me. But tell me, and I'll remember.'

'Make sure you do, because it's worth it. Make a mental note at least. Firpo versus Dempsey at the New York Polo Grounds. September 1923. More than 75,000 people saw the fight.'

'You don't say!'

I don't know if you have any idea how many people that is.'

'A lot.'

'Yes, a lot.'

'More than you can fit into Luna Park in Buenos Aires.'

'That's right, Verani.'

'More than you can get into the Argentine Boxing Federation on Calle Castro Barros.'

'Yes, Verani, a lot, lot more. Remember, back in 1923 they were fighting in an open stadium. You can't compare it to Luna Park, we're in another dimension. It's on a different scale altogether.'

'Without any disrespect to Luna Park, which is the temple of boxing.'

'Forget Luna Park, Verani, we're talking about a different dimension altogether. I get the impression you don't really grasp what I'm talking about.'

'You can think what you like. I'm not going to forget Luna Park, because it's the temple of boxing.'

'Seventy-five thousand souls, Verani: that's more than can fit into the Boca Juniors ground, or River Plate, if it comes to that. So don't insist on your Luna Park.'

'I will insist on it though, because it's the temple of boxing. And when Luna Park gets full, it's crowded.'

'Do you have any idea how many Luna Parks you'd need to reach the figure I mentioned?'

'It's quite simple, Ledesma. Don't make me do calculations, because I'll get confused. But when there's a crowd, there's a crowd, and in Luna Park you can get a real crowd. How many Teatro Colóns would it take to fill a Luna Park? Tell me that, can you?'

◆

Ledesma threatened to stop coming to the Touring Club. He said this was no way to have a conversation. I can clearly remember his abrupt, exaggerated gestures: by this time he could lose his temper quite easily, which led me to wonder whether even the most drastic descriptions of his famous argument might not be true.

He himself did not see that his conduct was in any way abrasive or authoritarian. He sighed deeply, peered through the dirty windowpane and complained that the noise in the street outside was never-ending. He also complained about Verani's outrageous comments. It's impossible to talk to him, he used to say, and I remember the phrase because it was me he used to say it to, as if I might be able to do something about it, or perhaps simply so I could be a witness: he wanted me to see that Verani was so narrow-minded that proper conversation was impossible.

And yet he never left. He would get as far as saying he was going; he'd even push back his chair, ask Mansilla for the bill, stand up and pick up his jacket to put it on. He didn't realise Quelita was staring at him from a nearby table. He accused Verani of being intolerant. Among many other things, he accused him of being a fascist. Verani didn't react. People at other tables were looking too. Ledesma had gone bright red in the face.

I would have liked to calm him down but had no idea how to. Fortunately, Verani didn't answer him back. Ledesma tried to explain: you lot, he said, without saying why he was using the plural, you lot think you always have the right to impose yourselves on everything. He was using the plural because he meant this wasn't a personal problem between him and Verani. No, he had a much bigger problem, and Verani was merely a symptom: people who were crazy about football, or boxing, or the music of Club del Clan, or Perón and Evita, always thought they had the right to impose their view. Either they did not know how, or did not want to occupy only the space (however big) that they were offered; they always wanted to take over everywhere. With their portable radios, their hit song 'Touslehead', their drums and marches, they left no room for anyone else. Totalitarians, Ledesma muttered, but luckily Verani said nothing. They're totalitarians, they push in everywhere. That's why you're so sure, he said to Verani (but in a calmer tone) that when Firpo was fighting Dempsey nobody had any possibility, let alone any right, to stay on the sidelines. You lot don't: you come with your radios, your noise, your drums, and don't allow anyone to be different. You can't tolerate it, he said. Anybody who doesn't want to know has no way out. You can see it in that Chaplin film: the radio and the loudspeakers all transmitting Hitler's speech. Everywhere: in every house, on every street, at every corner. There's one man who doesn't want to listen, but he can't avoid it. They won't let him not listen, they won't allow it. The radio, the loudspeakers, the megaphones. That's why there are so many megaphones in sport. And in fascism. They get everywhere, they push their way in, they steamroller everyone. It wasn't so much that Hitler used the radio: the two functioned in exacly the same way: invade, sweep everything away, flatten, crush: that's what both of them did. Two halves of the same totalitarian machine, which came together and fused. It's all very obvious in that Chaplin film. Hitler and the radio: they both used each other. They took over everything. Don't leave a single chink to escape through, or any hiding place: that was the slogan the leader of the masses and the mass media had in common. And you're doing the same, Verani, he said (but spreading his hands as if trying to get him to understand rather than to admonish him) with this absurd, totalitarian idea of yours that in a city like Buenos Aires everybody had to be part of an event, however important it might have been. I won't deny, he admitted, that the Firpo fight attracted a lot of people. As you've seen, I myself got caught up in it. But to jump to the conclusion that some poor guy locked in his hotel room must have been following something going on half a world away seems to me preposterous. And it's equally preposterous to think that if the poor guy killed himself, it was due to the fight, or that somebody else did him in for the same reason. A man has the right to stay alone in his hotel room, as an individual, a unique human being, with his private world and his private, personal motives for killing himself or being killed. There's no reason why that should be governed by mass hysteria, by what the masses do. He has the right to be caught up in his own world, and to die because of that. And if, my dear friend Verani, you can't accept (as Ledesma said this, he laid his hand politely on the other man's shoulder) that the news of the fight might not have invaded the privacy of that hotel room, then basically you're justifying – for example – Hitler invading Poland and forcibly annexing it to the Third Reich. And though the comparison may seem far-fetched, I assure you it isn't.'

Quelita started putting away her school things in her zip-up pencil case when she saw her father was about to leave: the compass, protractor, a Dos Banderas rubber, a Faber lead pencil, the two-coloured crayon, red on one side and blue on the other. But now she saw that despite his threats and raised voice he was not going anywhere, so she took everything out again, spread them on the table and silently went on with her homework.

◆

Nothing. Nothingness. Nothing at all. Nothing on nothing. Not a consideration or an awareness of nothing, just nothing (this isn't philosophy, it's boxing). His mind a blank, a complete blank. The little voice inside his head, the one everyone has and which talks to us all the time, has suddenly fallen silent. His mind a blank and his senses annulled. He hears nothing, feels nothing, sees nothing: nothing. Neither the twinkle of the floodlights above the ring nor the much weaker twinkling of the stars in the sky, way up beyond the lights. Neither the roar of the crowd (the astonished crowd has fallen silent anyway) nor the referee's count (he is dimly aware that Mr Gallagher is crouching down somewhere near him). And he doesn't feel anything either: neither the vertigo of the fall (he's no longer falling, he's already fallen as far as he can go) nor the pain of the single decisive punch to the face, nor the other blows he's received as he was falling. None of this. Nothing at all. Everything there was to feel or think has been annulled, and all that remains is this lack of everything. A moment in the fight, on that night of 14 September 1923, reduced to nothing, as if it had never existed. A similar gap, a similar moment, missing from his life. If at some point in the future he comes to write his memoirs, or more probably dictate them to a ghost writer, there will be many pages about tonight's fight, and among those many pages several will describe this fall. He will have to tell the story time and again until he dies; tonight, even, in only a few minutes' time, when the journalists come poking their noses around his dressing-room door, he will start to tell the story of the fight and his fall. Standing there in their suits that contrast so strangely with the usual bare bodies of boxing dressing rooms, they will listen to him, taking notes, writing everything down without taking sides, the neutral purveyors of a myth in the making. However attentive they are, they will not be able to write that at the heart of the scrupulous, detailed and careful story they are hearing there is an empty, hollow centre: a place of forgetting where nothing exists because nothing was registered, the place where Dempsey's mind was a blank, the second when he thought nothing, felt nothing. Nothing, nothing at all. What would these chroniclers raising their pencils do if Jack Dempsey suddenly spoke of this black hole where he saw and felt nothing? On the one hand, they might decide quite reasonably to write nothing, because nothing can come of nothing; on the other, they might insist they were there to chronicle the myth, and resolve that since there was nothing, what they write has to concentrate on that nothing, and treat it as if it were everything, or at least something. Awareness, memory, the senses: they can all accept these nothings, but writing cannot. Dempsey will understand.

◆

It's one in the afternoon.

I'm walking through the centre of Buenos Aires. I don't need to know Madrid to dismiss the idea that Avenida de Mayo could be like Gran Vía. That's simply a grandiose idea the capital's inhabitants have; if there is any similarity, it's because it's a poor copy. I'm from a featureless city, so I don't feel any local pride. Buenos Aires means nothing to me, and nor does Trelew.

I'm here to see Valentinis.

There's a lot to look at on this street, but I notice only one building. Ledesma often mentioned the Palacio Barolo. I don't know whether he liked it or not, but he found it interesting. It may have been that because of all the protuberances and excrescences that overwhelm the eye, he considered it unfortunate from an aesthetic point of view, but it definitely interested him (in fact he got Goffredi, who wrote a page on architecture for the paper and was a friend of his, to write an article about it). He was fascinated that it was 'programme' architecture, built to imitate the way Dante had structured his *Divine Comedy*. He was intrigued that there was a copy of the building in Montevideo known as the Palacio Salvo. The fact that for some years it was the tallest building in Buenos Aires concerned him less. With the Kavanagh Building, which replaced it as the highest building in the city around 1935, the height was important, because there the aim of creating a skyscraper is obvious. That is its whole reason for climbing skywards. But both the name and the shape of Palacio Barolo are different: it's beautiful and horrible at the same time; it's sinister and endearing. It probably is Dante-esque, although in a very different way to the one its creator intended.

I stop to gaze at it because that's what Ledesma would have done, each and every time he passed this way.

After that I go in search of a phone somewhere quiet, to do something Ledesma never did or would have done: talk to Valentinis. Ledesma lived and died happy in the certainty that he had solved the case of the dead man. To him, Valentinis did not matter.

I found Valentinis' number in one of those old address books that have the silhouette of a llama, vicuña or some such animal stamped on the front. The same address book which, years before, I had used to help Verani call and ask him for help. For a while, we went on ringing each other. Only very sporadically, two or three times a year (four at most) to find out what the other person was up to. We used to meet up whenever I visited Buenos Aires. I would have dinner at his place: Sandra would cook and we would have something to drink. Despite ourselves, our conversations always went back to the year of military service we had done together.

After a while, we stopped calling. I didn't call him and he didn't call me. For a long while I didn't visit Buenos Aires; when I eventually did, I thought of getting in touch, but in the end I never did (at that time I wasn't trying to get hold of him as I am now, to talk about the dead man at the City Hotel). So a friendship that had survived the years and the thousand or more kilometres between us gradually fizzled out.

Now I've found a public phone behind the staircase of a bar spread over two floors. I put in two tokens, dial Valentinis' number and, when it rings several times, wonder if he has moved. Then his wife Sandra answers: they haven't moved. She recognises my voice ('Roque, it's been so long!'). She hears interference on the line, and concludes I'm far away ('Are you calling from Trelew?'). She's delighted to learn I'm in Buenos Aires ('We must get together'). There's nobody on the stairs of the bar, so I can talk as if I were on my own at home. I tell Sandra I'm only in Buenos Aires for a short time ('I'm going back tomorrow on the afternoon flight'); she says I never stay long ('I'd love to see you'). I say the three of us should meet for a meal, I need to talk to Valentinis ('I don't know if you remember') about the ancient story of the crime or suicide that took place some time in the twenties. There's a lengthy silence on the line. When eventually she speaks again, Sandra sounds very different ('I thought you knew'). She's more serious, and speaks more hesitantly ('Augusto died almost a year ago'). Her voice is softer, but not necessarily weaker ('I swear I thought you knew'). Another lengthy silence, this time at my end of the line ('I don't know what to say') until Sandra insists, with the same enthusiastic voice as at the start ('You don't have to say anything. I want to see you').

◆

'Be a bit clearer, Verani. You're confusing me.'

'What d'you mean, confusing you? It's quite simple. You're the one who likes to complicate things.'

'For you, quantity is important. You don't distinguish between quantity and quality. And yet you're not bothered about numbers.'

'What can I say? I love crowds. Have you ever seen Plaza de Mayo or a football stadium completely packed? Whenever I see something like that, it moves me. All you do is count. I get tears in my eyes and pull out my handkerchief. You get out your calculator and start counting.'

'I know of only one case, just one, where it may be true that quantity is quality.'

'So you admit it then.'

'I'm talking about one single case.'

'But you admit it.'

'In this one case, yes.'

'All right, it's only one case, but then you admit it.'

'I don't know what it is you're thinking of. The case I'm talking about is Gustav Mahler's *Symphony of a Thousand*.'

'Mahler?'

'Yes, Mahler. His *Eighth Symphony*. Did you ever hear it?'

'No, never.'

'Come to my place and listen to it. It's known as the *Symphony of a Thousand* and it's really impressive.'

'Even so, the thousand you're talking about can't compare with the seventy-five thousand who went to see the Firpo fight.'

'Oh please, don't give me that.'

'Seventy-five thousand is a lot more than a thousand.'

'You don't say. And with that you think you're proving something? What you don't realise, because you're so pig-headed, is that Mahler's *Eighth Symphony* is known as the *Symphony of a Thousand* because that's how many people are involved in it.'

'A thousand people playing?'

'Playing and singing. It has an orchestra, a choir and soloists.'

'A thousand people.'

'That's why it's known as the *Symphony of a Thousand*.'

'Plus the conductor.'

'Plus the conductor.'

'A thousand and one, then.'

'A thousand, Verani, a thousand: the *Symphony of a Thousand*. It's a generic term, an estimate; there's no need to count them one by one.'

'But when I say that, you say I confuse you.'

'If you're right in saying that seventy-five thousand is more than a thousand, then you'd also have to admit that a thousand is more than two.'

'Two? Which two?'

'Firpo and Dempsey.'

'Two in the ring. Three, counting the referee. But how many more are there in the stands?'

'Seventy-five thousand, Verani. It was me who told you that.'

'And how many people fit into the Teatro Colón?'

'Not those huge, outlandish numbers you're so fond of.'

'I like crowds, not numbers.'

'You don't like numbers? Try this one: five hundred and nine thousand. What d'you think of that?'

'It's a lot. But what are we talking about?'

'You think it's a lot.'

'It sounds like a lot. But I don't know what it is we're talking about.'

'You're right, it is a lot. An awful lot. That's what they paid Jack Dempsey to fight Firpo. Five hundred and nine thousand dollars. What d'you think of that?'

'That he earned it.'

'Half a million dollars, Verani! That's crazy!'

'I say he deserved it. And they must have paid Firpo even more.'

'Why's that?'

'Because he knocked him out of the ring.'

'But Dempsey was the champion. And he won the fight.'

'That's why I said he deserved it.'

'The fight lasted less than two rounds. Which means that in five minutes Dempsey earned five hundred and nine thousand dollars. That's crazy.'

'I still say he deserved it.'

'A boxer? For getting in a ring and beating the hell out of some other poor brute for five minutes? What about Richard Strauss? How much do you think he deserved to get for putting on the performance of Mahler's *First Symphony* in the Teatro Colón?'

'That depends.'

'On what?'

'On the number of people who can fit into the theatre. If, like Dempsey, he could attract seventy-five thousand punters, each one of whom paid ten bucks at the box office, then he should get well paid, because there's a lot to go round. But if he can't attract so many, then he deserves to get less.'

'Life is simple for you, isn't it?'

'Yes, it is. If you put on a concert with a thousand people playing, and then another thousand turn up to listen, you can't expect to make much out of it. It's obvious Mahler wasn't Jewish. He was a disaster as a businessman.'

◆

So then I screwed up my courage to intervene. I never usually spoke: I was very young, a boy listening to the grown-ups, and so I never said a word. But that afternoon, after a lot of hesitation, I remember I decided to speak my mind. I took advantage of a silence (Ledesma was muttering to himself, and Verani was staring out of the window) to address them both. I had prepared and rehearsed what I wanted to say: I was determined not to stumble. I'm sure I swallowed hard, or cleared my throat, before I began. But when I finally spoke, I did so in a firm voice.

The fact is, I had an intuition, a sort of premonition that I needed to understand in order to explain it as clearly as I had seen it in my mind's eye. On the one hand, it seemed to me Ledesma was right. He was exaggerating a bit, it's true: he had gone too far. He did so because he was in a nervous state and because he wanted to be provocative, but beyond those histrionics, as far as I could see, he was right. Yet on the other hand it seemed to me that, without any clear idea of how or why, by plucking up my courage and speaking out in defence of Ledesma, I would also somehow justify Verani.

So I started to speak, slowly but surely. I told Ledesma that, to my way of thinking, things were more or less as he had said: that as far as sport, crowds of people, or the mass media were concerned, they could be arrogant and abusive. They were totalitarian in the true sense of the word: they infiltrated everywhere and took over everything. But this was precisely why Verani could be right too. If they were so bullying and disrespectful, it was not because Verani said so, or because of the way he said it. The fact that nothing could escape the Firpo–Dempsey fight that night in September 1923 was not Verani exaggerating: that exaggerated sense of its own importance existed in objective reality. He was not the one imposing the boxing match on everything else; it was because of its totalitarian nature that this was so. Therefore Ledesma was right, and Verani was right too. If Ledesma was arguing that the world inside that hotel room could escape from the pervasive intrusion of the world-title fight, that meant he would have to qualify his own hypothesis about totalitarian invasiveness. For him to win the argument against Verani, he would have to accept that Verani was right.

I didn't say this to keep them happy or as any judgement of Solomon. But I saw them nod in agreement, and realised I had convinced them both.

SEVEN

HE'S STILL NOT AWAKE, but he's starting to wake up. He's in that intermediate state that belongs as much to being awake as it does to being asleep. Some, or most, of us, react by putting our head underneath the pillow, flailing out blindly towards the alarm clock, hoping that its cruel clatter is a mistake or part of a dream, wishing it was still night and that the time to wake up had not really arrived. This is followed by a drowsy struggle that lasts more or less time depending on how great a sense of duty we feel. The circumstances in which Dempsey is confronting this limbo, where he's neither completely asleep nor completely awake, are of course very different. He's not in a bed, at home or in a hotel; nor is he in the narrow bunk of a ship crossing the sea or a train crossing the desert. No, not him: he is struggling between sleep and wakefulness under the eyes of thousands of people, and with two other people directly beneath him. It's the middle of the night, and he's outside the ring. Not a very pleasant place, it's true, but then he didn't choose it. As luck would have it, this is where he finds himself, and now he has to deal with the situation. He ought to wake up. Above all else, it would be good if he woke up. He knows there's something important he has to do. He knows this, even though, because of his momentary befuddlement, he cannot remember exactly what it is. This is the purest form of a sense of duty: it's an instinct, a reflex. He has to wake up. This certainty leads him to shake his head and try to open his eyes. Yet at the same time he wants to sleep. To relinquish the thread linking him to the world of the living, of those awake, and to give in to what he knows will be welcoming sleep. He feels so tired. So very tired. He has heard stories about soldiers who come back from the front. The Great War was terrible, and many soldiers came back full of stories to tell. Some of them had been forced to go several days without sleep. They had no drugs to help them stay on their feet: all they had was their fear of dying. Two, three, four whole days without a wink of sleep or the chance to take a quick nap somewhere. They reached a point, they said, when all they wanted to do was to sleep and sleep. It did not matter that the bombs continued to fall and the bullets went on whistling past: their only desire was to surrender to sleep, even if it cost them their lives. Death is like sleep, and looked at in this way, even death would be welcome. If they had not been so ragged, they would not have thought like this, but on the verge of exhaustion, when life, or staying awake, had become completely intolerable, their only possible desire was to sleep, whether only for a while or forever, a short time or for time out of time: to sleep. These are the far-off lands of extreme exhaustion. That's how Dempsey feels now. He is well aware he did not fight in the Great War. Not even in a little one. He has been fighting against only one man, however valiant; his only weapons were his gloved fists. Nor has he been fighting for years: not a hundred, as once happened in remote history; not four, as has just occurred in recent history. How long can the combat have lasted? A couple of minutes at most. Less than three, for sure, because that is how long a complete round lasts. And yet he feels and suffers the deadly weariness of the soldier denied sleep in the trenches or the relentlessly pursued fugitive. There is still a tiny voice, the last trace of discipline, whispering to him: it tells him to wake up, to get up. Now: right now. But his exhausted body is telling him something else. Like children roused early in the morning by their parents to go to school, his body is pleading with him for just that little bit more sleep. To let him sleep just a little bit longer. Let the whole world wait: school, teacher, Tom the school bus driver, Mr Gallagher the referee, the challenger Fripp or whatever his blasted name is. Half-asleep, Dempsey wants to go back to sleep properly. Half-awake, Dempsey has to be wide awake. Just as in every man, desire and duty struggle within him. Just as in the fight he is still part of, there is as yet no knowing which of the two will win.

◆

At a corner table of a bar in the centre of Buenos Aires, Sandra absentmindedly lines up a sachet of Ledesma sugar alongside another identical one I'm nervously twiddling between my fingers. I let it flop first one way and then the other on the impassive table. If I look out of the bar window, I can see the square tower of the City Hotel. It's also been used on the cover of a pop album. There it looks weird, unreal, as if it weren't part of this world here below. Seen through the window, however, it looks so normal it's disappointing. It looks plain, almost vulgar.

Sandra is not worried ('Augusto never knew about us, Roque, and if he did, he didn't care'). She gives me the same impression as always: that she has everything worked out ('Anyway, it doesn't matter now'). This time, as so often before, she inspires both trust and fear in me ('You have to understand, Sandra. I've only just heard the news'). I think she knows how to manipulate my mixed emotions too. ('He couldn't give a damn about anything, Roque, or anyone'). Just occasionally I'd like to see her have doubts ('He couldn't give a damn about anything. Didn't you realise that? All he wanted was to make fun of everything. And he succeeded'), to see her shaken out of her self-confidence. She was never at a loss or unable to cope: Valentinis was the only one who could drive her crazy ('I know he just laughed at everything, don't you?'). Sometimes she must have cried or been afraid ('He laughed at the whole damn lot, and especially at you and me').

It's two in the afternoon.

I tell Sandra that this time I've come to Buenos Aires specifically to find out about the crime that took place in 1923 ('Or the suicide, I don't know. That's what I'm trying to find out'). She leans back against the reassuring wood of the chair and drops the little sachet of sugar. She shrugs ('Augusto had a lot of fun with all that. A lot of fun'). I grow concerned ('What do you mean it was a lot of fun for him?'). She simply shrugs again ('Simply that, silly, didn't you say you knew he laughed at everything? Well, that made him laugh too'). My head starts to spin as I suddenly think that Valentinis could perfectly well have made everything up. It would be incredible, scandalous, but not impossible ('What do you mean he laughed at that as well?'), not for Sandra ('Just that: he laughed at it'), who, on principle, never ever shows any surprise ('But what kind of laugh? Because he had made the whole thing up?') but for me or for Ledesma and Verani, who for years had built up an entire world based on what Valentinis had said ('He just laughed, Roque. At everything. Why don't we go somewhere?').

Sandra is annoying me now. I'd like to get rid of her so that I can think this through calmly ('But why did he laugh? Because he had made it all up?'), but if I get rid of her that will mean I am stuck with no answers ('I didn't say that. I couldn't say that for sure in any way'). I want her to be quiet and yet I want her to talk, I want her to go and I want her to stay.

The three of us had managed to create something out of a crime that had come to nothing. To give it meaning. Many years had gone by since the event. And many more since we first learnt about it. And now that meaning risked being reduced to nothing again, to an absurdity. If Valentinis really had made everything up, none of what we had said or thought about the case meant a thing. Not a thing. What Ledesma had said right at the beginning could have been true: that there was a gap to fill in the newspaper and so the Trelew journalist had invented it. Or that the news was carried in a Buenos Aires newspaper, but had been elaborated on in Trelew. Or it might be that the dead man had existed and that the story was true, but without the extra elements Valentinis had added just for fun. All that might or might not have been the case.

Sandra grows impatient ('Why don't we leave here now? Let's go to Calle Viamonte'). So do I, in my own way ('I want to know whether all the information Augusto gave us was true, or if he made it up'). Sandra picks up the sachet of sugar again

('How would I know, Roque? It's so long ago'), shakes it between her fingers ('Besides, we didn't talk a lot about it'), producing a pleasant but rhythmless sound ('As far as I know, he always told the truth. He might have made one or two little things up. But I don't really know'). I'm still clutching my own sachet of sugar, which I now grip even tighter ('But there was a dead man'), as Sandra brings hers almost up against mine once more ('Yes, there was a dead man. There's always a dead man. Now Augusto himself is dead').

Well, I tell myself, if at least there was a dead man then not everything is lost, although Sandra doesn't seem at all interested ('Why don't we go somewhere else close by?'). If the dead man existed, then we would have to patiently – as patiently as we did all those years ago – sift through all the rest: to uncover what was true and what wasn't. That was the only way to be sure whether it had all been a waste of time or not.

◆

Quelita found long division with decimals hard. She did everything else well, and sometimes very well. She was an intelligent girl (very bright, as her father said) and had no problems with her other maths homework. She wasn't intimidated by big numbers or the different steps. After what was always a relatively short time, we would hear from the next table: 'Done it'. But she couldn't get division with a decimal point. I was no expert with numbers, but I did like explaining things. So one afternoon I found myself trying to help her understand what this point, which should have been at the end of sentences, was doing in her maths homework book.

The rule was simple, I just had to find a way to explain it. There are two parts to every division: the divisor and the dividend. Let's say the decimal point appears in the divisor. What you have to do is move it to the end of the number (and since it is meaningless there, you forget about it) through as many spaces as necessary. Then in the dividend you add as many zeros as you moved the decimal point in the divisor. Then you carry on as in any other division. Now let's take the case where the decimal point is in the dividend. You perform the same operation, but in reverse. Except that when you get the final figure, you need to re-insert the decimal point, counting the number of spaces you moved the decimal point in the first place. Luckily, she had no examples where there were decimal points in both the divisor and the dividend.

Verani followed all my explanations very closely.

Ledesma smiled at me and winked. He had asked us to treat Quelita normally, and never to show we felt sorry for her.

◆

Melody Nelson: a real bitch. The irredeemable whore, the inexorable whore: Melody Nelson. How many members can there be in all the different professional or semi-professional boxing leagues in the Union? Two thousand, five thousand, fifteen thousand, a hundred thousand? The Union is a huge place. And would that bitch Melody Nelson be willing to cavort with all of them, just like she was now cavorting with 'Buffalo' Dick? Was it enough for someone simply to be a boxer? Would she do it with all of them: with each and every single one?

How much effort you've put into forgetting Melody Nelson, Mr Gallagher. How much dedication. How much you've wanted a powerful flash of amnesia to strike you, an irreversible miracle of forgetting. What tenacity you've shown, Mr Gallagher, in your efforts to forget Melody Nelson. Years have gone by, and in those years there were whole days, whole months, when you didn't even think of her. Doris has been a good wife and mother. Sympathetic, understanding, careful, discreet, simple, prudent. Not a single complaint about good old Doris. So the years rolled by. Yet despite this, Mr Gallagher cannot ever be sure that while he is working as a referee, carrying out his difficult tasks, he will not be overwhelmed by the painful memory of Melody Nelson. Boxers inevitably remind him of her, and being a referee inevitably puts him in contact with boxers. Because, deep down, for Mr 'Slowest' Gallagher, a boxer is nothing more than the image of desire that bitch Melody Nelson harbours.

It's not that he thinks every boxer he sees fight has been making love to her. This one now, for example, who is standing so proud, gazing down at his toppled opponent, could not possibly have done so. It was totally, absolutely impossible, because he's nothing more than some primordial beast from one of those remote Latin American countries, brought here from his village and soon to return there, to tell all his friends about the amazing tall buildings in this great northern city. No, not with this one. But what has not happened is no comfort to Mr Gallagher, because although he knows it hasn't happened, he also knows it could well have happened, or could happen, provided the one single condition is fulfilled: that of being a boxer.

Sometimes he wonders what else he would fill his head with if he really did forget Melody Nelson. The memory of her takes over his entire mind. If he could only relieve himself of this constant burden, what might he not do with all that free mental space? He could devote all the time and effort he wastes on her on something much more productive. Who knows, perhaps he would discover he was an avid reader of adventure novels, or find unexpected pleasure in collecting watches, stamps or butterflies. If he wasn't thinking so much about Melody Nelson, who knows what might not occupy his thoughts? One thing is sure: he would become a more attentive, much more diligent man, a man with much greater powers of concentration than he is showing at this very moment.

◆

'I'm going to tell you a story, Verani. I'm sure it will interest you.'

'Go right ahead.'

'It happens on the afternoon of 26 August 1910, in a hotel in Leiden, Holland. Do you know where I'm talking about?'

'More or less.'

'OK. So on this summer August afternoon, in this hotel in a small Dutch city, two men meet.'

'Right.'

'Two great men.'

'Aha.'

'Can you imagine who they were?'

'No.'

'One of them, at least.'

'No.'

'All right then, hold your breath and I'll tell you.'

'Go right ahead.'

'As I said, two great men. One was Gustav Mahler; the other, Sigmund Freud.'

'You don't say.'

'Can you imagine, Verani? The greatest composer of the

turn of the century, and no less a person than the founder of psychoanalysis. The two men met on 26 August 1910 and held a lengthy conversation, one that lasted almost four hours.'

'The two of them in a hotel room?'

'No, I never said that. They met in the hotel, that's true. But afterwards they went out for a walk in the city. They strolled around and talked. A long, transcendental conversation.'

'Would you believe it?'

'And please, I beg you, don't lose sight of the stature of the two men I'm talking about.'

'I know, I know.'

'If you know, don't shrug your shoulders like that.'

'Pay no attention, Ledesma, it's just a nervous twitch.'

'None other than Mahler and Freud. Freud interrupted his holidays on the North Sea coast because, he said, he couldn't refuse a man as important as Mahler. Mahler had been in contact with him, wanting to see him. Freud sent him a telegram and they arranged to meet. The arrangement fell through four times: Mahler kept hesitating and cancelling.'

'He got cold feet.'

'No, it was something more complex than that. He was afraid of what he might hear, or worse, of what he might say. He wanted to meet Freud, and yet he didn't want to. Freud saw Mahler's reticence as a *folie de doute* that was part of his obsessive neurosis.'

'A what?'

'He was full of doubts, my friend. It's Gustav Mahler I'm talking about, not some country bumpkin. He didn't know what to do.'

'Poor guy.'

'Finally he made his mind up and confirmed the meeting. He travelled by train from Toblach to Leiden. During the journey he wrote letters: letters to Alma Mahler, his wife. He met Freud in Holland on 26 August. They were almost the same age, and from similar backgrounds. They got on well, they understood each other. They talked for four hours. Mahler and Freud. Gustav Mahler and Sigmund Freud. Just think how important such a meeting must have been.'

'I'm sorry, but, as I see it, they were just two guys chatting.'

'No, it wasn't simply a chat. It was a real session of analysis.'

'What does that mean? I can imagine an ordinary, run-of-the-mill Dutchman sitting at a table in a café just like we are now. He looks out of the window and sees them pass by. What does he see? Two guys chatting.'

'But it's more than that, isn't it, Verani? It's a psychoanalytical session, not just any old chat. We're talking about Gustav Mahler here. And Sigmund Freud, no less.'

'So?'

'Have you no idea what a psychoanalytical session with Freud implies? It's as though you, the sinner, wanted to confess, and had the pope as your confessor. The pope in person.'

'If you want to be amazed, go right ahead. To me they're still just two guys having a chat.'

'I must lend you *On the Interpretation of Dreams*.'

'Two men talking. Flesh-and-blood people.'

'Come back to my place one night. I've got some wine you'd like. And I'll put on Mahler's *Fifth Symphony*.'

'Two men talking. That's what they are, and nothing more.'

'You know what you are? You're thick-skinned.'

'And you know what *you* are? You're star-struck.'

'What did you say?'

'You heard me, Ledesma; you're star-struck. Like that comic-book character Cholula, mad about the stars.'

'How on earth could you say something like that about me?'

'Don't be upset, but it's the truth. If I came here with copies of *Radiolandia* or *El Gráfico* and started talking about all the stars in them, like Sandrini with Malvina Pastorino, "El Gringo" Scotta with "Oveja" Telch, what would you say? That I've gone mad over all those celebrities. That's what you would say. And the worst of it is, you think you're so different. Why? Because your celebrities are a musician and a psychologist. So what does that prove, Ledesma? You start dribbling with anticipation when you think of two such famous men together. You'd love to have their autographs: "It's for my daughter Quelita." I can just see it. So what's that, Ledesma? You're star-struck. Completely star-struck. You're just like that character Cholula: mad about stars.'

'Oh, my god!'

◆

Verani was anxious watching me help Quelita, and had difficulty hiding it. More than once he seemed to want to join in, but knew he couldn't do so without perhaps saying something that might embarrass him. Quelita didn't seem to notice him, but that had more to do with her sense of responsibility: when she sat down to study, she became so engrossed that nothing could distract her. It was only once she had finished her homework and her father had checked it that she tried to amuse herself, like any other girl of her age.

That was when Verani joined us. He knew lots of card games, and liked to teach them. Ledesma was not entirely happy to see his daughter in a bar like this shuffling the pack with unexpected skill. He might have accepted it in a boy, although even then he would probably have judged him too young to deal like a card sharp. But with Quelita it seemed all too rushed and inappropriate to him. Verani insisted, though, and finally persuaded him to be a little more flexible. He even argued (I'm not sure he was being serious) that games like Pontoon helped her with mental arithmetic. If Ledesma accepted this kind of argument without demur, it was either because he felt it wasn't really that important or because he was pretending to listen to Verani when in fact he wasn't paying him any attention.

Another thing the two of them often did was to explore the hotel. Strangely enough, Verani knew the place well: after all, there's no reason why someone living in a town should know anything about the hotels there, since, by definition, he is never going to stay in them. He would show Quelita all the secret places, the parts nobody ever visited, the internal courtyards, the unused exits. The corridor between the hairdresser's and the bathrooms, for example, had a nook hidden behind the broad main staircase. Nobody ever went there, and the only light was reflected from outside. All you had to do was to bend over and twist your body a little, and then you could hide in there without anyone seeing.

◆

'It's a pity you take your own superficiality for the superficiality of the world.'

'I don't get it.'

'It's quite simple, don't play the idiot: just because you see everything as flat doesn't mean the world is flat.'

'I still don't get it.'

'Only you could think that if Freud and Mahler hold a lengthy conversation on their own, for four hours, it's only interesting for entirely frivolous reasons.'

'I know, Ledesma, you already told me: to you it was a great event that a musician and a psychologist met to chat, and not Joe Schmoe with X or Y.'

'Are you being stupid on purpose? I couldn't give a damn if Ray Conniff meets up with Florencio Escardó. I'm talking about Mahler and Freud, my friend. Can't you get that into your head: Mahler and Freud. Got it?'

'Yes.'

'And Mahler was going through a real existential crisis.'

'Really?'

'Yes, a profound existential crisis. The artist and the abyss, Verani, the artist and the abyss. He didn't know what to do with his life.'

'You don't say.'

'Yes. The man of genius who rises with such ease to the sublime heights of the human condition, then suddenly falls prey to anguish, bewilderment, doubt. He doesn't know what to do.'

'But what happened to him, in practice?'

'In practice?'

'Yes.'

'In practice, my friend: problems with his soulmate.'

'The human soul is full of mystery.'

'Don't make fun of me, Verani, please, I'm not in the mood. Problems with his soulmate Alma, I said, not with his soul. Problems with Alma. Alma Schindler.'

'His lady wife?'

'His wife, yes. Problems with his wife.'

'So the guy goes and asks the psychologist for help?'

'That's your interpretation, not mine. We're not talking about a magazine agony aunt here, Verani. This is something completely different.'

'Whatever you say, Ledesma.'

'If you like, you can see it as Mahler going to see a psychologist.'

'Didn't he go and see Freud?'

'Yes.'

'And what was Freud?'

'A genius, Verani. A colossal genius. As big a genius as Mahler in music. And the two of them talked for four hours, walking the streets of Leiden.'

'So what did Freud say to him?'

'He told him that Alma, who was a good deal younger than Mahler, was looking for a father figure in him. That's what he said. And that he, Mahler, who had the habit of calling Alma by her second name, which was "Marie", was showing that he was fixated on his own mother. Marie was the name of Mahler's mother, you see.'

'It took four hours to tell him that?'

'Of course not, Verani. It took four hours to reach those conclusions. Four hours to elaborate on the ideas. Of course it only took five minutes to say.'

'Or less.'

'Or more, perhaps. But that's not the point, is it? The point is that Mahler, at the end of his tether, sought out Freud, and this brought about the extraordinary occurrence that two of the greatest geniuses the world has ever seen met one another.'

'And was it any use?'

'What?'

'Their talk.'

'The session?'

'Yes.'

'Well, yes, it was of some use. Some.'

'Some?'

'Mahler went back to Toblach full of enthusiasm. He thought that after such important insights things would be better.'

'And they weren't?'

'Not really, no.'

'No?'

'No.'

'No.'

'No. What can I say? No, they weren't.'

'Why was that?'

'Because Alma Mahler was intimate with Walter Gropius again.'

'What did you say, Ledesma?'

'What you heard, Verani, what you heard. Alma had previously had sexual relations with Walter Gropius, and Mahler found out. That was why he had been in such turmoil, not knowing what to do, and had wanted to talk to Freud.'

'So this Walter what's-his-name had it off with Mrs Mahler?'

'Please, can't you find a less crude way of putting it?'

'He screwed Mrs Mahler! What a snake in the grass that Walter must have been.'

'Walter Gropius, Verani. The founder of the Bauhaus, if that means anything to you.'

'No, but I do understand that the great Gustav Mahler turned out to be a great cuckold too.'

'If you don't watch your words, this is going to end badly.'

'What were you going on about, Ledesma, with your artist and the abyss, the sublime heights and all that other guff? It's just another story of a cuckolded husband, isn't it? Admit it, Ledesma. The sad story of a poor cuckold.'

'Do you know your problem, Verani? You bring everything down to your own level. And you haven't the faintest idea what the Bauhaus was.'

'Maybe not, but I know what faithless women are. I know a cuckold when I see one, and a musician, if it comes to that. Do you know what *your* problem is, Ledesma? You know about symphonies, lots of symphonies. But you don't know about tango. It's tango that you're lacking.'

◆

To Donald Mitchell, all of a sudden this seems like a foretaste of being dead. Not of dying, which isn't the same thing, but of being dead, dead and buried. That's how distant he feels from fresh air and the world of the living: the weight on top of him feels like being buried. It's easy for him to imagine that this is the marble tombstone laid on top of his dead body. He can even see the headstone with its inscription: 'Donald P. Mitchell, born New Haven 23.01.1902, died New York 14.09.1923.' This is what death will be like when it comes. To be down below, far down below, and to be unable to get back to the surface. Death is sinking into the ground, just like he's doing now, and being crushed there, like now. When he dies it will be exactly like this. He wonders anxiously if his life ends now, without the chance of reconciliation, whether his parents will feel sufficiently well disposed towards him to visit his grave and shed a tear or place a flower on it. That's what he wonders, and as he does so, he has to admit that death will not be like this, or at least not exactly like this, because it's obvious that when his life is over he won't be able to ask himself any questions: there will be nothing. Death is this, but without the possibility to think or ask oneself anything. This question he is asking himself about his parents must belong to life, what's left of it. Yet to be like this, here, crushed as if forever beneath an unrelenting weight, seems to him like being under a tombstone, like being dead. Even at this extreme, however, he manages to do something: he searches for a chink, finds it, stretches his arm out and lifts it out of this near-burial. There is a sinister aspect to all this, because as he finds himself crushed beneath the weight of this heavy body and thinks he has really been buried under a real marble slab, the sight of his arm groping and pushing its way upwards is like one of those horrific scenes where a ghastly hand rises from the earth, pushing open the coffin lid. It suggests one of two equally terrifying alternatives: the first being that the dead person has been resurrected and the Christian miracle has happened all over again. The buried body is struggling to return to everyday reality, as it has just returned to life, and is fighting its way out of the grave to which it was long ago consigned. The other and perhaps even worse possibility is that the person buried was not in fact dead, but was cataleptic or in a deep, deep sleep, and has just woken up to find himself wrapped not only in a shroud, but in a coffin and a tomb. When, to his horror, he realises this, he is desperate to escape, as who wouldn't be? The sight of Donald Mitchell's hand emerging and groping upwards could lead one to think all this, if he was doing it because he thought he was dead and buried; and yet his intention is much less other-worldly, far more ordinary and modest; he wants to reach out and touch his camera, which in the midst of all the falling and being crushed he found himself unwittingly obliged to let go of. He wants to lay his hand on this sorely-missed apparatus again, so that from this first certainty he can start to reorganise a world that suddenly seems to have crumbled all around him.

◆

Verani intercepted me in a quiet corner of the top floor of the newspaper. He confided in me that he didn't think he was going to make it in time. He whispered the words, squeezing my shoulder with his right hand as he did so. I pointed out I had no idea what he was talking about. He grumbled that the days were going by, and that he hadn't even started. He grew impatient when I asked: started what? He said he meant his piece on Firpo and Dempsey, the one he had to write for the special supplement. A week had already gone by and he hadn't even started. He had taken a few notes and made a rough outline from the things he'd talked about with Ledesma, which I knew about. The problem was that his mind was on other matters, he couldn't find the time to sit and write about the fight. The deadline was approaching and he wasn't going to make it.

For the first time he asked me directly something that until then he had only hinted at: that I write the article for him. He would give me what he was being paid for it, and was happy to add a few more pesos out of his own pocket. He would pay me, and would return the favour whenever I needed one.

I was non-committal.

♦

'Don't forget, Verani, that we're talking about a man who is close to death.'

'Mahler?'

'Yes, Mahler.'

'A shiver runs down my spine when you say that.'

'He meets Freud at the end of August 1910 in Leiden, Holland. He will die a few months later, on 18 May 1911, to be precise, in the Loew Sanatorium at Vienna, Austria. He was fifty years old.'

'Is that all?'

'That's all.'

'But when he saw Freud he didn't know he was going to kick the bucket so soon.'

'No, he didn't know, but perhaps he could sense it. Now you can say it if you like: the human soul is a mystery.'

'Too right it is.'

'Guess what happened only five days after such a terrible death.'

'No idea.'

'Only five days had gone by. It was 23 May 1911. Mahler's executor Emil Freund received a note. Can you guess who sent it?'

'No.'

'Sigmund Freud.'

'Freud to Freund.'

'That's right. And guess what it said.'

'No idea.'

'It was an invoice, asking for the sum of three hundred crowns for the consultation of the previous August in Leiden. A consultation that lasted several hours, he says. He doesn't say how many exactly. But he sent him an invoice for three hundred crowns.'

'A fortune.'

'Apparently, while Mahler was still alive, Freud hadn't asked for a thing. But as soon as he died, he sent an invoice demanding payment.'

'Did they pay him?'

'Yes, they did. There's an acknowledgment dated 24 October 1911. What a story, isn't it? For Mahler to die, and all the repercussions that had, and then a few days later an invoice arrives for an interview he had the year before, and from Sigmund Freud no less!'

'I'm not surprised.'

'You're not?'

'No.'

'You're really not surprised?'

'No. Wasn't Freud Jewish?'

'Yes.'

'Well, that's how Jews behave.'

'D'you think so?'

'Yes. They're terrible when it comes to money. As you've just shown, Ledesma, they'll try to extract money from the dead. From the dead! The Jews are tremendous, look how they tried to take advantage of a poor gentile.'

'That's an old chestnut, Verani. But do you know something? Mahler was a Jew too.'

'He was?'

'Yes.'

'Well then, I'm not surprised.'

'Not surprised at what?'

'Not surprised that he goes to see a psychologist for four hours, then leaves without paying.'

'He was born a Jew, but converted to Roman Catholicism in February 1897. It was almost impossible for a Jew to become a conductor of the court opera in Vienna. And that, above all else, was what Mahler aspired to. That was why in February 1897 he became a Catholic. And in April that same year, just a couple of months later, he was appointed.'

'What can I say, Ledesma? And he's one of your great men? A cuckold, a social climber and a turncoat.'

'Or rather: liberal, ambitious and clever.'

'No, no, no: cuckold, social climber, turncoat. And you know what? He got his comeuppance for being a turncoat. Because if he was born a Jew, he was always a Jew. He changed sides and got punished for it. Another Jew came on the scene and screwed him.'

EIGHT

I REMEMBER I LOOKED AT Sandra's hands ('You know what? I think I'll be off'). She notices and hides them ('You're leaving already?') because she feels that if I'm looking at them I'm not looking at her ('Yes. Time for me to be going'). When I was younger I never looked at hands: it's something I learnt as an adult. In those days I didn't even know my own hands. I didn't understand the meaning of that old saying, 'to know something like the palm of your hand', because I didn't know the palms of my hands at all.

It's three in the afternoon.

As confirmation that I really am leaving, I start to gather up my things. Sandra must think I'm taking my time on purpose ('Do as you like'), because she stops gazing at me and pretends she's not interested. What's holding me back is that I'm leaving with nothing; I'm more confused than when I arrived. I can see myself filling in the time I have left today and tomorrow, finding things to do until it's time for the return journey. I also see myself arriving back in Trelew empty-handed. Not that anybody is going to take me to task: Ledesma is dead, and Verani hasn't mentioned the matter in years. It's me who wants to know, and I find that the more I dig, the less sure I am.

None of this has ever mattered to Sandra, and still less now ('Go on, leave if that's what you want'). She also starts gathering her things, desperate to avoid it looking as if I am going and she is staying ('Let's go, why not? Let's go'). She does it so quickly it's as if she is the one leaving and I'm the one following her.

I can imagine she's not even that bothered about Valentinis' death. I can't think of any way to get her to feel that the other death, the unknown man who died almost seventy years ago, could be important for us, or for me. Perhaps it's not entirely true that Valentinis' death didn't affect her; perhaps that's just a front. Whatever the truth, she's in a bad mood, and there's no way I can return to the topic that interests me ('Didn't you say you were leaving? Well, leave then').

I suppose deep down I don't feel that Valentinis is that essential, and that's why I find it so hard to admit that with his death, or because of his death, the other matter has to be closed ('Can I ask you just one more question?'). I'm going to have to stay in Buenos Aires the rest of today anyway, and tomorrow morning, and I can't bear to think of wasting all that time ('Ask whatever you like: why not?'). One last thing, one last clue to hold on to ('Horischnik'). It's a name I blurt out, not a question ('Horischnik? What Horischnik?'). Sandra is the one who wants to leave now ('Horischnik, the one who played instead of the dead man') and pretends to be in a hurry ('Yes, the old man. What about him?') I was wrong to get her back up: she was never really interested, and now she wants to leave as quickly

as possible ('Did he really exist? I want to know if he existed').
I could never imagine Sandra with Valentinis, not even all the
times I saw them together.

◆

I remember that Ledesma accepted my argument, and that I
was very pleased he did. What for me was merely a suggestion
became for him a certainty: that the Firpo–Dempsey fight had
invaded the life (or the death) of the man in the hotel room, in
the same aggressive way that sport, big events and mass hysteria
did with any uninvolved individual.

This did not mean, however, that he finally decided to take a
real interest in the case. He thought I was right, but this didn't
increase his curiosity about what might have happened to the
dead man. Instead, he saw it as solving the mystery: the man
was the victim of popular culture. As Ledesma saw it, there
was no point determining whether it had been a murder or
suicide, because the same fundamental cause lay behind both.
He wasn't particularly interested in establishing whether the
man had been killed or had killed himself; in either case, it was
the Firpo–Dempsey fight that was the root cause, because the
man's life would have been saved had he managed to protect
himself from the event, and he lost it because he failed to
do so.

Verani tried to show him this was far too abstract a way
of solving the riddle. It was the same as arguing, for example,
that the reason behind every robbery or act of violence was the
misery and social inequalities born of capitalism. Not that this
was a false explanation, but it was too general: by explaining
everything, it explained nothing at all. A death is also always a

specific case, and the questions to be resolved about that death ought always to be concerned with its specific nature.

Ledesma did not see it that way. His reply was so furious that the two of us began to think he was putting it on. His explanation, he said, was the most concrete, the most specific, the only one possible. To deny the responsibility of what he now directly called fascism meant that any other suggestion was abstract, as it did not distinguish between the anecdotal and the essential.

◆

To add to his torment, they fight almost naked, showing their broad chests, muscular arms, taught thighs, the sinews where their shoulders support their necks, the sweep of their huge, symmetrical backs. Of course some parts are covered: their hands are encased in gloves, their feet in boots – boots like those gladiators wore, tall enough to cover part of their calves. And they also wear their ubiquitous shorts, pulled up over their stomachs to provide a smaller target, safeguarding their manhood.

Despite being covered like this, it's obvious they basically fight naked, emphasising that in this kind of combat what matters are their bodies. Manly, highly-trained bodies; there are no wooden sticks to wield and strike with, no swords which, despite being tipped, can still wound an opponent. Here the boxers' bodies are the only truth, the only reality: and this is precisely what the odd man out, Jack 'Slowest' Gallagher, would love to be able to forget.

He would love not to have to see or be so aware of the contestants' bodies, because they inevitably remind him of Melody Nelson and her weakness. This is exactly what she adores so much: this athletic vigour, this brute strength, the shiny steel capable of hurting without being hurt, the way boxers have developed their legs and arms, their necks, chests, the sheer breadth of their shoulders. It would be so much better to imagine a far less spectacular form of desire: to suffer (because he would still suffer) imagining that what Melody Nelson wants is a happy family with a good husband, a house in the suburbs with flowers and a garden, one or two dogs, two or three children, the latest model Ford, a hearth for the winter and shady trees for the summer. All this with someone who isn't him. That would be suffering enough. But as Mr Gallagher knows, that is not what Melody Nelson wants. He has a mental picture of a body that he himself has fondled in the night, trying not to make a noise and always worried they would be discovered: the sudden softness of flesh beneath the stiff corset, the mysteries promised by the rolled-up petticoat. That was what Melody Nelson was to him. What left when she left was this incomparable body. The only truth, reality. And what had she left him for? For those other strong, hard, sleek bodies: the bodies of boxers, yes: the body of a woman lost in a boxer's body.

As a referee, Mr Gallagher has to see all this. Not her: he doesn't have to see her with this one or that one. He wouldn't be able to bear it if he did. But he has to see these undeniable bodies, so painfully undeniable, so real; uncovered bodies, because they fight naked, or almost naked, and Mr Gallagher cannot help seeing them, partly because he's the referee and has to be sure there are no low blows or headbutts. He also has to touch them, to separate the two boxers if they try to tie each other in with their arms, he has to count to ten if one of them is knocked down, and then help him back on his feet while he raises the other's arm. He has to do all this, and as he does it he is mortified, because what he feels and what he sees in all this is Melody Nelson, her desire embodied, her desire for bodies embodied.

He suffers endlessly. He is mortified. He thinks: I should never have become a referee. Why did I do it? To see a boxer being knocked down (the way Jack Dempsey has just been knocked down) and to start imagining how Melody Nelson would lie alongside him, or on top of him? Is that why he's a referee? He suffers: yes, he is suffering. Yet he also gets enjoyment out of it. It's strange; he can't explain it. He suffers a lot, but he also enjoys it somehow. Melody Nelson: her soft, firm body, stripped of all her clothes and what little shame she posseses, fondling those bodies, wetting those bodies with her desire. Mr Gallagher feels his chest tightening with anguish, he can sense tears welling up in his choking throat. Yet down below, in his trousers, beneath his trousers, he can sense something stirring. He ignores the thousands of people crowded into the New York Polo Grounds; he doesn't allow that to prevent a certain stirring that might soon become visible. He even murmurs 'Melody'. Then her complete name 'Melody Nelson'. If anybody looked, they could see what was going on, but he doesn't care. He's a man, after all. Besides, everybody must be looking at Dempsey, who was knocked flying, or perhaps at the other boxer, the one who knocked him out of the ring. Mr Gallagher bends one leg slightly and turns to his left. There are photos of him in this position (from the back, fortunately for him). It looks as though he is kneeling to get a better view, and this is partially true. But only he knows the complete truth: he has shifted his position so that he can readjust what his vivid imagination has just caused to stir.

♦

'It's strange how, at certain periods, events seem to multiply. I don't know how to explain it, but there's a kind of concentration of events. In a certain more or less defined period of time lots and lots of things happen. Take, for example, that year, 1923. Look how many things happened then. You have your fight, I've got my concert. And Goffredi has his Palacio Barolo. I don't know if you've talked to Goffredi lately.'

'No.'

'Don't worry, I'll tell you about it. It's a fascinating coincidence. At the start of July, in that year 1923, mark you, one of the most famous buildings in all Buenos Aires was inaugurated. Just think of that period: Alvear was president, Argentina was apparently one of the most prosperous nations on earth, Latin America's most modern capital was constantly renewing itself. And in this flourishing atmosphere, the huge city gives birth to its tallest building: the Palacio Barolo.'

'The name's a joke.'

'It may sound like a joke, but what can you do – that was the owner's name. Don't dwell on its name though, that would be not to see the wood for the trees.'

'Barolo.'

'Yes, Barolo. It's a building conceived and built as a homage to Dante's *Divine Comedy*. How's that for an ambition?'

'I wouldn't want the wood to stop me seeing the trees.'

'Quite. The Palacio Barolo is situated on Avenida de Mayo, which is the most European of all Buenos Aires' avenues, apart from that other one in Palermo which comes out onto Plaza Italia and looks like the Champs Elysées in Paris.'

'So it's a very tall building.'

'Twenty-two storeys. If you look at it today, it hardly stands out from all the other tall buildings around it. But in 1923, and for many years afterwards, it was the highest point in all Buenos Aires.'

'Higher than the Obelisk?'

'The Obelisk hadn't been built then, Verani. What do you think, that Garay constructed it when he founded the city?'

'The Obelisk is beautiful.'

'You think so?'

'Yes.'

'Please, Verani, don't waste your time on that nonentity. I mean, when you go to Buenos Aires. Much better to go to the Square of the Two Congresses, commonly known as Plaza Congreso, and gaze in awe at the shapely exuberance of the Palacio Barolo.'

'Is it as beautiful as the Obelisk?'

'Why keep going on about the Obelisk? The Obelisk is as insipid as food without salt.'

'More boring than sucking a nail.'

'And that's what it looks like, an iron nail. It has nothing special about it.'

'And you're saying the Palacio Barolo does.'

'Yes, of course. A building conceived and built on the basis of Dante's *Divine Comedy*! That's something really special, don't you think?'

'Very special.'

'That's right.'

'Extra special, even.'

'Yes.'

'An extraordinary building.'

'Yes, it is.'

'Unique in the whole world.'

'Did you say "unique"?'

'Yes, in the whole wide world.'

'Well, I wouldn't go as far as that.'

'No, as you said, there are lots of obelisks. But there's only one Barolo.'

'I'm pleased you're so enthusiastic, Verani, but I wouldn't want to mislead you. Strictly speaking, it's not unique.'

'It isn't?'

'No.'

'There's another one like it?'

'Not like it: the same. Identical, Verani. What can I say? I'm sorry to disappoint you yet again.'

'So where is this twin?'

'Well, just across the river. In Montevideo.'

'Across the pond?'

'Yes.'

'Exactly the same?'

'Yes. Like Siamese twins.'

'Identical to this one that's so, so special?'

'Yes, identical.'

'They say Montevideo is a gloomy city.'

'Yes, it's sad, really sad.'

'Such is life.'

◆

He's also feeling around with his other hand. Crushed and blinded as he is, he has no other way of exploring where he is. But he doesn't stretch this hand out of the catacomb; instead he uses it to discover what is inside. If he could see, he would use his sharp eyes; as it is, he has to try to touch everything. By touching and feeling he discovers things. Now his fingers have met something, but he has no idea what. If he had been able to see, he would have known immediately what it was, but however sensitive his fingers are, they need more time. It's something soft but quite rough. It's flexible, and warm. If he twists his fingers, it folds over, if he pulls, it stretches. It's cloth: a sleeve. A jacket sleeve. So there must be an arm inside it. He feels with his fingers: yes, there is. A man's arm. If he moves down the arm, from the thicker part to the least thick, he will reach the wrist, and, further down still, another hand. He does this and can feel a wrist. On the wrist is a watch, a man's watch. If he could use his eyes, he could see what time it was; with his fingers all he can do is follow the edge of the strap and the watch face. When he reaches the hand, he can ask for help. For him, this is one of the ideas of what help means: one hand clutching another. He is not entirely clear what that means, but this isn't the moment to try to clarify what until now has been a confused feeling he has had. Is one hand clutching another offering help or asking for it? He doesn't know, and he doesn't care. Apart from anything else, it's the only chance he has. To find this hand and clutch it. This thought brings a glimmer of hope, but also a new concern. Donald Mitchell cannot get the image of a tomb out of his mind. And a tomb is a place where someone, the dead person, is alone, all alone. As everyone knows, we die alone, and we also know how lonely the dead are. And yet in this tomb, or what is almost a tomb and almost a death, there is someone else next to him. Who could it be? Who is it? Sometimes we are allowed company in our final resting place. But the only justification for that is love. Those who, out of love or resignation (if they're not the same people), have been able to spend a lifetime together often desire to be together after death as well. In order to cater to this wish, there are shared tombs (where, except in cases of double tragedies, one person arrives first and awaits the other) that convert this final resting place into the prolongation of their nuptial bed. Donald Mitchell finds all this moving, and with more time he might be overcome with emotion; but he cannot ignore the fact that in real life he is still a bachelor. He is and will continue to be one, at least for the foreseeable future. The fact is that he has never been in love, and he sometimes feels, or fears, he never will be. Be that as it may, in the situation he finds himself in, who is this other person lying underground next to him? Who is it, and what are they doing there? Donald Mitchell doesn't know: there's no reason he should. In fact, he is the thirty-six-year-old Kid McPartland, born in New Jersey, living in Manhattan, with features that give away his Irish ancestry as clearly as his name. He's one of the three judges for this world heavyweight title fight: his main task (but careful, it's not his only one) is to note down, round by round, the points each boxer has scored, so that if there is no knockout, the winner can be determined by totting up the scores he and the other two judges have awarded. This is Kid McPartland. What's he doing on the floor? It's very simple: Jack Dempsey, the world champion, fell on top of him just as he did on Donald Mitchell. And just like Mitchell, he was knocked flat and crushed by the weight. For the moment, at least, their destinies seem to be intextricably linked.

◆

'Please, let me explain, I wouldn't want you to get the wrong idea about either Barolo or me.'

'Explain away.'

'I think I need to explain why there's another building identical to the one I mentioned, which I called unique, and which I insist seems to me without compare.'

'Don't get so upset, Ledesma. We all know what Montevideo is: Buenos Aires, only smaller.'

'That's true, of course, but that isn't what I wanted to say. I need to explain a bit of history. The architect who planned and built the Palacio Barolo in Buenos Aires is the same man who soon afterwards did the same on the main avenue in Montevideo. There it's called the Palacio Salvo.'

'A much better name.'

'Possibly. So the buildings are the same because it was the same architect who designed and built them. They're not copies, and don't take anything away from each other.'

'It's as I was saying, Ledesma: Montevideo is like a smaller version of Buenos Aires.'

'I wouldn't insist on their size, if I were you. The Palacio Salvo is four storeys higher than the Palacio Barolo.'

'And why is that?'

'How should I know, Verani? Go and ask the architect: he's still alive.'

'He's had a long life.'

'He must be ninety if he's a day. The one who died young was Barolo.'

'Barolo.'

'Yes, Luis Barolo. He was the industrialist behind the Buenos

Aires Palace. He died in 1922, some months before the building was inaugurated. In other words, he never saw it completed.'

'Poor Barolo!'

'Yes, indeed. A typically Argentine case. I mean because of the way Palanti won him over. Palanti is the architect who built the building. One of those Italian wheeler-dealers, if you ask me. He convinced Barolo another war was about to break out in Europe. And guess what idea he sold him: that he could be the one to save the remains of Dante Alighieri. Dante was buried in Ravenna (and still is, I should add). Palanti succeeded in convincing Barolo that if there was another European war, Dante's remains would be in danger. Not just that: he persuaded him he ought to build a shrine where the ashes of the greatest bard Italy has ever known could be brought to Buenos Aires and kept safe.'

'Did the other guy think this was reasonable?'

'Yes; perfectly reasonable. Just like General Perón and Richter's projects for Huemul Island. Barolo backed Palanti's idea and paid for the construction of this sanctuary for Dante.'

'So where was it built?'

'What d'you mean, Verani? Don't you get it? The Palacio Barolo is the sanctuary.'

'There on Avenida de Mayo?'

'That's right! That was the plan. That's why the palace is a hundred metres high: because there are a hundred cantos in the *Divine Comedy*. And it's also why there are twenty-two floors: because most of the cantos have twenty-two stanzas. The ground floor is the Inferno. The first fourteen floors are built to evoke Purgatory. Between floors fourteen and twenty-two: Paradise. On the dome at the top there's a rotating lighthouse, which represents God.'

'Heresy!'

'Don't worry, there's no heresy. The building was inaugurated on 7 July 1923 with the blessing of the papal nuncio Giovanni Beda Cardinale. Among those present were Count Felizzano, the Italian ambassador, and the Argentine foreign minister of the day, Angel Gallardo.'

'Not Barolo?'

'Barolo was already dead.'

'And they never brought Dante.'

'No, of course not. For a start, war didn't break out – not in the twenties, at any rate. The plan to transfer Dante Alighieri's ashes was a product of nothing more than Mario Palanti's typically Italian flights of fancy, and Luis Barolo's typically Argentine credulity. But the palace was built. And given his name.'

'What happened to the Italian guy after that? I bet he made himself scarce.'

'He went first to Uruguay. Fortunately for them, I'd say: you should see how magnificent the Palacio Salvo is right next to Plaza Independencia. After that, he went back to Italy.'

'He went home.'

'Yes, he went home. To offer his services to Benito Mussolini.'

◆

Then finally something new cropped up. One afternoon. Valentinis called the paper from Buenos Aires. It didn't sound urgent, and his voice was neutral. He obviously didn't think he was telling us anything important: all he wanted to do was add a few more details to what he had already found out so we wouldn't think he had forgotten us. He didn't seem to regard the new information as crucial, except that it was very precise, and precision in these matters always suggests there could be some truth to it. What he had discovered in the judicial files were the dead man's personal details. Valentinis saw this as a mere footnote, and in a way he was right. But alongside all the other important facts, for us, footnotes could be the most revealing thing.

He asked to speak to Verani. He didn't know Ledesma was interested too. At that time, Verani regarded any call from him as urgent. He ran to the phone, knocking over a pile of papers or something similar on the way. I happened to be in the editorial offices: Verani waved frantically at me. Then, clenching the phone between ear and shoulder, he made a fist and scribbled in the air with his other hand: he wanted me to write something down. I grabbed a biro from one of the desks and picked up a scrap of paper. I went up to him.

Verani spelled out the words: Otto Stiglitz. Double T, T-Z. I asked him what they meant. The dead man's name, he said. He added a number: 52. His age. The name confirmed what we had already suspected: he was a foreigner. Valentinis knew the exact details. Verani listened, and told me. I wrote it down: Austrian, born in Vienna on 14 July 1871.

An Austrian in Buenos Aires in September 1923. Impossible not to think what we immediately thought: that Stiglitz must have been part of Richard Strauss's orchestra. When he wasn't playing or rehearsing, he spent his time in the hotel.

◆

'And the Palacio Barolo played a vital role in the story of the Firpo–Dempsey fight.'

'You don't say.'

'I do, Verani. Why else would I mention it?'

'How should I know? To make conversation?'

'Well, we're always conversing. But not just for the sake of it.'

'Of course, it's not simply idle chat.'

'You're probably wondering how a building, however impressive it might be, could play any sort of role in a boxing match.'

'Barolo: Ba-ro-lo, you called it.'

'You must be wondering.'

'Yes.'

'It's very simple. As I just explained, the Palacio Barolo had a lighthouse at the very top.'

'Yes. You said that was God.'

'Not me, the architect Mario Palanti did. But not that it was God – that it represented him.'

'It's the same thing.'

'No, it's not, but that doesn't matter. The thing is, the Palacio Barolo had this huge lighthouse at the top. A beam of 300,000 watts. And let me remind you: in those days, it was the tallest building in Buenos Aires.'

'The Obelisk hadn't been built.'

'Not yet. Well, because of its height and its powerful searchlight, the authorities decided they could use it to tell people the result of the world championship fight. Nowadays, Verani, in the 1970s, we know that news travels quickly. A lot of it arrives instantaneously. But transport yourself back then, Verani: it's the first half of the twenties. It's the modern world, obviously, the whole world is accessible, everybody is crazy about the new, the present and future are what matters. Modern times, Verani. Everyone is obsessed with all the technological advances. In hindsight, what is obvious about those years is that everything was just beginning, it had hardly got started. But people – ordinary people, I mean – already had this idea that things must be new. What does that mean, you may ask. It's very simple: that if Luis Angel Firpo and Jack Dempsey were fighting, Argentina wanted to receive the news live and on the spot, as we would say nowadays. Just imagine: all Buenos Aires, or almost all of it, was desperate to know the result of the fight. So what did the authorities do? They put two searchlights on top of the Palacio Barolo. Two huge searchlights, capable of sending out two clear, powerful beams of light. One blue, the other red. The agreement was: if Firpo won, the blue searchlight would be switched on. If Dempsey won, then it would be the red one. What d'you think of that?'

'It was a good idea. Blue is the colour of the Argentine flag.'

'Well, it's sky blue, Verani. Sky blue and white, not bright blue like the beam. Anyway, that's not important. People crowded the streets of Buenos Aires, peering up anxiously into the night sky. The suspense was tremendous. Just imagine, the whole city on tenterhooks. And then: what happened? At a certain moment just before midnight, what happened?'

'No idea. What happened?'

'What happened is that a beam lit up the night sky ... the blue beam.'

'The blue beam?'

'Yes.'

'The blue beam!'

'Yes!'

'So … Firpo won!'

'Yes, Firpo. Luis Angel Firpo. That's what the expectant crowds believed. There was immediate rejoicing all over Buenos Aires. An explosion of popular joy. Everybody cheered, applauded, blew trumpets, shouted. People jumped in the air, embraced each other. Some cried with emotion; others sang the national anthem. Firpo was the national hero.'

'He deserved to be.'

'Everybody celebrated: a noisy, heaving mass of people. Mass euphoria invaded the streets, the atmosphere was electric. Then all of a sudden, when nobody was expecting it, when it seemed impossible, something else happened.'

'What?'

'The impossible, Verani, the impossible.'

'Yes, but what impossible?'

'All of a sudden, another light shone out … the red beam.'

'The red beam?'

'Yes.'

'Dempsey's beam?'

'Yes.'

'Red like the stripes on the Yankee flag.'

'Yes.'

'So Dempsey won.'

'That's right, Verani. Dempsey won. We already know that. Minute after minute, the red beam shone from the top of the Palacio Barolo. In the streets, people realised the first one must have been a mistake. A dreadful mistake, which had given them a fleeting sense of hope. The red beam corrected the blue beam, cancelled it out. They were hoping against hope that the blue beam would come back and annul the red one. If someone had made a first mistake, then they might have made another one. Of course this didn't happen. The red beam stayed lighting up the sky: there was no denying it. It was so undeniable that the reports in the next morning's papers would merely confirm what everyone already knew: Jack Dempsey had won. For some time, the crowds continued with their deluded joy, but in the end, as with any unsustainable situation, the atmosphere changed, their hopes ebbed away. The streets fell gloomily silent. Heartbroken, the crowds began to disperse. Everybody went home without a word. It was winter, but not that cold: it was only a week before the start of spring.

◆

Yes, Stiglitz was a musician in Richard Strauss's orchestra. A cellist, Otto Stiglitz had been with the Vienna Philharmonic Orchestra for twelve years. He was not what might be called a principal player, because the first cellist was someone called Frederick Buxbaum (Valentinis had looked up the original concert programmes in the Teatro Colón archives). Nor was he just another musician. He wasn't a replacement player, he was a regular, with plenty of experience in the orchestra. Richard Strauss sometimes even stayed talking music with him.

He shared the room with Leopold Langer and Anton Weis (Valentinis had searched through the City Hotel registers) who were also stable members of the orchestra. The only musicians who had rooms of their own were the soloists: for example, Frederick Buxbaum, the first cellist, or Karl Freith, solo viola player; or Alfred Blumen, who had excelled in performing Beethoven's *Fifth Piano Concerto* on a Bechstein from Harrod's department store. Reasonably enough, Richard Strauss himself stayed in the hotel's main suite, which coincidentally had the same name as Beethoven's concerto: The Emperor Suite.

There were plenty of reasons, as well as the means, to ensure that Otto Stiglitz's strange death was quickly forgotten. Nobody wanted any scandal related to the Vienna Philharmonic in Buenos Aires: not the Argentine authorities, nor the organisers of the concerts, the other members of the orchestra, or indeed Richard Strauss himself. All of them preferred to see the matter hushed up. In cases like these, police interest is only lukewarm, and is quite easily satisfied. The Argentine and Austrian authorities combined to make sure the affair was closed before it had ever properly been opened. The official version was suicide, which was not entirely implausible. That way, nobody had the fact that a killer might still be on the loose on their conscience.

The transfer of the body posed a further problem, and another reason for things to be settled as quickly and quietly as possible. To repatriate the corpse would have raised legal as well as financial difficulties, not to mention the awkward question of having to store the coffin with the dead man inside for several days. And for what? So that he could be laid to rest in Vienna, where he was born. Somebody suggested that all musicians are citizens of the world, because music is universal, and that therefore a musician was at home wherever he found himself. Somebody else had a more practical argument: Otto Stiglitz was a bachelor. He had no wife or children; his parents were already dead, and he had been estranged from his only sister for a number of years, apparently because she was unhappy at Stiglitz not wanting to marry and have a family. As a result, nobody in Austria was going to claim the body.

Everything was arranged smoothly. The police closed the case, and the legal documents (the forensic tests and the scene of the crime reports) were archived. The press, which soon forgets everything, was allowed to forget this too.

Otto Stiglitz was cremated one windy morning at the Chacarita Cemetery in the city of Buenos Aires. The next morning, which was equally windy, a small procession made its way to the Fishermen's Club on a pier at the northern Costanera, also in the city of Buenos Aires. It was made up of some of the leading members of the Vienna Philharmonic Orchestra, including their conductor, the famous Richard Strauss, as well as a few grey local officials. Otto Stiglitz's ashes were scattered on the queasy waters of the Río de la Plata, where they soon dispersed.

◆

If the doctor had been there, leaning over him, or close beside him, what would he have said? In this case, the person Dempsey is thinking of is Jack 'Doc' Kearns. What would he say if he was beside him or leaning over him? He would ask him questions. The usual, obvious questions, the ones that helped determine how lucid or groggy a boxer was. The doc would ask him: what's your name, how old are you, where are we, in what city, what date is it today, what are you doing at this very moment (all this shouted in his ear). But since Jack 'Doc' Kearns was not there, and, for the moment at least, showed no sign of appearing, Dempsey decided to go ahead on his own. He was going to sort it out for himself, as they say. He was going to judge for himself how clear his mind was. After all, he knew what the questions were: every knocked-out boxer had heard them. Carefully, calmly, rationally, he went through them and told himself: my name is Jack Dempsey. I'm twenty-eight years old. I'm at the Polo Grounds in the city of New York. Today is 14 September 1923. And what I was doing was defending my world heavyweight champion title. The thing I love most in all the world. The only thing I have.

NINE

OTTO STIGLITZ WAS STAYING IN room No. 404. He and all the other members of the orchestra were put up on the fourth floor of the City Hotel. It's understandable that they should all have been together and have moved about en masse. But Strauss had adopted even stricter measures: nobody outside the orchestra was to have any contact with them. To this end, they went down to the hotel restaurant to eat an hour before the other guests (something that coincided with their European habit of dining early anyway), and rarely left the hotel except to be taken to the Teatro Colón. As the rehearsals and concerts took up almost all their time (they had performances on the 8th, 10th, 12th, 13th, 14th, 15th, 16th, 18th, 21st, 22nd, 23rd and 25th) they did little else but play.

Nobody apart from them was allowed up to the fourth floor. Richard Strauss had been particularly firm about this: since his musicians were the only guests there, it was not hard to prevent anyone else having access. The porters, lift attendants and maids all knew this, and strictly followed the instruction: nobody wanted to offend Strauss or disturb their illustrious visitors in any way.

Strauss and every single member of the orchestra must have thought that music was an art which created its own world. The main auditorium of the Teatro Colón could only have reinforced this belief: that of a world apart, where nothing from outside was able to enter. Strauss wanted the everyday life of the hotel to be as similar as possible to this. As a result, for the entire length of time they were in Buenos Aires, the musicians lived more or less completely isolated from the rest of the world.

◆

'Mahler and Strauss, who both faced rejection by the conservative tastes of their time, helped each other a great deal.'

'Good mates.'

'You could put it like that. But it's more than that: two great musicians, two great conductors, joined together by the same desire to break with the past and innovate, were united by the shared destiny of being misunderstood.'

'You already told me that. They couldn't get work.'

'Of course they could get work. You have to dig a little deeper to understand what their problem was.'

'So they could get some work.'

'No, it's not that. Try to understand that not everything in life is measured so crudely. Even in their own lifetimes, Mahler and Strauss were renowned.'

'Famous, in other words.'

'Something more than that, Verani. A film star like Sabu is famous. As I said, they were renowned. But certain what you might call avant-garde artists find it hard to gain proper recognition while they are alive. Their contemporaries don't understand, and so it is for posterity to do them justice.'

'Us, in other words.'

'We two and many more besides, of course. And to be honest, I'm not so sure about you, at least until you've been to my place and listened to Mahler with me.'

'So he wasn't popular at the time?'

'He was a great innovator. Of course, he didn't come out of nowhere: if you listen to Beethoven, you'll understand him, and Wagner and Brückner the same. But if you don't listen to anything, you won't understand anything. Yet even if you know where he came from, Mahler can sound new. Completely new. And that confuses people. He can even confuse us nowadays, even though we've had a Schoenberg or an Alban Berg since then, if you follow me. Just think what it must have been like in his own day. His music was really new and wasn't easy to assimilate. The same goes for Richard Strauss.'

'So they became friends?'

'I wouldn't quite put it like that. It sounds as though you're belittling them. As if they got together because they were in the same predicament.'

'And it wasn't like that.'

'Of course not. It's Gustav Mahler and Richard Strauss we're talking about here. As well as being composers, they were both orchestra conductors. That meant they could support each other's efforts. Not because they were good mates, as you put it, or because they felt sorry for one another. It was something very different, Verani: something to do with artistic affinity. It was music that brought them together: a similar concept of what music should be, and a similar frustration at the limitations of their era. They were writing music for a time which did not yet exist.'

'So they gave each other a leg up.'

'As a conductor, Mahler would include pieces by Richard Strauss in his performances. And Strauss did the same in return. It would be naïve to deny one reason for this was to help each other and help themselves. That's not what I'm saying. But at the same time, we can't reduce this extraordinary collaboration between two musical giants to a vulgar "giving each other a leg up". There was also genuine enthusiasm and true conviction behind what they did. The proof lies in the fact that Strauss, who outlived Mahler, carried on promoting his music even after his death. I mean, even though he knew he could not expect anything in return – not that he ever thought like that, of course. Mahler was no longer of this world (if, permit me a moment's emotion, he ever really had been) and yet Strauss continued to honour his music with much-admired performances. Let me remind you of something you already know: twelve years after Mahler's death, he put on his first symphony, known as the *Titan Symphony*, giving the first performance here.'

'Not here. In Buenos Aires. Nobody ever comes here.'

◆

Often – too often, Sandra doesn't bother to reply, or gives a meaningless answer. She knows it's irritating, and that's why she does it. Even more than anybody else, it drove Valentinis mad: he didn't want to shout at her, but he always ended up doing so. Once, unaware that he was parodying a tango, he even shouted: I'm leaving so that I don't hit you. It's just one of Sandra's little ways. More than once with me too she's tried to avoid answering or to change the subject. She gave up when she realised it didn't infuriate me. But now she's trying it again, possibly because she knows it's the last time we'll ever meet, or she realises there is something that interests me a lot (a lot more than her, that's for sure). I asked her about Horischnik, and she said nothing. She didn't say if he had existed or not. When I insisted, she started to polish the sunglasses she was about to put on with a rough cloth that must have scratched rather than cleaned them. That seemed to demand all her attention: the full amount of attention she could command.

We didn't say goodbye.

Now I'm going on my own into a café on Avenida Callao.

It's four in the afternoon.

I think about Abraham Horischnik. I tell myself: Sandra wasn't going to tell me anything that might arouse my enthusiasm. Not the way things were going between us. If she had wanted to upset me, she could have said openly that Horischnik had simply been another of Valentinis' inventions. She could have, and yet she didn't. I think I know the reason: Sandra is very good about keeping quiet or choosing not to say things, but she doesn't know how to lie. She's incapable of a deliberate, out-and-out lie (Valentinis knew this, of course, which was why he never asked her direct questions). If she didn't answer my questions about Horischnik, it was because if she had, she would have been obliged to admit that at least part of the story was true. Rather than admit that, she preferred to say nothing and so leave me with the doubt. But now I'm sure of it: if Horischnik had not existed, Sandra would have taken pleasure in telling me so. So I get up, go over to the bar and ask if they have a phone book. They say they do. I ask if they'll lend it me. They say they will. I go back to my seat lugging the huge tome. I open it and start searching through the letter H. I find the surname Horischnik: there are several. I look up Abraham: there's only one.

Seeing all the details lends a sense of reality to the name: a specific telephone number, an address, an avenue (Angel Gallardo), a nearby park (Parque Centenario), a real life. To my surprise, I realise that until this moment I had taken if for granted that Abraham Horischnik belonged to another era. By which I mean that he could not possibly still be alive. Ledesma has just died, Valentinis is dead as well, although I've only just found that out: all this had made it hard for me to imagine that, even though he is much older than them, there is no reason why Horischnik should not be alive.

I do a mental calculation. At the time of the concert, Abraham Horischnik was very young. Only a little over twenty: a sort of Argentine prodigy. Let's say he was at the most twenty-five. If he was twenty-five in 1923, that means he was born in 1898. Which in turn means that now he must be, or is, ninety-one or ninety-two. To think he *is* that old is much more comforting than to think he could be that old. So I scribble down the number from the phone book and decide to call it.

◆

'It's always a good idea to see great men as human beings.'

'If you like, I'll start: they were two ordinary guys, your average sort of person.'

'You're getting us off to a bad start, Verani. If you think they're just average sort of people, why not try composing the

Lieder von der Erde. Give it a go and then we'll see. Knock off *Salomé* any spare evening you have. Then come and tell me how easy it was, something any ordinary guy could do.'

'I don't know why you say we should try to see them as human if you immediately start getting mad at me.'

'It's just that if I give you an inch you take a mile. What I was trying to suggest was that, while we should recognise the exceptional genius of these men, we should also admit they had human weaknesses.'

'I have no problem admitting that.'

'I can see you don't. What I'm saying we should do is to admit that in some secret corner of his troubled soul, Mahler may have harboured, how shall I put it, a slight feeling of resentment towards Richard Strauss.'

'His great friend.'

'His colleague and associate, yes. We can't deny he felt a slight grudge against him.'

'The great Mahler?'

'Yes, the great Mahler. And he was great, despite everything. Great but human.'

'He'd acquired a bit of a grudge against Strauss, despite their artistic affinity.'

'The thing is, the whole of history, and the history of art above all, is riddled with injustices. As we've already discussed, Mahler was almost universally recognised as a wonderful orchestra conductor. No one doubted his preeminence. Things weren't so easy when it came to his own music, however: the music he composed. In addition to the intrinsic difficulties of his works, because of the audacity of their formal experimentation, they presented further problems due to their sheer size. A Mahler symphony (the *Third*, for example, or the *Second*) can last upwards of an hour.'

'Audiences got sick to the back teeth of them.'

'They became difficult to include in programmes. What new composers try to do is slip one of their works in among other well-known ones by established composers, which are what bring people along to the concerts.'

'See? Don't go telling me people don't matter.'

'But Mahler's were so long it was difficult to include them with other better-known works because on their own they took up all the time there was for a concert.'

'How long does a good tango last? No longer than three minutes. Four at most.'

'The contrast with Strauss is striking. Not that Strauss deliberately composed more accessible music. We know he didn't. But he was astute when it came to commercial matters, whereas Mahler was always so caught up in his all-encompassing world of music that he seemed oblivious to them. Strauss, on the other hand, knew about the channels linking music and money, and made sure they were open. Which also led to fame.'

'Fame is a mug's game.'

'They were different even in the way they related art to life. Their contemporaries said Strauss knew how to relax after work. In other words: Strauss knew how to live. Mahler didn't. Mahler lived for and through his work. He lived working. He never stopped.'

'That's not good.'

'But even he could see that the other man was having more success. It was true. The public, impresarios, other conductors, music critics, everyone praised him. In comparison (and we must understand he couldn't avoid the comparison) things weren't going so well for Mahler.'

'He was losing out to Strauss.'

'You could put it like that. He still had posterity. Mahler was aware of that, well aware of it. You can be sure he knew which of the two of them was the greater composer, the one who was really going to last. Mahler already knew he was the great composer of his time. He and not Strauss or anyone else. Him. And he knew it. He also knew, because history demonstrates it time and again, that it is posterity's definitive judgement which puts everything in its proper place. That would be when it became obvious Richard Strauss was a very significant composer, but Gustav Mahler was an exceptional one.'

'So why did he get so hot and bothered?'

'The musician composes for posterity, but the man, like all men, lives in his own time, Verani. And so, what did he see: in newspapers, Richard Strauss; in contracts, Richard Strauss; in the best concert halls, Richard Strauss; in music publishing, Richard Strauss. He could analyse things rationally and think to himself: for posterity, I'll be the one, not him. But he couldn't tell that to his guts. He couldn't stomach the present.'

◆

Ledesma was fascinated by that kind of hermetic, untouchable and untouched sphere. To him, music itself was the most perfect demonstration of this desire for autonomy; a world of pure form that was self-sufficient and needed nothing else. He liked the idea that this same need for self-sufficiency could be found in someone's life (like Mahler, for example, who was completely devoted to music and almost always unconcerned with anything else) or in a space (what is left of the outside world when one immerses oneself in the Teatro Colón concert hall?) or even in an everyday context (one entire floor of a hotel which is suddenly cut off from the rest of the world and becomes something quite different).

Otto Stiglitz's death meant that this sphere had been breached somewhere. Any other kind of death (more specifically, a death from natural causes) might not have had the same effect: after all, there is no way of foreseeing or preventing the collapse of a weak heart, or the changes to someone's brain if something is suddenly disconnected. But Stiglitz was found hanging from a leather belt, which only served to heighten the sense of rupture produced by every death. With this artificial death, which would not have happened if someone had not taken a hand in it, something from the outside had smashed the hermetic sphere and penetrated inside. It did not matter that, given the circumstances, the musicians of Strauss's orchestra found themselves in, it might reasonably be concluded that the person who had ended Stiglitz's life was a member of the orchestra or was very closely associated with it (which also applied, of course, to Stiglitz himself). No, to Ledesma that did not matter. A death of this sort demolished the smooth surface of the routine of rehearsals and concerts, the universe made up of music and only music.

It remained to be seen what could have been the cause of this invasion of a virtual ivory tower. To argue it must have had something to do with the Firpo–Dempsey fight was no more far-fetched than to establish any other kind of causal connection, and it at least allowed Ledesma to reach some kind of agreement with Verani. It was true that in Buenos Aires during those days the topic was, as they say, in the air. If something alien, from the outside, had penetrated the limpid crystal of harmonies and rehearsals, of rhythms and counterpoint, it could well have been related to the fight, and not in spite of its being on the outside and alien, but precisely because of that. This was what it was all about: what happens when two worlds which should not be in contact suddenly collide.

Ledesma remained convinced that there had not and could not have been any link between the life of a cellist in the Vienna Philharmonic and a boxing match between two brutes dedicated to beating each other senseless. Absolutely nothing. He would not yield in this, or give any ground to Verani: he even insisted the two were like oil and water, to show how incompatible he thought they were. All he would admit was that by some channel or other, something from one world had passed into the other, with the result we all knew about: Otto Stiglitz's horrible death. He was certain that if the common, vulgar world outside were to penetrate the sublime world of music, it would of necessity produce a catastrophe.

◆

The other hand lets go of his, and once again he feels lost. Lost twice over: lost because he has no idea where he is or how to get out, and lost because there appears to be no salvation. He is also lost because he feels like a sinner: every time something dreadful happens to him, he is filled with the vague sense that a god is punishing him for having behaved so shamefully in the past. The other person dropped his hand and escaped out of the side. He can't find any chink in the tomb and is still buried there. So he changes tack: he doesn't try to slide out anymore. Nor is he hoping that someone else will come to his aid. He tells himself determinedly: counter force with force. He pulls his arms back towards his sides: the opposite of what he has been trying to do until now. He presses his arms by his chest. He digs his elbows into the ground. Something hurts, but he tries to ignore it. He lifts his body, struggling to breathe, and manages to make a little room. Once he has done that, he uses the tight space to turn his hands over and raise them upwards, bent at the elbows. If he didn't have the heavyweight champion of the world on top of him, this might seem like an effeminate gesture. But since he is being crushed underneath Dempsey, the matter does not arise. The floor is his support, and Jack Dempsey is a world (a world weighing down on him just as the real world often weighs on wretched individuals). He flexes his elbows, tenses his forearms and spreads his hands on the boxer's profligate back. He counts to three (very rapidly: he gets to three in the time it would take someone else to get to one) and pushes. As hard as he can, until he's almost in tears. Dempsey doesn't budge. It's almost worse than trying to move a piano, a well-read person's library, a truck with jammed wheels or a railway engine. He tries again: nothing. He is making the same movement as if he was trying to raise himself from the floor doing press-ups. He starts with his hands by his chest, then tries to straighten them upwards. The difference is that when he does press-ups he is facing the ground, whereas now he is face up. Also, with press-ups, the strength in his arms is enough to move and separate his body from the floor, but now Jack Dempsey doesn't move or become separated from him. He tries again. He presses down with his elbows, tenses his hands and his clinging fingers. His teeth are about to chatter from the effort, he is ready to bring his knees up if and when there is room for them. And this time Jack Dempsey does shift a little. Yes, a little, even though it seems like a miracle, faith moving the human mountain. Donald Mitchell senses he is starting to raise him. Little by little, just like you might move a mountain. He feels he is a David toppling a Goliath. A Samson among the columns of the temple. He does not know there is somebody else (by the name of McPartland, the one who let go of his hand and managed to crawl out) who is now standing up and is also tugging as hard as he can to get Dempsey back on his feet. Donald Mitchell still thinks he is making all the effort. What's true is that he has got the worst of it, and that his part in the strenuous efforts to get the champion back on his feet is important too. He is succeeding in straightening his arms. He can't give in now. The image of an ant springs to his mind. At first, he sees it as derogatory: a bug, an insect, a mere fragile nothing. But then he reconsiders: he remembers something he once read in an old popular science magazine, where he learnt that an ant is capable of carrying twenty times its own weight. He has no wish, and there is no need, to actually carry Jack Dempsey, all he wants to do is literally get him off. But if an ant can manage weights up to twenty times greater than itself, why shouldn't he, however much of a weakling he is, be able to lift the giant Jack Dempsey, who must only weigh two and a half times what he does? Filled with this faith, he pushes and pushes.

◆

'Richard Strauss also knew the place each of the two of them would occupy when it came to writing the definitive pages of the history of music. He saw that very clearly. He therefore admired Mahler and tried to collaborate with him as far as possible, to prevent the sniping of his mediocre critics from completely demoralising him. For his part, he was gratified by the success he was quite rightfully enjoying in those years, and showed he could be generous. He felt honoured by the recognition and friendly gestures Gustav Mahler made towards him. Mahler really appreciated him. In certain circumstances, in fact, his was the only opinion that truly mattered. Mahler was capable of being scornful about anyone else's criticism, even those of such an eminent authority as Hans von Bulow. But he was always interested in Strauss's comments, and felt them deeply.'

'So Mahler also had a good opinion of him.'

'Of course he did. The thing was that at the same time he harboured somewhat contradictory feelings. Basically he was very fond of Strauss: he had respect, gratitude and great fellow feeling for him. But he was also slightly resentful. He kept it to himself, of course, he tried to control it and didn't shout it from the rooftops.'

'I get it: in the daytime, with everyone around, he was all smiles. But in bed at night, it kept him awake. Tossing and turning under the blankets, unable to get Strauss out of his mind.'

'He expressed his feelings in private correspondence. For example, after many bitter rejections, in October 1903 Mahler began to win some recognition. He conducted one of his symphonies in Amsterdam, for example, and it went really well. He wrote to his wife Alma: "I'm much more successful than Strauss, even though he's very popular here."'

'He couldn't stand his success.'

'Yes, it stuck in his throat. Or rather, he couldn't get it out of his mind. And yet at the same time he appreciated Strauss and did all he could to support him, such as fighting tooth and nail against the censorship over *Salomé* in Vienna.'

'He had mixed emotions.'

'Yes, he felt both things at the same time. Through all those years, Mahler was gripped by a sense of troublesome animosity or rivalry towards Strauss. Of course he never allowed any of this to seep out.'

'Strauss hadn't the slightest idea.'

'No. To the end of their days they were always on the best of terms. Or rather, until the end of Mahler's days, because he was the first to die.'

'Before Strauss.'

'A long time before. If you remember, Mahler died in May 1911. One of the last satisfactions he ever had was to receive a note from Strauss asking after his health. And I've already told you about all that Strauss went on doing on Mahler's behalf, even after his regrettable death. In fact, Strauss lived on another thirty-eight years. A lot of time went by, a lot of things happened: the Great War, the first performance in Vienna of *Salomé*, becoming conductor of the Vienna Opera, his big tour of South America. In January 1933, Hitler came to power. In November of that same year, Strauss took up the post of president of the Reich's Music Bureau.'

'How nice.'

'Richard Strauss always said that art was above politics.'

'You don't say.'

'He left the post after a series of arguments. Among others, because he wanted to put on music by Mahler and the authorities would not allow it. After that came the Second World War, which lasted six years. At the end of the conflict, the Third Reich was finished and Richard Strauss left behind the oppressive cold and hunger of Germany to seek refuge in Switzerland.'

'Nicely done too.'

'Now imagine it's the evening of 28 December 1946. Strauss is visiting the house of his friend and future biographer Willi Schuh. He spends some time browsing in his library. Then, all of a sudden, he finds something.'

'What?'

'A book.'

'Of course! But what book?'

'Alma Mahler's memoirs. Naturally enough, he starts to read them. After all, it's basically about his friend Gustav. Thirty-five years have passed since his untimely death. Thirty-five years of honouring his music and their friendship. Now, in December 1946, Strauss flicks through the pages of Alma Mahler's book and guess what he finds.'

'What?'

'A series of terrible letters where Mahler said all kinds of harsh things about him.'

'No!'

'Yes. Alma published them without compunction. And so, thirty or more years later, Strauss discovered what his friend had really thought of him. From that moment on, he looked on an entire period of his life (the most important, we could say) in a completely different light. The whole story of their cherished friendship changed its meaning overnight. All alone in Switzerland, Strauss learned everything that Mahler was careful not to tell him during all those years when they were the greatest of friends. He read it in a book that thousands upon thousands of others would read, although Mahler was a long way off, had been dead many years. There was nothing he could say or do about it.'

'So what did Strauss do?'

'Just that: nothing. He closed the book, left it on a table, stuck his hands in his trouser pockets and stared out of the window at the harsh grip that winter had taken on the landscape.'

♦

The best way to forget Melody Nelson is to think of her. Doing the opposite, never thinking of her, has proved a failure. Sometimes he managed it for several hours; he had even spent almost entire evenings without thinking of her once. But inevitably, sooner or later, for some chance reason or for no reason at all, the memory of her returned. If he was with boxers, it was almost instantaneous. But it also reappeared as if out of the blue and with no obvious cause. Once he travelled for nearly two hours back to Manhattan from Coney Island and didn't give her a single thought; and yet as he was crossing the East River, without realising it, without knowing how, she was suddenly on his mind again. His huge efforts never to think of her were doomed to fail; apart from anything else, they meant he had to think of her at least a little.

Since this initial idea proved impossible, he hit on another strategy: to think of her as much as he could. To surrender to the inevitable rather than fighting it. To give in and emphasise it to the maximum; to force himself to think of Melody Nelson. To devote his best and worst thoughts to her, and to do so both when he had something concrete to think about and when he was thinking of nothing in particular. The thousand and one ways of thinking about Melody Nelson: remembering, reconciling himself, making a decision, and so on to infinity. Until finally he was so full of her that he had enough. Stuffing himself until he could take no more. He was so stuffed he almost suffered from mental retching, if such a thing exists. He gorged on Melody Nelson until he felt his head was going to explode. And then, with surprising ease, he forgot her. From thinking too much about her, he turned a somersault and dismissed all thoughts of her. Where once she was everything, now she was nothing.

Mr Gallagher returns to the real world with the relieved expression of someone who has been very sick and all of a sudden finds himself cured. There's also something in his expression of a person who has slept and dreamt a lot, but suddenly wakes up and finds none of it was real. He looks around at everything with innocent eyes: everything he sees surprises and moves him. Now, for example, what does he see in front of him? There's a challenger, who's called Firpo, and who is obviously keen to see what he thinks is the end of the bout. What else? The champion, Jack Dempsey, knocked clear out of the ring. What else? Thousands of spectators. And him: the referee. The fight referee. As much a protagonist as the man who landed the punch and the man who was knocked down.

◆

Ledesma had no doubts. The only possible option for a cellist from the Vienna Philharmonic Orchestra was to know nothing about boxing or its implications. As Ledesma saw it, there was no other possibility: a man who dedicated himself to perfecting his musical technique, so successfully that no less a celebrity than Richard Strauss was conducting him, could only view the crude confrontation between two boxers as totally alien.

At the same time, however, Ledesma admitted that on the night of 14 September 1923, Otto Stiglitz had died because of the world championship fight between Jack Dempsey and Luis Angel Firpo. I wondered how he could reconcile these two opposing convictions. Ledesma replied with what was his fundamental belief: that it must have been to do with a wager. As he saw it, the channel between the two worlds that explained the death of Stiglitz in his City Hotel room was a bet on the Firpo–Dempsey fight.

A gambler's passion is for the wager itself, rather than whatever is being bet on, and still more than the amount or thing being staked, which sometimes may even be nothing. People will bet on anything, even betting nothing, provided they can make a bet. The attraction lies in forecasting, challenging, taking the risk, in winning or losing. The attraction comes from the bet itself, and has nothing to do with whatever it is that is being wagered on. For example, there could be a dog ambling down the middle of a not very wide and not very narrow street. Two men see it go by. One of them says: 'Twenty bucks says that when the dog leaves the street, it will climb the pavement on this side, and not on the far side.' The other man accepts, and the bet is made. It's blindingly obvious that neither man is remotely interested in the dog, or in the pavement it's going to climb onto. They are simply the excuse for the bet, and that's enough.

According to Ledesma, that is what Stiglitz must have done. He must have been as horrified by boxing as any other well-educated person would be. And yet, if he was a gambler, a fight that everybody was talking about must have seemed like a good excuse to indulge his passion. Gambling combines feelings, chance and a calculation of odds; in other words, it's a combination of pure intuition and mathematical calculation.

Perhaps it wasn't so strange that a musician should see an affinity between his profession and the desire to speculate about something yet to happen.

While it is possible to bet nothing, it is more usual to bet something. Often, in fact, people bet a lot. Some of them risk an expensive watch, a car, even a house, and then the giddy sensation every wager brings is redoubled by the dizzy feeling that something so valuable could be lost. Stiglitz must have bet something of really great value. The Firpo–Dempsey fight might have meant nothing to him, but whatever he wagered must have meant a lot. An Austrian musician who happened to find himself in Buenos Aires could not have cared less if it was Firpo or Dempsey who won the fight. He probably didn't even know who they were. But whatever he did bet, on whichever of the two contestants, had to be so vital that if Stiglitz won, the man who lost chose to kill him rather than pay up, and if he lost, Stiglitz preferred to kill himself rather than hand it over.

◆

Has he lost? So he's lost? Does everything that's going on mean he has lost the fight? Dempsey is awake. His back is hurting, though he has no idea why. He also senses that someone is tugging determinedly at his arm, but he doesn't know why they're doing that either. His mind is still not clear enough for him to see or think: this is a photographer, that's one of the judges. For now he can simply feel and glimpse things. He does not really know what's going on. Though at least he knows that he doesn't know, and that, even in these circumstances, means real progress. He can ask himself certain questions, and if he doesn't know the answers, he is aware that he doesn't. The most insistent of these questions is if he has lost. From what he can glimpse, from the way everything was smashed and shattered, from the way he flew through the air and fell so drastically, he wonders whether it wouldn't be best for him to conclude that he has already lost the fight. It may well be that the world heavyweight championship fight is over, and he is the only one who doesn't know it. It may be that he, Jack Dempsey, the world champion, is no longer world champion, even though he is still Jack Dempsey. He doesn't know. He doesn't know what is or isn't. He likes being called champ; over time he's got used to it. But perhaps that's no longer true. Overthrown kings and soldiers stripped of their rank also lose their titles. If the fight is already over – something he can't be sure of, but which wouldn't surprise him – that means that he, Jack Dempsey, is no longer the world champion. It's strange: it had come to seem so natural to him. Now the champion must be the other guy, the Wild Bull from he can't remember where. That is if he has lost, if the fight really is over. But that's not certain. What's certain is that he fell. But falling doesn't necessarily mean losing. Not if he gets up. So he is going to get up. And once he's on his feet, he'll see what he can see: whether his opponent is crouching, fists ready to finish him off once and for all, or is already being carried shoulder high, cheered by the crowd, showing off for photographers and public alike the glittering belt which, until before tonight's fight, belonged to him. Jack Dempsey. For the moment, he doesn't know. Being a boxing champion was the most important thing in his life: his childhood dream, the goal of his youth, the triumph of his adulthood. But for the moment he has no idea if he is the champion or not. If he has lost or not. He doesn't know: it's all a question of time. That's what boxing is, a question of time.

Three minutes each round, a minute's break, ten seconds for a knockout: it's all a question of time. Contrary to appearances, this ennobles boxing rather than diminishing it. After all, isn't death, in relation to the life it brings to an end, also simply a question of time? A boxer who's been knocked out loses when his allotted time runs out. So does every man who dies.

TEN!

WHEN A MAN HAS WON everything from someone, everything or something equivalent to it, then his life is in danger. Any life that becomes too important is in danger. When it reaches that point, killing that person becomes a possibility.

◆

The instant. Donald Mitchell's old obsession: the instant. The definition of photography that most pleases and convinces him: photography as the art of the instant. The one lesson that life has taught him: that the course of history can be stood on its head in an instant.

◆

When a man has lost everything, or something equivalent to everything, he feels his life is worthless. And it may well be that what he feels is objectively true. So then killing himself becomes a possibility.

◆

'Did you know there's a film of the Firpo–Dempsey fight?'

'No.'

'Well, there is. Of course, it's not very clear – remember it's from the 1920s. But it exists.'

◆

A man can bet a lot or a little. He can also bet everything, or something equivalent to everything. When be bets everything, or its equivalent, what he's really betting is his life. The real gambler always bets his life. That's why, although it is morally repugnant, Russian roulette is the most genuine form of betting: it's the purest, most authentic sort of wager.

◆

'And do you know what someone did with that film?'

'No.'

'They took a stopwatch and counted how long Jack Dempsey's knockdown really lasted.'

'How long he was knocked down for?'

'Exactly. From the moment he fell backwards through the ropes to the moment he climbed back into the ring.'

'And how long was it?'

'Seventeen seconds.'

'How long?'

'Seventeen seconds.'

◆

Abraham Horischnik is still alive, but he doesn't live at the address the phone book gives. For the last two or three years he's been in an old people's home in the Flores neighbourhood. The people living in his old apartment are happy to give me his new address. I write it down.

It's exactly six o'clock in the afternoon.

◆

In his mind he hears his mother's voice, on one of those distant early mornings in the east. She shouts hoarsely at him: 'Time to get up, Jack.' Time for school – which he never finished anyway. His mother shouting in the early dawn light: 'Get up, Jack.' It was an unforgettable part of the rituals of his childhood, the ones that always stay with you. That's why, so many years later, and in the middle of the night, it's his mother's voice he hears. Her words, not anyone else's: 'Time to get up, Jack.'

◆

'D'you know what seventeen seconds mean?'

'Yes. A very long time.'

'Exactly. Not in every case, but definitely in this one. And d'you know what that very long time means?'

'No.'

'It's very simple, Verani. It means that, strictly speaking, in all fairness, Firpo won the fight against Dempsey.'

'Our man.'

'Yes. If things had been done properly, at the tenth second the referee should have called a knockout and declared Firpo the winner.'

'But he didn't.'

'Of course not. Heaven knows where his mind was at that moment. Didn't I tell you: seventeen seconds went by!'

199

'Yes. And in the end, it was Dempsey who won.'

'In the end, yes. In the end Dempsey was the winner.'

◆

Everybody has something like an internal clock. This explains how, for example, a farmer will wake up at exactly 4.30 in the morning without needing to resort to any mechanical reminder of the time (that horrible ringing of an alarm clock) or any natural one (the shrill crowing of an anxious cock). Another example might be the way a school teacher knows the exact moment when the forty minutes of a class are up, without having to look down at his wristwatch or peer out of the window at the church clock opposite. We all have this internal clock: the ability to measure the passage of time without having to consciously think about it. In this way, we can calculate hours, minutes, even seconds. Mr Jack 'Slowest' Gallagher, a boxing referee by profession, also has this kind of chronological reflex. His internal clock, which at this precise moment is ringing like an alarm clock. It's telling him there's a time he should be marking at this very moment. That means his clock is working, but he cannot understand why or for what reason. It's like a warning going off without him hearing it, or one that he hears but does not register, or that he registers but does not recognise, or recognises but does not understand, or understands but does not react to in time.

ELEVEN!

HE KNOWS HE SEES THINGS as a photographer. He is aware of that. He looks and frames. He takes a second look, then presses the button. He sees images in his mind and is able to capture them: fixed, properly composed, the lines and shapes fitting in well. He looks and sees as what he is: a photographer. But in addition – and he is aware of this too – he has a cinematic imagination. He has realised this too. Part of his mind responds not merely to photographic but also to cinematic form (the cinema of his day, but also the cinema to come). It's only thanks to this that he can understand what is happening, or the way he is experiencing it. While the champion was falling, it seemed as though everything was happening more slowly. Slowed down, and in a kind of sonic vacuum, with only a whistling or buzzing sound in the background. Dempsey fell in slow motion. At some point in the future it will be hard to believe that when a man falls out of a window, or a car plunges over a precipice, this isn't how it happens. Donald Mitchell has this slow motion camera in his mind and memory. That was why Dempsey seemed to fall so slowly and silently. Now he is getting back to his feet, two things missing until now return: the sounds of the outside world, and the normal speed at which things take place.

◆

It's seven in the evening.

The word 'geriatric' is nowhere to be seen. There's a big sign on the railing outside, a smaller one on the door, and on the wall a ceramic creation that also shows the address and name of the institution. They use other expressions: 'old people's home', 'residence', or 'senior citizens' centre'. No room for the truth.

I ring the bell and, while I'm waiting, look around: straggly trees, uneven cobbles, old houses so typical of Flores, the unlikely remains of what had once been tram tracks still visible at the street corners. I'm so absorbed that when the woman appears, she startles me ('Good evening'). An ageless woman, really ageless, who somehow has something of the night about her, although it's still daylight in the street and the lamps haven't yet come on. ('What can I do for you?') Whenever I'm nervous, I start rubbing my hands together ('I'm looking for Abraham Horischnik'), and that's what I'm doing now. It's only at this point I realise she is dressed like a nurse. I cough ('Does he live here?'), she sizes me up without saying a word, openly calculating if she needs to tell the truth or not. Eventually she sighs ('Yes'), and acknowledges me ('Who wants him?').

Doing my best to sound trustworthy, I explain who I am and why I'm there. She asks me to wait ('Stay here a moment, will you?') then disappears the way she came, without opening the door or showing me in. This time it's her neutral voice that occupies my thoughts. Finally, she reappears. This time she opens the door properly, which leads me to think I'm going in. I'm wrong ('Señor Horischnik says he's tired. They're just serving supper, and he says he's going to bed straight afterwards'). Hoping I sound more anguished than demanding, I insist, explaining what it is that has brought me here. Again, I'm wrong ('Señor Horischnik says he's not interested in talking about that anymore'), and again I suddenly find the door shut in my face.

◆

It is only now that Jack Dempsey understands where he is and what has happened to him. In fact, what he understands, or rather confirms, is where he is: outside the ring. He deduces that he must have been sent flying there by that other brute whose name he can't remember. He looks around: everywhere there's consternation, amazement or fear, the expression of people who have seen something they shouldn't have seen, or seen something happen that shouldn't have happened. The radio commentators are still speaking (their medium demands it), searching unsuccessfully for the words to describe what has taken place. Jack Dempsey stands up. He's already completely upright, and yet he can still feel the evidence of his fall in his body. A man is sprawled at his feet: he's groaning and flailing about with his arms. If Dempsey had trod on his foot in a tramcar, or in a narrow corridor, he would even now be excusing himself. In fact, he has crashed on top of him with all his weight, and yet he can't think of anything to say to him. Of course, the circumstances explain and justify this rudeness. There's another man beside him. This one is standing up, and he knows him. Despite the dishevelled hair, twisted bow tie and crooked glasses, there's something familiar about his face. He's one of the judges, Dempsey thinks he's called Kid, Kid something or other; he's a judge with a boxer's name. He's holding Dempsey's arm. At first Dempsey is perplexed, but then understands. This man has been helping him get up, by grabbing hold of his arm at the narrowest point just above the glove and pulling as hard as he can. It's time for him to let go now, because Dempsey is finally back on his feet. But he doesn't want to offend him by tugging his arm free or swatting at him with his free arm. No, he mustn't do that, this good fellow was only trying to help him when he was under no obligation to do so: in fact, he was under an obligation (which in this case he ignored) *not* to do anything of the kind. And on top of that, he is one of the fight judges. Supposing the fight goes on (and with a glimmer of hope, Dempsey is beginning to realise he has not yet lost) and that, however improbable it may seem, it reaches the final round without either of them being knocked out. If that happens, this man will be responsible for a third of the crucial decision about who has won and who has lost. One third of the final decision on points will depend on him. The hand is helping Dempsey, but it's impossible for Dempsey or anyone else to know what he is thinking. Perhaps he is already coldly calculating how many points to deduct. Ten, in this sport as in all others with the same scoring system, means perfection. Anyone knocked out of the ring obviously cannot hope to score that. But how far off it will Dempsey be? Two points? Three? Four? Or five? Dempsey would love to see from the judge's face how many he is deducting. He peers at him, but can't tell a thing. His brilliantined hair is sticking up in spiky tufts. His eyes are rolling, his jaw has dropped. It's impossible to tell from his face if he will help Dempsey in the same way his hand has been doing. If the fight does go on, Dempsey tells himself, I'd better knock the other guy out.

♦

No gambler, absolutely none, not even the most apathetic or embittered, would bet on a draw. Not merely because of a question of probabilities (far fewer bouts are drawn than are won or lost) but also because it's unsatisfactory for the price of a victory to be the lack of a victory: that for somebody to win a bet nobody has to win.

It was this kind of argument which led Ledesma to conclude that Otto Stiglitz must have bet on one or other of the boxers, rather than on neither of them. All he had to work out now was which one. Once he knew that, he would also by inference know if Stiglitz had been killed or had killed himself. Since Dempsey had won, there were two possible alternatives: either Stiglitz had bet on the champion, had won and been killed; or he had bet on the Argentinian, had lost and committed suicide.

He could picture the scene: Otto Stiglitz at midnight, leaning out of his hotel bedroom window. He also took into account where the City Hotel was situated: half a block from San Ignacio Church, and an equal distance from City Hall. From there, if he had a room facing the avenue, it would have been impossible not to see the beam from the top of the Palacio Barolo. Although nowadays there are buildings in the way, in the 1920s there was a clear view of it, so that Stiglitz would have instantly known the result of the fight and of his wager.

Verani was convinced Stiglitz had bet on Dempsey. A foreigner would always bet on a foreigner, he said. Ledesma disagreed; he took Verani to task for yet again over-simplifying things by supposing that all foreigners are the same or similar. An Austrian and a North American, he explained, were completely different. Anyway, he pointed out, given the situation the orchestra members found themselves in at the hotel, it was most likely that Stiglitz had made the bet with another musician: in other words, with another foreigner. That being the case, either of them could have chosen the champion or the challenger.

Yet Ledesma somehow also thought that Stiglitz must have bet on Dempsey, even though he could not explain to himself why. Perhaps unintentionally he was arguing backwards: he thought a crime was more likely than a suicide, and so concluded Stiglitz must have bet on Dempsey. Then he realised that in fact there were four, not two, alternatives. As he himself had pointed out to Verani a few days earlier, before the red beam flashed out from the top of the Palacio Barolo, the blue one had been shown by mistake. For a moment, Stiglitz must also have been convinced that it was Firpo who had won the fight. He could have been killed, or even have killed himself, before the second beam corrected the first. A death need not take very long; everything could have been over and done with in the few minutes between the first and second beams. So then the reasoning as to the link between the meaning of the bet and the meaning of the death was not only doubled, but reversed. Suicide meant a bet on Dempsey. A bet on Firpo signified that a crime had been committed.

◆

'Historians have suggested what I think is a very graphic image to describe the relation between Mahler and Strauss. It's this: Mahler and Strauss were like two moles who collided while digging tunnels in opposite directions. What do you make of that?'

'It's very graphic.'

'But do you understand it?'

'I think so. More or less.'

'It's very clear. There's no doubt that in more than one sense Mahler and Strauss reached the same point. By following a course that was not so evident to their contemporaries. That's what is meant by the tunnels and the moles, you see?'

'Yes.'

'They reached the same point, but hadn't got there in the same way. In fact, they were burrowing in opposite directions. But for precisely that reason, they ended up meeting.'

◆

In among all the blur of heads, there's one that stands out: Jack Dempsey's. If he stretches out his neck from up in the ring, Mr Gallagher can see it. It's rising out of the mass. He sees it rising, sees the lights glinting off it. Mr Gallagher is surprised. It's only now that he realises how final he had considered the champion's unheard-of disappearance outside the ring. He understands now that, for him, that was the end of everything: after all, that was what a defining moment was. After that, there is nothing. And there couldn't be any more defining moment, for a boxer or in life in general, than being knocked completely out of the ring. In boxing, the ring is everything: the outside does not exist. Anybody who goes outside the ring no longer exists. If they do, that's that: it's the end. That is what Mr Gallagher has been unconsciously thinking all this time. But now he discovers he was mistaken, and still is to some extent. Dempsey is on his feet. That means this isn't the apocalypse, the final judgment day: life goes on, the world goes on, and so does the fight.

TWELVE

HE OUGHT TO HAVE COUNTED; he ought to be counting. He didn't, and still isn't. It's a straightforward rule: if a boxer is knocked down, the referee counts. He is well aware of the rule, but hasn't applied it. He hasn't counted, and still isn't. A question flashes through his mind: how could this have happened? He cannot imagine how he forgot this, precisely this – to count from one to ten when one of the boxers has been knocked down. And yet, almost immediately, he realises why. Boxing means the ring: that's all there is to it. Anything that is outside the ring, or goes outside the ring (in this instance, Jack Dempsey) is necessarily therefore outside boxing. As a result, the rules of boxing (this one, for example: the count over a fallen fighter) no longer apply. This, in a confused way, is what must have happened to him. In order to ease his conscience, that is how he rationalises it: his mind was completely occupied with the ring (in other words, his error was not one of a lack of attention, but of concentrating too hard), so nothing outside the ring interested him. He forgot Dempsey because he was no longer in the ring. He didn't count because there was nothing to count, nobody to count over. Looked at in this way, he doesn't think he made such a huge mistake. It's not his problem if Jack Dempsey was knocked outside the ring. No, his problem is what is happening now: Jack Dempsey is standing up and climbing back inside.

◆

'Look what a coincidence. D'you know the name of the gym where Luis Angel Firpo trained for the fight against Jack Dempsey?'

'No.'

'He was in New York and not Buenos Aires, remember.'

'I remember.'

'So do you know what it was called?'

'No.'

'Prepare to be amazed. It was called the "Abasto" Boxing Club. Just like that, in Spanish.'

'Abasto, like the central market here in Buenos Aires?'

'Yes, Abasto. Don't you think that's incredible?'

'Yes.'

'To travel the length of the continent and arrive at somewhere called "Abasto". At 53 Siskind Avenue, in the heart of Queens.'

'Life's full of surprises.'

'Isn't it just?'

'Yes. And I can imagine, Ledesma, that while he was training there Firpo redoubled his efforts knowing that all the time Carlitos Gardel was peering down at him from heaven.'

'Who?'

'Carlitos Gardel, Ledesma. The criollo songthrush. The black-haired boy from the Abasto. The king of tango. Didn't you say Firpo trained at the Abasto?'

'Yes.'

'Don't tell me then that Carlos Gardel wasn't looking down on him from heaven.'

'Sometimes I wonder about your sense of history, Verani. We're talking about 1923, right?'

'Yes.'

'So what heaven are you talking about? In those days, Gardel was as fit as a fiddle. Fit, strong, chubby-cheeked. More alive than most. He didn't die in that plane crash in Medellin until 1935.'

◆

Full of admiration, they gently and shyly pat him, prod him. They touch him with their hands like gypsies, as if to prove it's him and not a ghost who is rising and getting ready to fight again. Their gentle prodding, born of devotion and incredulity, shows him the way back. They are indicating something: the steps up to the ring. Partly with their help, partly thanks to his own efforts, Jack Dempsey reaches the steps. He recognises them. Of course he does. Four short planks of dark wood, veined with cracks and with nails sticking up here and there. Surely he has just climbed them? He calculates it must have been only ten minutes ago, or twelve at most, that he climbed up them into the ring. He looked different then: he had his gown on, and his hair was neat and tidy. His head wasn't throbbing, and there was one less knockdown in his boxing record. He strode up the steps, the proud champion, slipped through the ropes and bounced on his toes on the canvas. Then he raised his arms, first to one side, then the other, rousing the motley crowd. Then came the anthems: he sang his and ignored his opponent's. After the famous *Star-Spangled Banner* and the unknown *Broken Chains*, he stripped off everything apart from his boots, gloves and shorts, and prepared to fight. To do his job. Now he's climbing the same steps again. This is the one and only time in his boxing career that he will have to perform this brief ceremony twice over. He's climbing them again, but he's a different person. He's not wearing his dressing gown. He's not going to salute the motley crowd. Or sing. He's not filled with that special sense of expectation brought by new things: a first day at school, newly-weds, a brand new car, a suit fresh from the tailor's. He's not starting anything new: he's doing everything for the second time. Absolutely everything. What does that mean? The fight for the heavyweight championship of the world, the most prestigious title in boxing.

◆

Valentinis called the newspaper late one afternoon. I was no longer there; nor was Verani. Our working day was over, and, as usual, we had gone with Ledesma to wait for it to get dark at the Touring Club Hotel Café. The only people left in the newspaper were those who had to close that day's edition. In 1973, all the news was about politics, not sport, which was Verani's patch, and still less culture, which was Ledesma's responsibility. I closed the archives at six. They left their pieces finished at more or less the same time. So when Valentinis phoned, none of us were there.

A rather ambitious youngster took the call. Nowadays he's a section head but back then he was just starting out. Valentinis insisted so much that he had to talk to us, and refused to be patient and call back the next morning, that in the end the kid agreed to come down to the Touring Club to tell us. He may even have run the two blocks, because when he arrived he was out of breath.

The Touring Club is run by two brothers. The younger one lent me the phone. He raised his eyebrows when I said I needed to call Buenos Aires, and shook his fingers as though trying to dry them, in an admonishing gesture. I dialled and waited. The phone only rang once, then I heard Valentinis at the other end. He tripped over his words he was so anxious: I had to shout to calm him down. He was in a real hurry: he had found out several things he thought we should know. What he had told us before was true: the members of the Vienna Orchestra lived more or less cut off from the outside world on the fourth floor of the City Hotel. But something else was true as well: a small number of Argentine musicians, all of them members of the resident orchestra of the Teatro Colón, had been allowed to join those directed by Richard Strauss.

It was Gino Marinuzzi, at that time director-general of the Colón, who had won this concession. He knew that any contact with the Austrian maestros was bound to benefit the young local musicians. He achieved quite a lot: they could go and take part in all the rehearsals, attend the concerts in the best seats and meet and talk with their European colleagues in the slack periods at the City Hotel.

When Otto Stiglitz was found hanged in his room, his death presented Richard Strauss with many problems. Some were legal, some moral, some diplomatic. But there was also one specifically musical difficulty. There were a certain number of stand-in musicians for the orchestra. One of these cellists could fill in for Sitglitz in all the concerts except one. Gustav Mahler's music was so powerful (even overblown in some places) that it demanded the presence of every available musician. The other concerts the orchestra still had to perform could be covered easily enough, but not the Mahler (sometimes there were musicians who went on a tour simply to play Mahler's music). In order to put on Mahler's *First Symphony*, Strauss needed each and every one of the musicians in the orchestra. With Stiglitz dead, he was one short.

Any less demanding conductor would possibly have agreed to the symphony being played with one less cello. It would have been easy enough to persuade oneself that nobody would notice. But not Richard Strauss. He would have spent the entire night unable to listen to anything but the lack of that instrument. Faced with the problem of a missing cellist, Strauss began to worry. Then he remembered the handful of young Argentine musicians who were always around: they seemed so curious, so keen to learn, so anxious to help.

He asked if there were any cellists among them: there were three. Strauss devoted an hour of his time to giving them an audition to choose which of them would replace Otto Stiglitz. All three were good, but one was better than the others: the youngest, the one who at first had seemed the least promising. His name (Abraham Horischnik, of course) became engraved on my memory.

◆

Donald Mitchell needs to know, as quickly as possible, if his camera is still working. He found it on the floor close beside him, apparently intact. In order to be sure there is nothing seriously wrong with it, he will have to wait to develop the photos he's taken and verify they weren't damaged in any way. Still, he can do some kind of check in the meantime. If he takes a photo straightaway, he'll be able to tell whether the mechanical part of his apparatus works, or gets stuck and doesn't respond. Not that he can afford to waste a photo just for the sake of making sure everything is OK. He can never forget he has limited means and materials. He has to find a photo that's easy to take but is worth taking. That's going to be difficult because, at this precise moment, there is no fight (if by fight we mean two men squaring up to each other). Donald Mitchell is beginning to worry there is nothing for him to photograph, when all of a sudden he sees something. It's probably not an image of any great journalistic value: it doesn't bear witness to anything; it doesn't prove, document or illustrate anything. Yet its strength is its human interest: it's the engrossed face of the fight referee. Donald Mitchell has never (and although he doesn't yet know it, never will again) seen such a lost, utterly bemused expression on anyone's face.

◆

I left, knowing I would be back. An hour later, I was there again.

It's eight in the evening.

I haven't devised any strategy for improving my chances compared to the previous time. I'm simply being stubborn: ring the doorbell again, explain who I am and say I would like to see old man Horischnik. Nothing has changed: I don't have a better idea or a more persuasive argument. I merely want to insist, to try again. The succession of obstacles put in my way meant my journey had been a waste of time. I had been about to leave altogether when I suddenly changed my mind completely and went the other way entirely.

Even with usually undemonstrative people, this kind of change of mind can be quite frequent. In a rare coincidence, something similar must also have happened to Horischnik. I arrive at the same house as before. I ring the bell. A woman very similar to the earlier one appears at the door – they look so alike I could confuse the two, but it's not her. I introduce myself and explain why I'm there. She disappears, then shortly afterwards comes back to the door. As she does so, she invites me in, because old man Horischnik ('Don Abraham is expecting you') has agreed to see me.

THIRTEEN!

WHAT IS MOST STRIKING ABOUT Abraham Horsichnik are his hands. Not merely because I know he is or was a cellist (how long does a cellist have not to play for until you can say he no longer is one?) and because all his art was or is in his hands. There is that, of course, but there's also something more. His hands are the only part of him which don't seem to have aged. The rest is what you might expect from a man of over ninety: he's stooped, shrunken, his face and neck are all sagging flesh, his eyes have a weary look to them, his head is completely bald, with white patches on it. He shuffles as he walks along. But there is something different about his hands: they still retain a vague sense of power and strength. His hands are the same as they always were.

I watch while he finishes eating. Then he comes over to me. He's very friendly: he tells me his name, I tell him mine. He asks what I know about him, and why I've come to see him. We go and sit on some straight-backed armchairs in an almost empty room. I don't want to bring up Otto Stiglitz yet: I think it's too soon to talk about death. I say I know he played with Richard Strauss, the great Richard Strauss, more than seventy years ago. It must have seemed almost miraculous, extraordinary, to have been given such an honour when he was so young, just starting out on his career as a musician.

He stares at me and asks if that is what I want to talk about. I say it is.

He starts to ramble on ('Richard Strauss was a calm, affable man; he gave very precise, quite strict instructions. Like most front-rank conductors, he wasn't very approachable, but he wasn't unfriendly either. I saw him rehearsing lots of concerts with the Philharmonic at the Colón, but I only played in one: Gustav Mahler's *First Symphony*. Mahler is very special to me, perhaps because, like him, I am a renegade Jew. Strauss knew him very well, which impressed me a lot. Above and beyond what Strauss represented in his own right, I detected in him something of Mahler's mysterious aura. It was more special than, for example, being under Bruno Walter's baton. Walter had also been very close to Mahler, but as his disciple. His favourite disciple, possibly, but a disciple all the same. Strauss, on the other hand, had been his equal. He talked about Mahler in the same way Mahler could have talked about him. It was curious: Strauss showed great interest in the personality of each of the composers whose music he was going to perform. This awareness of the artist's character seemed to him relevant to help understand his music. He talked a lot about Beethoven, Brahms, Mozart, Schubert, Berlioz, and of course he had even more to say about Mahler, because he had been friends with him, and knew him well. But the strangest thing was that although the orchestra played several of his own pieces: *Don Juan*, *Don Quijote*, *A Hero's Life*, *Salomé*, the *Domestic Symphony*, the *Alpine Symphony*, those were the only occasions he let the music speak for itself and said nothing about their author. Strauss didn't like talking about himself'). All at once the old man falls silent. He looks at his watch.

It's nine o'clock.

He glances at me as if he suddenly remembers who I am, or as though he were watching me arrive. He goes back to the start of our conversation. Asks me to remind him of my name ('My name is Roque Alfaro'), who I am ('I'm a journalist from a newspaper in Trelew') and how I found him ('I've known about you for years'). It's common knowledge that old people have an excellent memory for the distant past. He does remember ('So you must be a friend of that young man'), he snaps his fingers ('the one who came to ask questions for a Chubut newspaper, what was his name?'). I say yes, I was his friend, that we did our military service together and stayed in touch, but in the end, partly because we lived so far from each other and partly because these things always happen, we drifted apart. I tell him that anyway Valentinis died a couple of years ago. Horischnik shrugs and wearily mutters some words I can hardly hear ('We all have to die some day').

◆

Jack Dempsey flexes his muscles and looks around. As he does so, the crowd roars excitedly. Dempsey flexes his muscles, and as he does so he appears not only to grow in stature but to have completely recovered. It looks as if he is doubly erect, standing there massively, more upright than a man can be by simply standing on his feet. That isn't why he flexes, however. He stretches in order to get a good look around. The stirring cheers of the crowd in the background and the shouts of encouragement from the spectators nearer to him act like a tonic on his fighter's body. All this helps, and in his mind he thanks them for it, as he will do out loud later to the pressmen. But he doesn't want to plunge on blindly, like a bull let loose in the ring, and charge in a rage. It's the other man who is the Wild Bull of the Pampas, not him. He wants to get a clear idea of how things stand. He flexes and surveys the scene. In the ring he spies the challenger, the man with the Italian name and the fearsome punch, and the referee, Jack 'Slowest' Gallagher, who is well-known in the trade and is not such a bad sort. They're all there apart from him. And it is this uncomfortable feeling, that there is something missing and that it is him, which gives him the final push towards climbing back into the ring.

◆

'Don't imagine, Verani, that Strauss left Argentina empty-handed.'

'I guess not. I expect he left with a sackful of dough.'

'Don't be so crude, my friend. That's not what I'm talking about.'

'No? What then?'

'Come home and you'll find out.'

'I can't imagine what you're talking about.'

'About music, Verani. Music, the supreme art. Years after this second visit to Argentina, Strauss composed a small piece whose first chords are unmistakable for any Argentine. D'you know why?'

'No idea.'

'It's very simple. Because they are the opening bars of the Argentine national anthem.'

'You don't say.'

'I do.'

'"Hark you mortals to the sacred cry"?'

'No, that's the beginning of the sung part. I mean the very first few bars: "Ta-ta, ta-tan." That bit.'

That's wonderful, isn't it?'

'Yes.'

'And how proud Vicente López would have felt.'

'Vicente López? You mean Blas Parera, don't you? He composed our national anthem.'

'Of course, Blas Parera. Blas Parera.'

◆

Although obviously it is very rare, the rules of boxing do provide for the eventuality of a referee losing count. Several different possibilities are contemplated: he may slip, stumble or fall at the precise moment of the knockdown; the boxer, as he falls to the canvas, may take the referee with him; or the attacking fighter may be so carried away that he goes on punching his fallen rival, forcing the referee to intervene to try to stop him. In all these cases (and others) the referee may lose track of his counting. It's provided for in the rules. At the same time, a solution is offered. One of the three ringside judges is meant to mentally start counting as soon as one of the two fighters is knocked down. He does not have to count out loud, but the referee knows he is doing so. For example, if a boxer is knocked down and the referee hasn't begun the count for one of the reasons given above, he will have to start somewhere in the middle. To do that, he will need to look over towards the judge chosen to help him, and somehow (by openly asking him or by raising his eyebrows or holding up all his fingers) query him about how many seconds have gone by since the knockdown began. In response, the chosen judge will hold up one or two hands (hopefully, one will be enough) and clearly indicate with his erect fingers how many seconds have elapsed, and at what point on the scale from one to ten the referee has to renew the count. So Mr Gallagher peers towards the spot where the judge he needs, Kid McPartland, is to be found (or ought to be found). He finds the place, but the judge isn't there: all he can see is a toppled chair. Mr Gallagher searches desperately among the throng of people crowded at the ringside. He can't see McPartland anywhere.

◆

Just as I am doing now, but seventeen years ago, Valentinis went looking for Abraham Horischnik. Just like me, he was greeted with such a curt refusal that he thought any change of heart by the old man would be impossible. One difference, which may or may not have been important, is that Valentinis went to visit him when he still lived in his apartment on Avenida Angel Gallardo, closer to Parque Centenario than Avenida Corrientes. On that occasion he didn't have to struggle to get past nurses, but had to try to make himself understood over a faulty intercom.

Horischnik twice refused to see him before eventually agreeing to an interview. He said it had to be short, because talking tired him. He showed Valentinis into a dark, dank apartment, where the only pleasant surprise came from the music being played on a brightly-coloured record player. Valentinis came straight to the point: he mentioned Otto Stiglitz, or rather his strange death; he told the old man that he knew the facts surrounding it had been downplayed and hushed up thanks to the intervention of the people organising the tour and Richard Strauss himself. He also revealed that by searching through the old registers at the City Hotel he had discovered that a certain number of young Argentine musicians had access to the floor reserved for the Austrians. This discovery had changed his firm belief that once the Vienna Philharmonic Orchestra had left Buenos Aires all traces of the affair must have disappeared into thin air. He then consulted the archives at the Teatro Colón, where an employee with a Basque surname told him about the Argentine cellist who had played on the evening Mahler's *First Symphony* was performed.

After that, Valentinis told him about us, the journalists down in Trelew. He explained Ledesma's theory: the story of the bets on the Firpo–Dempsey fight. At that precise moment, the record came to an end. There was a scratchy sound, then the needle lifted and, with the jerky docility of a robot, the arm returned to its original position. The record player switched itself off, but Abraham Horischnik got up to put on another record. He took time choosing one and placing it on the turntable. Then he carefully put the other one first in its cellophane cover and then in its cardboard sleeve.

When he had done all this, he resumed the conversation. He admitted that everything Valentinis had said was true. The isolated Europeans, the Argentines allowed in, the hushed-up death, the wager: it was all true, the whole truth. So then Valentinis pointed out that the question of the bet raised various equally plausible possibilities, and asked Horischnik if he knew which of them was correct.

◆

Donald Mitchell presses the button, and apparently takes the photo. So it seems, at least: he can detect nothing wrong with the mechanism, nothing seizes up or refuses to move. The flash goes off. The button bounces back as it should. He begins to feel a photographer's pride. He knows (because he knows what he saw) that it will be a good photograph. Not as a document, to be published alongside the report of the fight, but as something he only dimly intuits: that a photograph can also be appreciated for its aesthetic qualities, like a painting. It's not always a matter of showing the world as it is, or an event as it took place.

FOURTEEN!

BUT THE PHOTO WON'T COME OUT. Donald Mitchell doesn't know this yet: there's no way he could. The photo he has just taken of the fight referee's bewildered face never comes out; nor do any of the others he has made throughout this seemingly endless night. But nobody can rob him of the profound emotion he felt each time he framed an image of what was happening in front of him and decided to take and keep it. That quiver of excitement at each successive present instant is his forever. Yet nothing of it will survive as a past he can recover and revisit even as time unfolds and passes.

◆

This was what had happened: that afternoon, in the build-up to the fight, the musicians began to discuss boxing. It was something foreign to almost all of them, but, as so often happens, this was precisely its attraction. After all, travellers are looking for the unknown rather than the known. And these men were travellers. They knew nothing about boxing, but talked about it with all the enthusiasm of beginners. To bet, intuition is as good as expertise. So they started placing bets. Austrians and Argentines challenged each other, accepting each other's wager.

Abraham Horischnik remembered it clearly: Otto Stiglitz backed Dempsey. He did so for various reasons, some of which he did not reveal. A US champion fighting in the United States with a US referee: that was enough for him to be willing to bet on what was likely to happen in New York that night.

They had finished their concert by the time the fight started. Stiglitz leaned out of the window with the others, looking towards Avenida de Mayo. Horischnik was one of those who, like Stiglitz, stood staring up at the sky, waiting for the beam of light. Finally it appeared, and it was blue. Otto Stiglitz admitted defeat and withdrew to his room. When the red beam shone out to cancel the first one, a group of three or four of them went to tell him there was no need for him to be upset at having lost: his boxer had won. Horischnik was also part of the group which made its leisurely way (leisurely because they did not think anything so terrible was at stake) up to the room to give Stiglitz the good news.

They arrived, pushed open the door and discovered, to their horror, that Stiglitz had hanged himself. Understandably, they all rushed to try to revert the terrible situation: they cut down the belt, lowered the body to the floor, tried to massage the neck and made several unsuccessful attempts to revive him.

They tried to reverse the course of events, but life had passed inexorably into death. In the end, they had to accept it, and they notified the authorities.

◆

There he is, at last: the one with the bow tie and glasses. At this very moment he is struggling to straighten them both. He's also trying to smoothe down his dark pinstripe suit, which has been soaked and crumpled. Mr Gallagher tries to catch his eye. At first, the other man is so distracted by his efforts that he seems unaware of what is going on. Then, almost by chance, his eyes meet the referee's. The latter's are asking a question; his own are full of surprise. Even though he hasn't completely recovered from his bemusement, he can feel his hands rising to his side. How many fingers is he going to raise? In other words, how many seconds should he indicate? For the moment, both his hands are visible. What does that mean? That he's showing the referee all ten fingers? No, he can't be doing that; he shouldn't be doing that. No, that's not what he's doing. He's not holding up ten fingers. He is telling him, insofar as someone can do just by using his flat hands, how he feels overwhelmed by all that has happened: the heavyweight champion of the world fell on top of him (him and the other guy who had been next to him) and all but crushed him. Then he had to struggle to help him back onto his feet, comfort him, help him recover. He had to clear a way for him, and then show him the way to take. It was impossible to do all that and count at the same time. Kid McPartland tries to explain, or at least convey, all this to Jack Gallagher by holding his hands horizontally level with his waist. What he is trying to say is: 'What can you expect?' His gesture has a double meaning that hasn't occurred to him: don't count on me, it says.

◆

'The fight was so important in Argentina, Verani, that *Crítica* newspaper had set up a special radio transmission for it.'

'You don't say.'

'It's true. You've heard of *Crítica*, haven't you?'

'Of course I have.'

'So you know about its constant efforts to modernise Argentine journalism.'

'I do.'

'And back in 1923, no less, it set up a special radio-telegraph link with the United States.'

'Real pioneers.'

'You said it. They put the amateur radio ham Horacio Martínez Seeber in charge. They hired a direct line via the International News Service.'

'You don't say!'

'Yes. They set up a complicated re-transmission relay between the United States and Transradio Internacional, based in Villa Elisa, La Plata.'

'Villa Elisa?'

'Yes, sorry to be so prosaic. Villa Elisa. It's a place like any other.'

'I suppose it is.'

'The fight was transmitted first to Transradio Internacional in Villa Elisa, from there to Radio Sudamérica, and then to Radio Cultura. Radio Cultura was the one people tuned into.'

'Radio what did you say?'

'Radio Cultura.'

'Aha! Well then, don't try to tell me it's only music played in Teatro Colón that is culture.'

'You always take things too far.'

'No, I'm telling you how things are.'

'Anyway, apart from purely anthropological considerations, we've got used to calling everything "culture". The poisoned arrow fashioned by the clumsy hands of an Indian is also culture. It is no matter that these Indians are only halfway between being mere animals and demonstrating the dignity of human beings. The simple necklaces they thread with fragile glass beads are culture too. So don't think you've caught me out by showing that the word "culture" (which just happens to have been the name of the radio station) has become confused with the bread and circus of a boxing match.'

◆

Ten o'clock.

Horischnik has grown tired of the hard, upright backs of the armchairs in the downstairs room: he can't relax in them. As if there was some mystery about it, he leans over and asks in a whisper if I still have some time or if I have to go. I tell him I have time ('Until my plane leaves tomorrow, I've got all the time in the world'). He says we would both be more comfortable if we went up to his room.

As was to be expected, his room is spartan, with no pretensions or accumulated junk. There are two beds, two chairs, a wardrobe, a mirror: that's about it. Until a few days earlier, Horischnik had been sharing it with an insomniac old man who never complained. One morning he was found lying dead in his bed, still without a word of complaint, still with his eyes wide open. He was taken away that same afternoon, and since then Horischnik has had the room to himself.

I see him rummaging among his things. He asks me if I like

to play dice, and to be polite I say I do. He motions towards the table and chairs, and adds three new things to the scene: a tumbler with a set of dice, a notebook and a blunt pencil. He says how pleased he is that I can stay ('As you know, we old people don't sleep much'). He sits in a chair and invites me to do the same.

More at ease now, I decide it's time to bring up the question of the dead man. At first Horischnik hesitates, but then boasts about how well he can remember it even after all these years. I somewhat tactlessly point out that, like him, the dead man played the cello ('Yes, the cello. He played the cello. And in German, his surname means "goldfinch"'). He shakes the tumbler carefully, but doesn't immediately throw the dice.

I say that a death like that must have been very inconvenient, causing a scandal that had to be hushed up. He shrugs ('These things happen'), but admits that at times Richard Strauss seemed to find it all too much. I conjure up the picture of a genius irritated at being bothered by mere earthly matters ('No, it wasn't really like that. But don't imagine he shed any tears for him'), and ask if Strauss ever considered cancelling the concert. Horischnik hands me the notebook and pencil and asks me to write down our scores ('Cancel concerts? Never. Only two things kept Strauss awake: the first, making sure the press didn't get to hear about it; the second, finding a replacement for the missing musician').

I haven't written with a pencil since I was a child, and yet I immediately recognise the smell of the sharpened wood and the tug of the graphite across the paper. Horischnik apologises for going first ('Strauss had three of us Argentine cellists to choose from. I went to the audition confident I was the best'). I write two initials at the top of the page: an A and an R. I draw a line under them, then another vertical one to divide the sheet in half ('Although it's not for me to say it, I was particularly brilliant that day, so he chose me').

Horischnik throws the dice: two threes, two ones, one two.

He throws a second time: a three, a six and a four.

He goes again: a one and a four. ('Today I can say to anyone willing to hear: I played Mahler in the Teatro Colón, conducted by Richard Strauss'). He tells me to write down three threes, and I do.

◆

His right foot lands directly on the second step, and his left one on the fourth: he has no need of the other two. Skipping, jumping, Dempsey climbs back larger than life into the ring (and in the ring, back to the fight). His eagerness to renew the combat is plain for all to see. He looks restored, he bounds up the steps: no one who's been defeated could appear so confident. It's true that the effects of punches and pain can be indirect, even labyrinthine: you think you've overcome them when suddenly they crop up again (in the break between rounds, Jack Dempsey, still fighting, still champion, talks drunken nonsense). For now, though, he looks alert and alive: this is no swan song. True, he was knocked out of the ring. But now he's back, with the determined look of someone who's where he's meant to be.

FIFTEEN

HE DOESN'T SO MUCH GRAB the ropes as push them apart. He is feeling strong. A weak person holds on, seeks support from anything that might help him stay upright or prevent him from stumbling. A strong man ploughs straight ahead, pushing obstacles out of the way. That's what Jack Dempsey does with the ropes: he doesn't try to cling to them, but pushes them aside so he can return to his rightful place. Get out of my way and let me through. He might just as well be brushing away flies, branches or insignificant individuals. He doesn't even notice these trifling obstacles: his mind is set on reaching a goal that does not allow any obstructions along the way. That goal has a name: Luis Angel Firpo, and although Dempsey's fragile memory can't remember it (all he can dimly recall is a nickname: The Wild Bull of the Pampas) he is well aware that he is the goal and knows where he will find him. He's not climbing back into the ring to see what's going on. No, he's climbing back in the knowledge that he is marked with an indelible stigma: that of having been knocked from the ring by a fateful punch. He's climbing back to avenge the insult, to confront this big bull with an Italian name, to mete out a punishment and a defeat which might still not be enough to erase the humiliation.

◆

Valentinis saw it in purely commercial terms: for him, it was all about money. After all, bets were a kind of transaction, even if they involved a greater dose of anxiety and risk. To kill yourself because of a lost bet means you must have staked a very large sum. Someone who despises his own life and has no qualms about losing it might well decide to kill himself for nothing. But they wouldn't do it because they had lost a small amount in a bet over a boxing match. In order to justify the effort of first tying a belt to a light fitting, then putting it round your neck, climbing up onto a chair and kicking it away, the amount of money lost must have meant ruin, a ruined life that was no longer worth living.

Horischnik let him talk. Valentinis went on with his reasoning: it was likely that a musician with the Vienna Philharmonic would be well paid. Even in those years, still so badly affected by the misfortunes of the postwar period, they would earn a good salary. Even so, they were probably not made of money, as the saying goes. Nor was Otto Stiglitz a soloist, or an orchestra principal. Then again, even if he had been rich, there was no reason to suppose he took huge sums with him on a tour of the far-off countries of South America – but if the person taking the bet was Argentine, he would demand to be paid immediately.

Horischnik blew out his cheeks. He told Valentinis his argument was flawed. Each link might fit with the one before and the one after, but the general premises he was starting from were wrong. To understand the death of a musician you had to understand precisely that: he was a musician, which meant that a different kind of pride and scale of values applied. Stiglitz, it was true, was not made of money. On the contrary, he had just made three or four bad decisions back in Austria which had left him heavily in debt. So heavily in fact, that he had little possibility of repaying the money: even if he had been a soloist, it would have taken several years of his salary; even an orchestra conductor (which he was not and never would be) would have needed several years to pay them off.

Stiglitz was still preoccupied with these problems that night in Buenos Aires when he chanced to meet a wealthy and extremely patriotic Argentine. Like a true believer, this man was convinced that Argentina was a superior nation in every area. The arts, sport, economy, climate, science: to him, this young country was the best of all (it was prospering as the United States was, but did not suffer from the same vulgarity). Stiglitz found it easy to provoke him by suggesting Luis Angel Firpo was going to lose the fight that night. The Argentine accepted the challenge, and gave his own reasons for thinking Firpo would win. When, soon afterwards, their argument became a wager, the sum involved was very large indeed.

Stiglitz didn't have a cent, but he couldn't allow this extraordinary opportunity to pass him by. So he took his big decision. He didn't for a minute consider the possibility that Dempsey might lose. He was convinced he would win, which explains why he took a decision that would cost him his life. The rich Argentine bet an inconsiderable part of his considerable fortune. Otto Stiglitz bet the only thing he had: his cello.

◆

'By the way, Alma Schindler was a composer too.'

'Mahler's wife?'

'Yes, Mahler's wife. She composed as well.'

'Was she good?'

'I must admit, I don't know.'

'You don't have any of her records?'

'I'm not sure there are any.'

'So she didn't get very far.'

'Not in music.'

'There you go then.'

'The truth is, Mahler had something to do with that. When they began their relationship, Alma still had musical ambitions. Who knows if she was any good …'

'Who knows.'

'He, on the other hand, was better than good – he was a real genius, and was very conscious of the fact. So one fine day he confronted Alma Schindler and brutally presented her with how he saw things: one of them (she) was a promising amateur; the other (he) was an outstanding genius. Between daily life and art there are often, if not always, insoluble differences that demand sacrifices. Mahler had a very clear idea of which of the two of them should sacrifice their musical career. And he told Alma this equally clearly.'

'And she accepted?'

'Yes, she did.'

'A classic case of a downtrodden woman.'

'To some extent, yes. But only to some extent. The same couldn't be said of her bedroom adventures.'

'She liked a romp, I think you said.'

'That's one way of putting it.'

'She was hot stuff.'

'If you want to call it that.'

'See what I mean, Ledesma? Life is full of surprises. As an artist, she lost out, but she took her revenge as a woman.'

❖

His apparatus for capturing images also halts time. If he photographs it, each moment that was meant to pass by is held forever. Not that Donald Mitchell knows this: he's a photographer, a man of action, not a photography theorist. He does sense it, though, and the clarity of his intuition is just as valid as a reasoned argument or reflective analysis. For him it is nothing more than an impression, but it's a well-founded one. He knows that when he takes a photo he is pinning down a fleeting, unique moment, and that when he develops that image in the future and looks at it, he can return to that instant and bring it into the present. Each photo prevents time dissolving all those things which, if they had merely been seen rather than photographed, were destined to vanish along with failing memory. He doesn't know this, and could not explain it, and yet whenever he takes a photo he feels something of this emotion. Which is why, when later he tries to develop the photos he has taken tonight and discovers nothing has come out, he senses that there are certain gods of time (he knows nothing about Cronos, or any of their names) who have wreaked their revenge on him for what had seemed to him entirely innocent audacity.

❖

Now it's my turn.

First throw: two fours, two fives and one one. I keep the fives.

Second throw: two ones and a three.

Last throw: a five, a three and a six.

I write my score: three fives, total fifteen. I pass the tumbler to Horischnik ('When you start out on your career you have only one ambition: to be a soloist. And your greatest dream is to take the lead in a concerto for cello and orchestra – Dvorak's, for example, although that's not the one I like best; or to be completely on your own up on stage playing something like the Bach *Cello Suites*, so you feel like Pablo Casals; or accompanied by, say, a Schnabel, if you'll allow me to choose, in a performance of Beethoven's *Sonatas*').

He has his turn: three fives, a two and a three.

He throws the dice again: one three and one one ('But of course only the chosen few can reach such heights, and even they have to wait years to get there').

His third throw: a five and a six. Four of a kind. I write it down. He hands me the tumbler.

It's eleven at night.

My first throw: two threes, a six, a four and a two.

I throw the dice again: a four, a two and a one.

A third time: a five and two fours. All I score are two threes.

I hand him back the tumbler.

He rolls the dice: two fours, one one, two threes ('So there I was, still very young, with an opportunity I was unlikely ever to get again').

He has his second turn: a six ('It didn't matter how brilliant my career might be in the future. I was never going to have another opportunity like that one').

His last throw: a three. Full house.

I write it down and take the tumbler. I ask him about the fight ('Yes, the Firpo–Dempsey fight'), and how it penetrated into the closed world of music and the orchestra.

The old man shrugs. He twists his mouth and his whole face looks different. He points to the tumbler, urging me to throw the dice.

I throw: three ones, a five and a six.

My second throw: a four and a five.

My last go: a two and a three ('Why do you think the fight was so important?').

I note down three aces. Hand him back the tumbler. I stare him in the face, but his gaze is concentrated on his hand and the sound of the dice rolling around inside the tumbler. I remind him that Stiglitz killed himself because he lost a bet, or thought he had: he had backed Dempsey to win.

He throws two fives, two ones and a four.

He throws again: a six, a two and a one.

His last throw: two threes, one one. ('Yes, of course, I remember. All that stuff about the bets. What a lot of nonsense!') He tells me to note down two fives, then appears to hesitate because it's so little ('Yes, all those bets'), but finally says yes, I should write down two fives, and hands me the tumbler for my go.

◆

Jack Gallagher sees him coming back into the ring and is astonished. He looks so tall, so big, so solid, so renewed, so sure of himself. He looks every inch the champion; he's so determined, so glowing, so concentrated, that he is truly astonishing. Dempsey is staring at him. He obviously expects him to do something. Something specific or something vague, but something! After all, simply by being in the ring he is the incarnation of the rule of law and justice. He has to do something. So Mr Gallagher reacts: he goes over to the boxer and stretches out an arm and a finger. He lets the arm drop, but his finger is still pointing upwards. He chooses a random number between one and ten, and as his arm swings downwards, he peers straight at Dempsey and shouts hoarsely 'Four!'

HE PAUSES FOR EXACTLY A SECOND, then, with the same voice and the same gesture, still staring Dempsey in the face, he cries 'Five!' Dempsey hears him and nods. To some extent he accepts the warning and the number. But the expression on his face is so resolute that even while he is accepting it, he is also objecting. OK, if they want to count over him. That's understandable. But they should also accept the evidence of their eyes: he's back in the ring, he's on his own two feet, he's ready to resume boxing. He's not befuddled in any way, he's as fresh as when he first wakes up in the morning, as fit as at the start of the fight. OK, so they have to make some sort of count. But there's no real reason now for them to go on doing so. Mr Jack 'Slowest' Gallagher is a professional referee and an intelligent man, so he soon gets the message. If, by any chance, merely to be prepared, the next number was taking shape in his mind, that is where it would stay, a virtual, abstract number that would never issue from his mouth. Mr Gallagher doesn't shout 'Six!' Not now, not ever.

◆

'And not only that. Outside the *Crítica* newspaper offices they set up powerful loudspeakers so they could broadcast news of the fight instantaneously.'

'You don't say.'

'I do.'

'And people crowded around.'

'They did indeed.'

'When you say it, I can almost see the scene. Can you imagine it? I can: crowds thronging Avenida de Mayo outside the newspaper.'

'You're right to say you're imagining it, Verani, since imagination and the historical truth are two different things. Back in 1923 *Crítica* newspaper was still in Calle Sarmiento. It hadn't yet moved to Avenida de Mayo. And Calle Sarmiento is quite a narrow street.'

◆

He could also think of it like this: a photo is not a memory, it's a way of avoiding having to remember. If you know there's a photo of something, it becomes possible to relieve the memory of any effort to retain it. Since photos exist, there is no need for memory: there is nothing that has to be saved from oblivion. Whenever you wish, all you have to do is look at the photos, and what existed in the past is there once more. No evocation can be more perfect than the one created by a faithful reproduction of what took place. So oblivion can take its course: there is nothing that a photograph is unable to rescue.

For this same reason, however, if there are no photos – as there aren't tonight – it will be thanks only to the efforts of memory that something remains of all that has happened. When he realises this is the case, Donald Mitchell will try to recall his memories, to fix them so that they become permanent. For now, though, in his ignorance, he insists on frantically choosing images and pressing the button.

◆

Naturally, Richard Strauss knew nothing about all this. He would not have allowed it, even if the reason for the bets had been a worthy or prestigious one, which it plainly was not. The way the bets had been placed by all the musicians turned the hotel into a low dive; they were like sailors in port, lowly suburban factory workers, or criminal layabouts who drink beer and bet on whatever the future might bring.

Those placing the bets knew perfectly well they would be rebuked if it ever got out. They therefore kept very quiet about it, making sure it seemed nothing was going on. They hid every one of the wagers made, so that Richard Strauss would never guess what was happening in his entourage. When they leaned out of the windows to see which beam was going to flash from Palacio Barolo, they were careful to make it seem as though they were only vaguely interested, and were so successful that they gave the impression they weren't interested at all.

They were equally cautious after the fight, when they had to hand over everything that had been wagered: banknotes of various currencies, heavy rings, precision watches. In this discreet, concealed operation, Otto Stiglitz had gone too far. He had been so sure he was right (as in fact he was) and could not lose, that he had gone too far. Even if a musician is absolutely convinced there is no risk, he should never stake his instrument.

He shouldn't do it, for the same reason that he wouldn't walk along a railway line even though he knew there were no more trains running on it.

Yet Stiglitz did: he wagered his cello. He did it in one of those moments of daring or madness you only think better of when it's too late. If Richard Strauss had found out what he had done, he would have been thrown out of the orchestra, even if Dempsey had won the fight and Stiglitz his bet. The shame was not in having lost his instrument, but in having bet it in the first place. The loss of his cello simply meant he would not be able to hide his initial decision, which is where the real disgrace and humiliation lay.

He could have endured any other kind of loss. As an Austrian, husband, father, friend or colleague, Otto Stiglitz was able to rise above any other betrayal apart from this one, which denied him his existence as a musician. His own stricken conscience was enough to mortify him, and would have been enough to lead him to suicide. But there was also Strauss: Richard Strauss. The famous conductor with whom he sometimes even discussed music. What he also had to face was Richard Strauss's harsh condemnation. It was as certain as the carrying out of a death sentence (as certain as death, but inspiring an even greater terror in him). A cellist without a cello: that meant he was already nobody. Strauss's reprimand, his dismissive scorn, would merely serve to confirm his nullity. A withering look from Richard Strauss was worse than death. In order to avoid it, Stiglitz killed himself.

◆

He's suddenly struck by a disturbing thought: why does the other man, the challenger, the boxer who's sent him flying so far out of the ring, look so despondent now the bout is about to resume? Dempsey only has to look at him to see that he's intimidated, apparently pursued by all kinds of demons. If he weren't a boxer, and therefore by definition brave, Dempsey might even say he's scared. How can this be? From the outside, everything points to the fact that he should win. Tonight he's the hero, he's the one who's done great things. He should look arrogant, ready to go in for the kill, he should be the cool and calm executioner. Yet on the contrary, it's plain from his expression that he feels threatened. What makes him so hesitant, when he should be carried away with the euphoria of knowing he is on the point of victory? Why has he got his gloves up in a defensive position, rather than holding them out in front of him for the final assault? Jack Dempsey can't understand it. He stares at him, and he can't understand. There is, however, a valid explanation. Firpo was convinced he had won the fight. What Dempsey, however unclearly, sees as 'on the point of victory', a victory about to happen, was for the other man a victory that had already been won. All that was left was his moment of glory. Firpo had already won, and felt he was the champion. With Dempsey knocked out of the ring, there was no other possibility: his victory was a fact. Now Dempsey is back in the ring. Firpo glances at the referee, thinks he hears him call out a ridiculous number, and grasps that the fight is continuing, that he has to fight on. He sees Dempsey restored, sees him tall and proud as a champion. This is something that in future years the cinema will show time and again: one man riddles another with bullets, finishes him off completely, is satisfied he's dead and breathes a sigh of relief. Then all at once the presumed dead body somehow recovers and gets to his feet again. The person doing the killing goes rigid with fear. Something similar is taking place now. Jack Dempsey got up and climbed back into the ring. They have to carry on fighting. All the champion has to do is what he immediately sets about doing: he slows things down, holds on, puts his arms around and blocks the other man, keeping him in a clinch, not allowing him to punch, playing for time until the gong sounds. As soon as that happens, he knows he has a respite: an entire minute when he can rest, black out, talk nonsense, take deep breaths, make sure he's completely recovered, be born again as a new man. This is the first break, at the end of the first round. It's true that the climax of the fight is already over. But like some symphonies, some boxing matches do not end with the climax.

◆

It's midnight.

I throw the dice: two fours, two sixes and a two.

I throw again: a five.

My third throw: a one. ('That friend of yours, Valentinis. He talked too much. He preferred to hear himself talk rather than listen'). I note down two fours: not much.

Horischnik gives the tumbler a good shake ('He came one afternoon with that story about the bets. He was in a hurry to tell me it; he was pleased with himself, thought he knew everything. It was only as an afterthought that he asked me for my version'). He rolls the dice: two threes, a four, a five and a six.

He throws again: a five.

His third throw: another five ('The fact was that the story about the bets suited me fine'). He asks me to write down two threes for him, but I tell him he's already filled that line. He knows he's already got four fives: I confirm it. Irritated, he tells me to cross off the two four of a kinds ('You can imagine how easy it was to convince that young fellow the story of the bets was true. He was already convinced when he came to see me').

My turn: a four, two threes, two sixes.

I throw again: a two.

My third throw: a one. ('All I did was reinforce his imaginary version of what had happened. I added a couple of details that would increase his sense that it was all true. I let him leave satisfied that the suicide story was the right one, because he thought Dempsey had lost').

I hesitate, and finally note down two sixes. As I hand Horischnik the tumbler, I ask him what it was that Otto Stiglitz bet that night. The old man takes the tumbler as if he can't understand the question, then starts furiously shaking it ('You don't understand. Either that, or you don't want to. There were no bets that night. Nobody bet a thing'). Eventually he throws the dice: two sixes, two threes, one one.

He throws again: a six, a three, a two.

His third throw: a six and a two.

He asks me to note down four sixes. I do so, then ask him what really happened that night back in 1923. If it was true that he met Stiglitz and Strauss, that he went to the hotel and played Mahler at the Colón ('Of course I played. It was the most important night of my life'). I insist, asking him again what really happened that night ('Somebody died, didn't they?'). Horischnik tells me to roll the dice ('Of course somebody died').

I throw the dice: three fours, a one, a two.

I throw again: a three and a one.

My third throw: a four and a two.

Four of a kind. I write it down. ('Look, my friend. What happened is very simple. Terrible perhaps, but very simple').

◆

He throws the dice: two threes, a five, a six and a one. He hesitates, then chooses. Rolls the dice again ('I wanted to play with that orchestra, at any cost'). A six ('Conducted by Richard Strauss, no less! At any cost'). He throws again: a four. Full house ('Gustav Mahler, conducted by Strauss, with the Vienna Philharmonic Orchestra. I was ready to do anything, absolutely anything, to play that night').

My throw: three twos, one one, one four.

My second throw: a two and a five.

My third throw: a six. Four twos.

The old man takes the tumbler and shakes it, concentrating hard ('Yes, I was prepared to do anything to play that night'). He lets the dice rattle for a long while, then finally rolls them.

SEVENTEEN!

'**WILHELM KIENZL SAID: "MAHLER WORKED** against the grain of his time; Strauss worked with it."'

◆

His arguments will be success and a fortune. But not only do his parents not appreciate these aspects of life, they suspect they are simply a cloak for mere ambition and greed. They could only forgive him if he was truly sorry for what he had done. But this is and always will be impossible: Donald Mitchell is not proud of what he has done, but seeing the consequences and the way his life has taken a turn for the better, he is never really going to feel sorry.

◆

'Gustav Mahler said: "I am, as Nietzsche put it, a man out of joint with his time. That is true above all for the kind of works I write. Richard Strauss is the true contemporary. That's why he is able to enjoy immortality in his own lifetime."'

'When did he say that?'

'In August 1906, when he was travelling by train to Salzburg. He was sharing a sleeper with Barnard Scharlitt, a citic from the *Musikalisches Wochenblatt.*'

'And the guy published it.'

'Yes he did, but not then. It came out in the *Neue Freie Presse* on 25 May 1911.'

'Five years later.'

'That's right, almost five years after the conversation. And exactly one week after Mahler's death in the Loew Clinic in Vienna. Just as his own immortality had begun.'

◆

Before allowing him to resume the fight, he takes hold of his gloves. It's a typical gesture before he signals the restart: catching hold of the boxer's gloves and holding them steady. That's when the referee also checks the fighter has really recovered (making sure his eyes are focussed, that his mouth isn't hanging open or his nose bleeding badly, or he's unsteady on his feet) and he isn't sending him to the slaughter. Dempsey's eyes are clear, and he focuses them directly on the referee. Jack Gallagher finds it hard to resist their intense scrutiny. There's something else as well: he can feel the energy in his fists. Between his hands, he can feel them coursing with energy. He holds them briefly and notes it. With this he knows, from his instinct and experience, what everyone else will only know a few minutes later: that Jack Dempsey is going to win.

◆

Quelita had finished her homework and was wandering around the bar. She was bored. Childhood is a time for games and amusement, but there's also a lot of boredom in the long, empty hours. She came over to our table and said she wanted to explore all the nooks and crannies in the hotel where nobody ever went. Ledesma told her to be quiet and to do her homework. She pouted: she'd done it all; she was bored and wanted to explore the places in the hotel where nobody ever went.

Ledesma puffed out his cheeks. Verani said: 'I'll take you. Come with me.'

They disappeared down the corridor.

◆

Oh, yes, now he remembers. His name is Firpo. Luis Angel Firpo. It's an Italian name, but he's not Italian. He's from somewhere else. It doesn't matter where. Whatever his name is, and wherever he comes from, he's going to beat him.

◆

It's exactly one o'clock in the morning.

The dice roll: five fours. Five fours in one throw of the dice. Five of a kind.

Horischnik smiles. I press the pencil against the paper to note down his huge score ('What can I say? Well done'). I know we'll go on playing, even though he's already beaten me.

He picks up the dice and puts them all back in the tumbler. He passes it to me in a friendly way ('I'm not going to deny it; I'm a lucky man') and tells me to put all my heart into rolling the dice.

◆

'Wouldn't you like to come home one evening? We could share a few glasses of wine, some cheese, listen to some music together.'

'To tell you the truth, no, I wouldn't.'